SURFACES
OF A
DIAMOND

SURFACES
★ OF A ★
DIAMOND

A Novel by
Louis D. Rubin, Jr.

Louisiana State University Press
BATON ROUGE AND LONDON   1981

LIBRARY OF CONGRESS CATALOGING IN PUBLICATION DATA

Rubin, Louis Decimus, 1923–
Surfaces of a diamond.

I. Title.
PS3568.U26S9   813'.54   81-6034
ISBN 0-8071-0897-9   AACR2

For Max Steele
and for Joan and Manning

PART ONE

I.

In the spring of 1939, in the city of Columbia, South Carolina, I
went to a movie. I was fifteen years old, and I was in Columbia to
attend a scholastic press convention. The movie was not one that I
might ordinarily have chosen to see, but my companions wanted to
go, and I was so pleased to be there and in their company that I
willingly went along with them.

The movie was about some young women who were student
nurses. One of the nurses was rebellious and resented the restrictions placed on her opportunities to be with her male friends. After
a while came an incident in which she had made plans for a date,
but was scheduled for night hospital duty. She asked another student nurse, a widow who had a small son back home, to take her
place.

The widowed nurse was seated in the hospital room at night, in
front of a low-silled open window, and was reading a letter from her
child. She was blond and very sweet-looking. Absorbed in her reading, she was smiling at the contents of the letter. Across the room a
patient was asleep in a bed. She was lying on her side, and her face
was hidden, and she was breathing heavily, so that the bedclothes
moved up and down.

Suddenly the patient opened her eyes and looked about the room.
She was a middle-aged woman in a black nightgown, with a round,
full face, and her eyes were wide with an insane rage. Meanwhile,
all unseeing, the young nurse sat by the open window reading and,
from time to time, smiling happily at the letter.

The woman in the bed sat up, her large eyes burning in madness,
her face contorted, glaring at the nurse and the open window beyond. The nurse read on.

Abruptly the woman bolted from the bed and sprang for the
window.

The next scene showed the funeral services for the nurse, and the
shame and grief of the other nurse who had asked her to take her
place in the hospital room so that she could go out with her boy-
friend. As I watched I berated myself for having gone to such a

3

movie. I tried to shut my eyes and not look at the screen, but the image of the insane woman stuck in my mind and the suspense of the story drew me back to it.

Ultimately the young nurse redeemed herself. There was an emergency call for nurses to go to the scene of a train wreck. A passenger train had jumped the tracks on a railroad bridge and the coaches had tumbled down into a flooding river. They were half submerged, and the current was powerful, and some injured passengers were trapped inside. Despite the rising water and the possibility of being trapped and drowned herself as the current threatened to overturn the half-submerged coaches, the young nurse went down into a Pullman car with a doctor.

Inside a compartment in the car, with the water rising higher each minute, the nurse and the doctor struggled to extricate an unconscious passenger. Then just as the doctor bore the passenger out of the coach to safety, the coach gave a lurch and the young nurse was trapped within the compartment, unable to extricate herself and with the exit now shut off by the rising river water. She groped at the window, seeking in vain to open it. Finally, unconscious now herself, she was reached and carried to safety.

When it was over and we left the theater and went out onto Sumter Street, it was as if I had emerged from a subterranean pit. The life of the bright afternoon daylight seemed fragile after what I had just experienced. I could not drive from my thoughts the look of the woman in the hospital bed. There was a heavy, sickening fleshiness to her, with her full face, wide round eyes, and the black nightgown, that was terrible in its menace. I wondered what could have caused the woman to become so distraught.

I tried to think of what I would do if I were ever trapped in a railroad coach underwater. There would be air to breathe at the top of the coach; I would try to make my way out by crawling from upper berth to upper berth. Or else try to find a buoyant cushion, perhaps a suitcase, and wait to be rescued. Or . . .

That was in April, toward the end of my junior year in high school. Of the series of events that took place that spring and summer, and that I want to tell about, it seemed to me in later years that the movie I saw in Columbia was the signal for them to begin. It was as if all the necessary elements were there waiting, and an incident was required to set them into motion. Once that occurred, everything else followed as in a sequence.

When I look back at that time, now that I am a middle-aged man with children who are themselves older than I was that spring and summer, I see much that I could not recognize then. What I see are meanings that were not then visible. It is with the light of what I have come to know that I want to tell about that time. But for its own sake, as it happened, and not as prelude to any future. It will be very difficult to do, because it is not an easy thing to remember what we did and thought, let alone who we were, without seeing these in terms of what we later came to be. It is difficult to understand why at the age of fifteen we took some things as seriously as we did. Such things—a high school press convention, a baseball coach, an assignment to write a story for a newspaper, a dance, a date, a piece of music heard on a phonograph—how very unexceptional in themselves they now seem, and did only a few years afterward for that matter. Yet to tell of those things without re-creating their importance at the time would be to misrepresent and even falsify them.

It is only when I can see the pattern in the apparent randomness that their full significance can emerge. And I see, too, the importance of other things that at the time I thought were unimportant by comparison. Yet if I were to relate these from a perspective of now, I would be distorting what they meant then.

Neither in memory, nor in the interpretation of its meaning for the present, does the truth of our experience lie. It is in the shaping of the lineaments of memory into patterns that will reveal their own meaning that experience becomes real. The way to possess it is to make it into a story that will be authentic because so much did not happen in that way at all.

In a grove of oaks a quarter-mile from our house there was one tree that stretched far out from the shore. So perpendicular was its branching that I had only to scramble up the several rungs I had nailed on the trunk, and then step out along a thick limb, holding to an overhead branch for support, to a place where the bough divided and formed a natural seat, well away from the shore and twenty feet above the marsh grass. There, with my back against one limb and my feet anchored on a lower branch, I was screened on three sides by trees and branches, and open only to the marsh and the Ashley River. Secure against observation from land, it was a concealed place, to which I might retreat whenever I pleased, as effectively masked from sight as if I were far away, in another country.

I went there frequently that spring. I came home from school, ate my mid-afternoon dinner, and then if I were not to play or practice baseball I took a book, set out from our side yard, made my way around the Rittenhouses' house with its picket fencing, then across the Cartwrights' backyard, and along the dirt road that led into the grove. I left the road where it turned eastward, followed a narrow path toward the shore, slipped downstream along the riverbank for a dozen yards, and climbed into the tree. I even thought of making a rope ladder that I could pull up after me so that I might be completely safe from intrusion—though from whom or what I should not have been able to say, since no one knew I was there, or cared. The area around me was deserted. At home my father was still asleep, taking his afternoon nap. He was retired from business because of illness, and took a nap every afternoon. My mother was reading a magazine or working in her flower garden. Tommy Rittenhouse was still at Palmer Military Academy. Sometimes I might hear a car bumping up Peachtree Street, or the hammering from a new house under construction a half-mile off to the east, or the southbound Boll Weevil or perhaps a freight train crossing the river on the Seaboard Air Line trestle over toward town. But no one except myself ever came into Devereaux Woods during the daytime.

By rights I should have taken along a textbook to read, for my studies were not going well. But I did not want to be reminded of school, not even of my work on the school newspaper, which had always been my principal interest. I did not want to think about anything important—my schoolwork, my father or mother, or whatever. I wished to withdraw into a place of my own imagining, in which nothing that might require any commitment could intrude.

The book I brought with me might be a work of history, in particular the Civil War. I had already read all the books on that subject in the school library, but the shelves of the public library contained hundreds of Civil War books, many of them old volumes that comprised the memoirs of the leading generals and others. I read General Longstreet's *From Manassas to Appomattox, Advance and Retreat* by the Gallant Hood of Texas, the *Military Memoirs of a Confederate* by E. P. Alexander, and others on browning, foxed paper and bound in faded cloth, in which the soldiers of the southern cause described the heroic operations in which they had taken part.

I imagined that I was a Confederate hero—a young brigadier general, the youngest in the war, leader of a brigade of South Carolinians who, after the victorious assault upon Fort Sumter, entrained northward with General Beauregard to join the army being assembled in Virginia to fend off the invading northern hosts. "On to Richmond!" was the cry as we clambered aboard the railroad cars for the journey to the front. At other times I envisioned myself as the captain of a blockade runner, a swift, low-silhouetted craft that on moonless nights crept out of Charleston Harbor to sneak past the patrolling Federal gunboats stationed beyond the harbor bar and sped off to Nassau to take on a cargo of rifles, ammunition, and other materials of war urgently needed by the beleaguered Confederacy.

I did not read very much fiction at this time, but sometimes I would bring a novel that interested me, one of the Rafael Sabatini tales of adventure perhaps, or *Ivanhoe* or *Kenilworth*, or the Sherlock Holmes stories. I liked books about heroic deeds, far off in time and place from my own life. Sometimes, too, I brought along a book of poems, which I read and, confident that no one could overhear me, recited aloud. I liked the *Barrack-Room Ballads* of Rudyard Kipling, and tried to imitate the cockney English pronunciation. My favorite poem, however, which I did not need to read in a book because after having to memorize it in grammar school I knew it by heart, was an "Ode" by Henry Timrod. I especially liked the final stanza:

> Stoop, angels, hither from the skies!
> There is no holier spot of ground
> Than where defeated valor lies,
> By mourning beauty crowned!

It was about the Confederate dead in Magnolia Cemetery, over across the city on the Cooper River. Several times when my father had driven us through the cemetery on Sunday afternoons, I had seen the graves of the soldiers that the poem described.

Usually, though, I did not read for very long at a time. I watched the marsh and the clouds, listened to far-off sounds of the city, and sometimes thought about the things I wanted to do when I grew up. I wanted to be a newspaper reporter, to travel, to own a boat and explore the harbor and the coast up and down the Inland Waterway, to be a writer for the movies in California like my Uncle Ben and know famous actors and actresses, to be a major league baseball player and hold down the first base position for the New York Giants, to be a foreign correspondent, and be rich and famous.

Sometimes I thought about women, and how I would like to possess them, this girl or that, and would imagine that a girl might come strolling out in the woods and would see me, and invite me down to the bank along the shore, and guide me into her. Dreaming giddily then of sexual intercourse, I might wrench spasms of pleasure from my body, until, spent, I sat silently looking out at the marshland and the river beyond.

But most of the time my thoughts followed no sequence and provoked no such response. Instead I thought idly of many things, and watched the patterns of light and shade that the sky and clouds worked on the marsh, and let the minutes drift by one after another, in drowsy sequence, with no thought of time. I gave in to an absent lethargy, as if carried along in a tidal sweep of water, suspended, making no motion to direct myself shoreward, buoyed by the flow of the river, a floating plank being conducted passively toward the sea. I was fifteen years old, and it was as if a torpor had settled upon me.

The afternoon went by, and I stayed in my high place, suspended over the marsh, until the angle of the light began changing and it was time to make my way home. I extricated myself from my perch and stepped along the limb to the fork of the trunk and lowered myself to the earth. Back along the path and the dirt road I walked. Mr. Cartwright was working in his garden. By now Mr. Rittenhouse would have come home from his drugstore and was watering his lawn, or Tommy might see me passing and call to me from his window. When I reached our gate my father, long since risen from his nap, was working on his fruit trees. I walked up the front steps, across the porch and into the living room, to read the evening paper, talk to my sister, and listen to the baseball scores over the radio, until it was time for supper.

✳

Saturday afternoon Tommy Rittenhouse came over to our house and wanted me to catch baseball with him. I got my first-base mitt out of the closet, and we walked through our yard and over to his house. We never threw baseballs in our yard, because my father was afraid a ball might get away and hit one of his temple orange trees or rose-bushes. I did have a basketball backboard in one corner of the yard, but that was permissible, because the ball never went very far. We took up stations in Tommy's yard and began loosening up, tossing easy at first and then harder. After a few minutes Tommy began spinning a few curveballs. He had a pretty good curve, though be-cause of his size—he was only about five feet four inches tall, con-siderably shorter than I was—he could not throw with too much ve-locity. I could handle anything he threw with my first-base mitt.

Mr. Rittenhouse was watering their front lawn, along the edge of the Cartwright property, and after a time he came over to watch. "How you making it, Omar?" he called to me. "How's the old soup-bone?" He was a large man, over six feet tall and weighing at least two hundred pounds, and in the summer he was the coach of our team in the Neighborhood League. We were the only team with an adult coach. He had volunteered to do it the summer before, and he was going to coach us in the summer ahead. He had a hearty way about him, but he took baseball very seriously. Last summer, when we had lost out for the pennant, he had been disapppointed and had argued with the umpires repeatedly.

Mr. Rittenhouse was a prominent businessman in Charleston. He owned the biggest drugstore, Rittenhouse's Pharmacy, located at King and Wentworth. My father had known him for years, from the time when he too had been a well-known businessman. He played in the Saturday night poker game in our basement, and he always brought two new decks of Bicycle cards from his store. He was a good poker player, and my father said he won every week. As our baseball coach he was also successful, for our team usually won. He brought a bag of chewing gum from his store for each game, and when we won he treated us to soft drinks.

Mr. Rittenhouse watched Tommy throwing to me, and occasion-ally halted him to demonstrate things. After fifteen minutes or so he told us to stop throwing. "You don't want to strain your arm," he told Tommy.

"I'm not tired," Tommy said.

"I don't care. It's early in the season and you'll get a sore arm."

We stopped throwing and went up to Tommy's room. Tommy was not a student at Charleston High School like I was; he attended Palmer Military Academy, where he was a year behind me in school, though we were close to the same age. He had been sent to Palmer because his parents decided that he needed the discipline of a military school. Palmer had no baseball team, so Tommy played only in the summer. It was a summer sport for me, too, for I did not go out for high school baseball. It would have interfered too much with my work on the school newspaper, and probably I could not have made the team anyway.

Tommy liked to throw with me when I was available, even though his father had a catcher's mitt and worked with him all spring long to get him ready for the season. We played games, calling balls and strikes and imagining that we were pitching for major league teams. I was lefthanded and my control was erratic, and Tommy usually won, because whenever he walked a couple of batters he would ease up and begin to throw strikes regularly, which I could not do. In an actual game, against batters, the easy pitches would have been feasted upon, but since we had no batters and used strikes and balls to determine the outcome, he grooved the ball across the plate for strikes and outs.

We looked at his baseball scrapbook for awhile, and talked about the pennant races, which were just getting under way up north. Tommy had actually seen some major league games. Each summer his family went on a vacation trip to New York and Boston. He had official programs from Yankee Stadium, the Polo Grounds, Ebbets Field, and Fenway Park, and on his wall were pennants for the Yankees, Giants, Dodgers, and Red Sox, which his father had bought for him at the games. He also had a baseball in a glass case signed by all the players on the 1937 Yankees. I had never seen a big league game myself, though I had watched the Atlanta Crackers and the Richmond Colts when visiting my cousins in those cities, and several of the players I had seen were now in the majors.

"Do you want to throw some tomorrow afternoon?" I asked as I was leaving.

"No, I can't," Tommy said. "After church the old man's going to take me fishing at Edisto Beach."

My own father was not a fisherman, and I envied Tommy. In addition to coaching our team in the summer, Mr. Rittenhouse hunted and fished, and frequently took Tommy along with him. My father had no interest in such things. Before his illness he had played golf and several times had taken me along, even though I was only six or seven then, but nowadays he went out to the links only once in a long while, with our neighbor Mr. Herbert Simons, and never invited me to go.

When I arrived home my father and mother were both at work in the garden. My father had on an old undershirt, which he usually wore around the yard except in cold weather. He had a canister over his back and a handkerchief tied over his nose and mouth, and he was spraying the temple orange trees.

"Don't come too close!" he warned me.

I made a wide detour and went on into the house.

Since my principal ambition was to be a newspaperman, I had fixed up my desk in my room to resemble a newsroom. On the wall I pinned clippings, photographs, and unusual headlines. Over the desk I hung a light bulb with a green metal lampshade. With a coat hanger and a block of wood I had fashioned a copy spike, on which I impaled carbons of the stories I wrote. I always wore my hat when I worked at my typewriter, as I had seen newspaper reporters do in the movies.

My Uncle Edward, a bachelor who lived downtown, was city editor of the afternoon paper, the *Evening Post*. On Saturday mornings after attending services at the Temple I usually went by the newspaper office on Meeting Street. In the *Evening Post* newsroom there was a long table against one wall on which were piled the newspaper exchanges received from other cities, and I borrowed a pair of scissors and looked through them all, in search of pictures for my baseball scrapbook. I knew several of the reporters and would talk to them a little, and sometimes I would go into the telegraph room and examine the stories coming in on the Associated Press and United

Press teletype machines. Usually I exchanged a few words with my uncle, but never at any length, for he was on the taciturn side.

When I first entered high school, I lost no time in joining the staff of the school newspaper. Soon I was writing stories, helping to edit copy and write headlines, and each month when it was time to put the paper to bed, going down to the printshop and helping to lay out pages, correct galley, cut and rewrite copy. The afternoons at the printer were what I liked best. The smells and sounds of the shop intrigued me. When, at the close of our labors, the paper came off the press I opened the pages, still warm and the ink not quite dry, and examined the edition I had helped create. Afterward, riding home on the bus, I read through all my stories, which now that they had been given substance in columned type seemed no longer to be merely words and sentences that I had used to tell a story, but finished artifacts, achieved and independent.

I could write. It was the one thing I was good at, the sole accomplishment that enabled my parents to take pride in my achievement. My father mailed off copies of the papers to our relatives, with the stories I had written prominently marked. And because I was interested in sports and wrote some of the stories about the athletic teams, I found that the players and even the coaches treated me with respect—a respect that increased when I began writing accounts of the high school boxing matches and the football, basketball, and baseball games for the *Evening Post*, which because it had no full-time sportswriters was glad to publish my stories instead of having to rewrite the accounts from the morning paper.

There was no question of being paid for writing such articles. Only the morning newspaper, the *News and Courier*, paid space rates to its correspondents, and the sports editor of that paper had shown no interest in employing me to cover any athletic events for him. My mother did not understand why I spent so much time writing stories for the *Evening Post* when I received no pay. But it was enough for me to have my stories published in the afternoon paper, often with a by-line indicating my authorship.

Sometimes, following a night basketball game or a boxing match, I went downtown to the newspaper office, installed myself at a typewriter in the deserted newsroom of the afternoon paper, and wrote my story there so that it would be ready for editing the following morning. At such times I felt myself to be the working newsman I aspired to become. The typewriters in the city room were old, and several of them were identical to my Underwood No. 5 at home. I liked their loose action, which seemed especially suited to my two-fingered, hunt-and-peck technique. I had taught myself how to type on my father's Royal portable and on my eleventh birthday had been given the old Underwood No. 5. There was something about it that seemed professional to me, and I enjoyed using the machines in the newsroom for the same reason. From time to time one of the reporters or deskmen on the morning paper, whose newsroom was just down the hall, would come walking past as I worked, and sometimes pause to chat for a minute. Occasionally, too, the sports editor of the morning paper, a cadaverous man named Billy Ball, who wrote a daily column, "As the Ball Bounces," would see me at work there, but he only nodded distantly and passed on.

Often when I covered the high school athletic events for the evening paper I sat alongside a tall blond-headed boy named Paul Munro. A grade ahead of me in school and a year older, he was the sports editor of our school newspaper. He lived downtown, near Colonial Lake, and his father was a banker. It was Paul who was employed to write up the games for the morning paper. Although I would have liked that privilege myself, I was not jealous of him, for he was a better sportswriter than I, and he wrote about athletics, which was his chief interest, with an authority and terseness that I could not equal. What I did envy was his self-assurance, the conviction of his own ability and worth, which did not involve any conceit or arrogance whatever, but only quiet confidence in his knowledge and judgment.

Although good humored and possessed of a dry wit, he did not ordinarily talk a great deal—did not seem to feel it necessary, as I did, to tell what he was thinking, make comparisons and other observations, and discuss his own doings. He had a way, which I often found myself attempting to emulate when I was with him, of seeming to be ironically skeptical of whatever was going on, and to view his experience with an amused tolerance. Yet at the same time he regarded his role as sportswriter with a high professional seriousness that left no room for frivolity or carelessness.

In the company of Paul or others like him, I felt sometimes that I was a kind of poseur, that I was pretending to an independence of thought and judgment that I did not really possess. I sought to maintain a pose of confidence and to appear self-sufficient, self-contained, a little cynical. Yet too often I could not refrain from talking more freely about myself.

Early that fall my father had approached the city director of playgrounds about a part-time job for me, and the director had spoken of a position that would soon be opening up as official scorer of the Municipal Basketball League, with the added responsibility of writing accounts of the games for the morning newspaper. I was so delighted at the prospect that I told Paul Munro about it, as if it were not merely a possibility but a likelihood. The next day my father reported that the director of playgrounds had decided that I was still a little too young for the job. I was embarrassed at having spoken of it to Paul. To my chagrin, when the season opened I found that it was Paul who had been given the position.

My failure to get the job at the basketball games was disappointing to me for another reason. Over the winter my mother had grown critical of my failure to get a part-time job and make money. When she came up to my room and saw me lying on my bed reading, I was taxed with the example of my cousins in Richmond, who were adept at earning money even though still in school and not much older than myself. Several times she suggested that I apply for a newspaper route after school, or a weekend job as usher at a movie theater.

Neither prospect appealed to me. I dreaded the public soliciting that would have been involved in going from house to house each week and collecting for the newspapers, and I also wanted to play baseball and, during the school months, to work on the newspaper. And as for being an usher, the thought of having to escort people to seats in a theater was appalling, particularly now that some of my own classmates had begun to take girls to the movies. To encounter some of the boys on the newspaper staff or players on the varsity athletic teams, with their dates, while I was dressed in an usher's uniform with a little round hat on my head, and to have to lead them down the aisle, flashlight in hand, would embarrass me.

My mother used various arguments. I could save money for a vacation trip. I could buy things that I wanted. I could set up a bank account of my own.

"You'll soon be wanting to go out with girls," she said, "and you'll need money."

"No I won't," I responded at once. I did not want to discuss it with her. Several of my friends had begun going out with girls, my sister, who was a year younger than I, was always talking about dates, and I was beginning to feel that it was expected of me.

One of my duties as feature editor of the high school newspaper was to oversee the preparation of a monthly gossip column that chronicled the romantic doings of various students, based upon reports from their friends. It contained items such as, "John Connolly has been playing a great deal of tennis lately. Could it be a love match with B. J. J.?" or "What was Earl Mazo doing over at the J. C. C. the other evening? Ask Rita V., she knows." Since our high school was for male students only, I seldom knew the girls who were mentioned. But during the past year the names of some of my own classmates had commenced to turn up among the items that I collected for the column, and I realized that going out on dates with girls was no longer something that only boys older than myself did.

My mother seemed to have grown more nervous and distracted. In the past it was always my father who had been nervous, anxious; his long illness, his enforced retirement, the recurrence of nervous spells that kept him under medication had left him frequently disturbed and dispirited. It had been my mother who on most occasions was the steady one, even-tempered and unexcitable. But now she seemed to be more tense and to become quickly exasperated.

A day came in April when I arrived home later than usual after working at the print shop getting the school newspaper ready, and she was very angry, more angry that I had ever known her to be. She threatened to forbid me to work on the newspaper when we had to go down to the printer's. In the past both she and my father had always been amenable to my activities on the school paper, even pleased. In the past, too, I had sometimes come home late, without any such response from her. I was alarmed by her anger, and as soon as I could safely do so I asked to be excused from the supper table and hurried up to my room.

An hour or so later my father came upstairs to see that the windows were closed, because it had begun raining. I handed him a copy of the newspaper we had just produced, with my stories marked. He glanced through it. "You wrote a lot this month," he said.

Later in the evening I wondered whether, now that her anger had subsided, my mother might not be regretting her loss of temper. So after a while I went downstairs, feeling resentful, yet wishing to have the breach mended. But my mother and father had gone to bed early, and the living room was dark.

The copy of the school newspaper that I brought from the printshop was to be the last regular edition for the school year. The present session was the one-hundredth in the history of Charleston High School, and to commemorate it, instead of the usual May number, there was planned a centennial issue, *Charleston High School 1839 –1939*, to come out late in May, printed on heavy coated paper, with many more pages than usual. Because I was not a senior, I was given no editorial post, but it was my assignment to write the lead article describing the program and celebration. When the assignment had been given to me, the faculty adviser, an English teacher named Charles Minot Legaré, had made it clear that I should consider it an honor. I had worked on the newspaper since my freshman term. I was the ranking member of the staff in the junior class, and the assumption was that next fall, when I was a senior, I would become the editor in chief.

To write the story, I would have to interview the school principal, Mr. Strohmeier, for the details. It would not be the first time I had gone to his office to get information for a story. The principal was a friend of my father's; they had grown up together. On the first occasion that I had encountered him when I was a freshman, he had recognized me and asked after my father. "If you can be the man your father was, my boy," he said, "you'll do all right."

I went to see him soon after getting the centennial assignment, but that day Mr. Stohmeier was in an impatient mood and dismissed me peremptorily, with very little information and the statement that I would have to wait for additional details. I should have gone back a few days afterward, hoping to catch him when he was in a better mood and then kept returning to his office until I had secured the material I needed. Yet I put it off and made no move to prepare the story. I told myself that since the deadline was still several weeks away I would wait a little longer and then get the material from Mr. Strohmeier.

I took to going out in Devereaux Woods to my perch in the tree almost every afternoon when I came home from school, though sometimes I caught baseball for a while with Tommy Rittenhouse. If my parents noticed that I was not staying around the house, they made no comment.

There was, however, a rough moment at supper one evening when the subject of the press convention that I was to attend the following weekend came up. My mother declared that with my grades as low as they were, I ought to be made to stay home and study. I objected that as the likely editor of the newspaper in the year ahead, I was expected to go.

"Your schoolwork comes first," my mother said.

"But you told me I could go," I argued.

"You don't deserve to go on a trip. You lie around wasting your time when you ought to be studying."

"I'll study. It won't hurt me to be away for three days."

My mother made no reply.

"I've got to go." I was beginning to be alarmed. Having to inform Mr. Legaré and the others that I was not to be permitted to go to the convention after all, as if I were still a child, would be humiliating. "You promised me that I could go!" I declared. "You're breaking your promise!"

"Don't talk to your mother like that!" my father interjected.

My mother said nothing.

"Can't I go?" I pleaded. "Please?"

"We'll see," my mother answered after a moment.

My school work *was* going poorly, and had been for some months. It was not because I did not try to study. Every evening after supper I got out the textbooks and went through the following day's assignments. The trouble was that I could not make myself concentrate on them. I would look up a Latin declension or conjugation, translate the words, and five minutes later was unable to remember the grammar. By the next morning, in class, I had forgotten the definition itself. With geometry it was almost as bad. When I sought to focus my mind on the problems I soon found that my attention had wandered far away, and I would be thinking, instead, of Mr. Strohmeier and imagine him asking after my father, or about Paul Munro and the sports editor of the morning newspaper, Billy Ball, or about working in the printshop, or any of a hundred different things instead of the numbers and figures on the page in front of me, only to realize, a few minutes later, that I had let my attention wander again. Finally I would give up, tell myself that I would do the work tomorrow when my mind was fresh, and turn on the radio and begin reading a book.

2.

Mr. Rittenhouse called the first meeting of our baseball team for Saturday afternoon. He wanted to hold it in the morning, but I had to go to confirmation class and services at the Temple every Saturday morning, and so did Jack Marcussohn, who was our third baseman. The meeting was to take place in the Rittenhouses' basement, so I telephoned Jack the evening before and told him to come home with me after services and have lunch at our house.

The confirmation class at the Temple consisted of the two of us and one girl. Although we had been elevated from the Sabbath school routine in the adjacent tabernacle, which my sister still had to attend, we met for an hour with the rabbi, Dr. Raskin, in his office at the rear of the Temple and then went to the services. Our actual confirmation would not come until the year following, when we would be sixteen.

What we did in the confirmation class was to talk about successive chapters in a book entitled *The Essence of Judaism*. None of us was an especially diligent scholar, and occasionally Dr. Raskin would become exasperated and say, "How can you be good Jews if you don't want to know what your religion means?"

Ten minutes before time for the services to begin, Dr. Raskin dismissed us. Each week either Jack or I was expected to help him with the handling of the Torah during the services. This week it was my turn.

The nod to come up to the altar always came just as Dr. Raskin read a passage in the prayer book beginning "Who shall ascend into the mountain of the Lord, and who shall dwell in His holy place?" "Kohn," Jack whispered as I arose to go.

I walked up the aisle and onto the dais, helped Dr. Raskin divest the smallest of the several Torah scrolls of its silver breastplate and ornaments and its tight-fitting velvet jacket, then took a seat in one of the high-backed, plush-covered chairs while Dr. Raskin wrapped the chain of a silver pointer around his hand, unrolled the scroll, and began reading from it. When he was done, he turned to me, and I handed him first the velvet jacket and helped him pull it down over the scroll, then the ornaments, and after that I took the Torah back to my chair and held it in my lap while he read from the Bible.

The Torah was not heavy, but as always I felt awkward holding it while in public view, because it reminded me of a little baby, with the bottom of the wooden spools the feet, the velvet jacket its dress, the breastplate a bib, and the ornaments its cap. I felt as if I were being asked to take charge of an infant and hold it upright. Meanwhile Jack Marcussohn was making covert faces at me, and I tried to keep from looking at him for fear of breaking into laughter.

To add to my difficulty in keeping a properly reverent expression on my face, after a minute there came through the half-opened stained-glass windows the sound of band music, which meant that Jenkins Band, an organization of musicians from the local Negro orphanage, had set up operations just down the street at the corner of King and Hasell, and was embarking upon several rousing numbers while a guard of young blacks passed the hat among the Saturday morning shoppers.

As if that were not bad enough, the number that the band chose to render was the "National Emblem March." I dared not look at Jack, for I knew, and knew very well that he knew, the universally recited paraphrase of the refrain:

> Oh the monkey wrapped his tail around the flag pole,
>> And caught a bad cold
>> Up his ass hole . . .

So I sought to avert my glance, but could not resist the urge to look toward him, and so I did—and he was grinning and rolling up his eyes. I looked away, but too late. I bit my lip, stared down to keep from laughing, but could not suppress a giggle.

After the services we walked over to Wentworth Street and caught a bus uptown, had lunch at my house, and then went over to the Rittenhouses'. Before Mr. Rittenhouse had taken over as coach, we had never had any team meetings. But evidently he intended to do things in much more organized fashion during the coming summer, for he had sent us all letters inviting us to the meeting, and telling about how we were going to win the Neighborhood League pennant.

Tommy Rittenhouse and I had organized our team back when I was only twelve years old. We called it the Rose Garden Rebels, the general name for the northern portion of the city, and we played pick-up games with other teams in town. The year before when the Playground Department announced that it was setting up the Neighborhood League, we decided to enter it. There were five of us who constituted the team's nucleus—Tommy and myself, Junie Fox, Mac Miller, and Johnny Harriman. Junie was the best athlete, and this spring was playing on the high school team. He had grown very tall over the past two years, and was now six feet and weighed close to two hundred pounds.

The rules of the Neighborhood League were that each team had to draw its players from a single designated local neighborhood, and that nobody older than sixteen could play. Shortly after the last season had begun, Mr. Rittenhouse had offered to be our coach. I thought it would be a good idea, because he knew a great deal about playing baseball. I asked the others about it, and they agreed with me. We had several boys on the team who were neither very good players nor especially reliable in showing up for all the games, so it was not long before Mr. Rittenhouse invited Jack Marcussohn and Dave Gregg, who lived on Hampton Park Terrace, to join us.

I had been more or less in charge of the team when we played pick-up ball, in the sense that I arranged for games and set the starting lineup, and when we moved into the Neighborhood League, I continued in that role. Once Mr. Rittenhouse took over, however, my role as captain was limited almost entirely to going out with the other team's captain before each game to review the ground rules with the umpires.

The meeting was held in Mr. Rittenhouse's game room. It was a large basement room, with pine-paneled walls, and on them were framed photographs of him when he played in college and the Municipal League, and also some later ones showing him at various local civic functions, with the mayor and the governor and others. There was a trophy case displaying a half-dozen or so silver loving cups, plaques, and medals he had won during his playing days. He also kept his shotgun and rifles in a large cabinet with glass doors, and his fishing tackle was over against one wall.

Everyone except Johnny Harriman was present for the meeting. Mr. Rittenhouse gave a talk about the importance of team effort, and everybody being alert and involved in the game at all times. "We're going to be a running, hustling ball club," he said. "We're going to force the other team to make mistakes, and we're going to take advantage of them when they do." Although it was still a month before the season began, we would practice twice a week, he told us, and everybody was expected to be there except Junie Fox, who was on the high school team and would join us when the school season was over.

"Now we've got to keep in perspective what we're doing," he declared. "What we want to do is to have fun—and winning's the most fun of all. So we're going out to win, and that means first of all, having a winning attitude. I don't want anybody on this ball club who doesn't want to be a winner, and isn't willing to work hard to win. If you don't want to win, now's the time to get off the team."

My own feelings, as I listened to his speech, were somewhat mixed. I enjoyed playing on a team that was well organized, and last summer I had liked the things that Mr. Rittenhouse had done to make us play better as a team. He had instituted signals and taught us how to back up throws, take relays from the outfield, use a cutoff man, how to shift to right or left against various batters, and other things that would not have occurred to us. At the same time, however, I sensed that the team had become mostly Mr. Rittenhouse's instead of ours.

If his speech bothered any of the other boys on the team, they gave no sign of it. After Mr. Rittenhouse set up a practice schedule and reviewed the signals we would be using, he served ice cream and cokes, and everyone seemed to be satisfied.

After the meeting was over and the others had gone home, Tommy and I went outside and played a little catch. During the meeting Tommy had said nothing. Once I had glanced over at him while his father was speaking, and he was looking out the window.

After supper that evening I rode downtown on the bus to my Uncle Edward's apartment, to listen to music on his phonograph. He owned more than a hundred albums of classical music and an expensive Capehart record player. Five or six sides could be played, one after the other, providing as much as twenty-five minutes of music, so that I could read while listening, without having constantly to stop and change records. My uncle also had a libary of about a thousand books, the majority of them on Greek and Roman history, archaeology, philosophy, and painting.

I made a point of arriving at his apartment a short while before he would be leaving for the Saturday night poker game held in our basement. My uncle was a man of few words, but he seemed to like me, sometimes telephoned to tell me when he was going out for the evening during the week so that I could come and listen to his records if I liked, and always gave me a little change before he left for the evening.

That evening I told him that I would be going to the state press convention in Columbia the following weekend. He nodded.

` "Didn't Uncle Ben work there once?" I asked.

"I believe he did," my uncle said. Like Edward, Ben had begun as a newspaperman, but while Edward had remained in Charleston all his life, working on the *Evening Post*, Ben had held jobs on various newspapers, moving from Birmingham to Fort Worth to Denver to Jacksonville to Atlanta to Columbia, until his plays had begun to get produced on Broadway and he gave up newspaper writing.

"Didn't you ever want to work on other papers, like Uncle Ben?" I asked.

"No," he said. "One newspaper's about the same as another."

He was older than my father, but younger than Ben, who was now a film writer for RKO Pictures and lived on the West Coast. In his younger days Uncle Edward had tried his hand at writing fiction. In the apartment he had occupied before moving to his present lodgings a year earlier, there had been a wicker bookcase containing numerous magazines, each with a short story he had written. They were printed on pulp paper, bore such titles as *Blue Book*, *True Adventure*, *Ainslie's*, *Munsey's*, and *Dime Detective*, and the coarse paper had turned brown and brittle. They were mostly adventure and detective stories, with tricky plots. When he moved to his new apartment, on the second floor of a small house, he had evidently thrown them all away. Once I asked him why he stopped writing stories, but all he said was, "I grew tired of it."

He also used to read many of the current western, adventure, and detective magazines, and when he was finished with them he would pass them along to my father, who in turn handed them on to Mr. Simons. But copies of these were no longer to be found in his apartment, either. The magazines he now read were *Harper's*, *The Atlantic Monthly*, *The American Mercury*, and *Forum*.

My father, who in any event was not much of a reader, had found the change in taste not to his liking. "Edward goes in for all that highbrow stuff now," I once heard him remark to Mr. Simons.

After my uncle left for the game, I selected an album, the First Symphony of Brahms, and as the first record dropped into place I began reading a book I had brought along, a biography of Nathan Bedford Forrest by a man named Andrew Lytle. I had already more than half-finished it, and I took up the story where I had left off, following the Confederate cavalry in the campaigns against the invading Union Army in Tennessee, Alabama, and Mississippi.

When I listened to music, my thoughts seemed to go wandering off into little byways and directions. But when I read while I was listening, the book occupied just enough of my attention so that I could follow the music carefully along its way. I heard the music and I kept with my story, and neither got in the way of the other. I heard every note of music very clearly and was very much aware of the pattern of the symphony as it developed.

When I finished the biography of Bedford Forrest, it was only about 10 P.M., nearly an hour before I would have to leave for home. I looked around for something else to read. I discovered a volume entitled *The Royal Road to Romance*, by Richard Halliburton. Just as I began to read it, the symphony I was playing came to an end. I replaced the records in the album, and I took up a new album of the Eroica Symphony, which was lying out on my uncle's reading table, and loaded the records on the machine. Then I settled back to read.

The book was a travel book, about journeying to far-off places, and no sooner had I begun to read than the music seemed to bear me aloft and conduct me on a journey. The symphony had a quality of something outside and beyond everyday life. It seemed to propose great distances and faraway scenes, and to move through them as if to demonstrate that it could be done. But not as if it were going along the ground, as in a train trip. Instead it seemed to view the country, traversing from a remarkable elevation, superior to obstacles or interruption, with a tremendous sense of command and mastery of its journey.

Moreover, it was not merely the travel, as such. What it seemed to suggest—more than that, assure me—was that I was certain to make a journey myself. I would some day know for myself what the music knew—or things comparable to it, because it did not insist upon specific vistas, not even those in the book, which I soon put down and forgot.

I had the sense that the music was telling me that however inept and without talent I might now consider myself, the time would come when I should be able to move with purpose and assurance along my own chosen route. And if, as the music seemed also to suggest at times, there would be disappointments and setbacks, such things would only be taken up and made part of the journey. So I listened, imagining along with the music, on and on, until the last record had been played and the phonograph turned itself off with a click.

Now in the silence the sense of the music still reverberated in the room, which as I gazed around at the bookcases, the desk, the typewriter, the Japanese prints on the wall, the open windows that gave out upon the night, seemed to have a glow of its own, and its furnishings to take on a richness and solidity of detail that enabled me to see them as distinct objects, possessing body and dignity.

In listening and responding to the music, I felt as if I had become engaged in an excursion, though to where and for what purpose I could not have said, for the music had not informed me of that. It had only told me that I was already underway.

When the uptown-bound Rutledge Avenue bus drew up at the corner of Calhoun and Rutledge, the doors swung open, and I hopped aboard. But as I turned toward the aisle, I saw, seated several rows back, Paul Munro and a girl, Janice Bryan, who lived on Versailles Street several blocks from my house.

I had sometimes thought that if ever I came to invite a girl to go on a date with me, it would be this girl. She was a friend of my sister's, and we exchanged brief greetings as I hastened by, making sure to take a seat well back in the bus, away from them. Obviously they had been on a date to the movies, and now Paul was escorting her home. It was, after all, Saturday night. While I had been spending the evening by myself at my uncle's, listening to music and reading, others my age were going to the movies with girls.

As the bus rumbled northward along Rutledge Avenue, passing College Park and through the Seaboard Railroad crossing at Grove

Street, I realized that Paul and Janice Bryan would also be getting off at Versailles Street, and we would be walking in the same direction. I did not want to intrude upon their date, but at the same time, if I hurried off up the street ahead of them, it would only call attention to my embarrassment.

I thought of staying on the bus and riding up to the end of the line at Herriott Street, and getting off at Versailles on the way back, but I was likely to run into Paul who would be waiting for the bus to go back downtown when I got off. As the bus passed Maple Street, I kept trying to think of what I would do and say when the time came to get off.

Just before we got to Peachtree Street I pulled the bell cord, and the bus ground to a stop. As I reached the door, Paul and Janice turned around toward me. "Goodnight!" I said, and stepped down into the street. It was a few blocks farther to walk this way, but as I stepped along in the darkness I felt as if I had escaped from a trap.

★

The Municipal League season opened Sunday afternoon, and I went with Tommy and Mr. Rittenhouse to see the doubleheader at College Park. When Mr. Rittenhouse went with us, we always sat in the stands along the third-base line, because he used to be a third baseman.

College Park was located across Cleveland Street from the playground at Hampton Park where we played our Neighborhood League games during the summer. At the far extremity of left field, bordering on Grove Street, were the tracks and the pink stucco passenger station of the Seaboard Air Line Railway, and Rutledge Avenue lay just beyond the right-field fence. To hit a home run over the right field fence into the trees along Rutledge Avenue was a relatively short poke. A ball hit to left or left center, however, might sail on and on and still come to earth within the limits of the playing field, for there was no left-field fence. Stroked over the fielder's head, a well-hit ball could roll all the way to the Seaboard passenger station for an inside-the-park home run.

When the games were slow and one-sided, with the sun bearing down and the dense foliage of the trees in Hampton Park blocking any slight breeze that might blow in off the river a mile away to the west, I played a secret game. I tried to catch sight of the Boll Weevil arriving at the Seaboard Station. It was a small gas-electric combine, painted black with smudged white stripes, containing operating cab, baggage compartment, and passenger coach all in one, with a single day coach coupled behind. Early each afternoon it came to Charleston from Hamlet, North Carolina, and after a lengthy wait at the station out beyond left field it departed for Savannah.

I tried to keep my eyes fastened upon the station area when it was time for the Boll Weevil to arrive, hoping to actually see it pull into the station. But I never saw it arrive. The ball game would reclaim my attention, and when I remembered to look, the train would already be there. Then I would resolve to watch it depart, but again my attention would be diverted, and later when I looked again it would be gone.

If it had been a freight train or had been pulled by a steam locomotive, I could have heard it, of course, but the sound of the gas-electric engine could not penetrate the noise of the crowd. As trains went, the Boll Weevil was not very impressive. Actually there were two of them, one operating each way daily between Savannah and Hamlet. The Charleston service of the Seaboard was only a branch line. I knew that the Seaboard had full-fledged passenger trains with steam locomotives, coaches, and Pullmans, but they operated on the main line that crossed through the state of South Carolina well away from the seacoast, stopping at Columbia. Perhaps the next weekend, when I went to Columbia for the state scholastic press convention, I might catch sight of one.

To travel northward or southward from Charleston it was necessary to go up to the North Charleston station, ten miles from the city limits, and board one of the Atlantic Coast Line trains, while anyone who wished to travel to Columbia and Cincinnati rode on the Southern Railway. The only persons who patronized the Boll Weevil were those who wished to get to or from the various little towns and stations in the Low-country, or in the eastern part of the state toward the North Carolina line. Sometimes when I saw the Boll Weevil waiting at the small stucco station, however, I wished that I might board it and ride all the way to its terminus at Hamlet.

Although my attention might wander away from the playing field, Mr. Rittenhouse watched the game closely, and frequently he noted faults that he called to Tommy's attention, so that Tommy would not make the same mistakes. "He's throwing across his body," he said of one pitcher. "See how he strides too far to the right, so that he has to come across his body with his pitch? That's why he's missing with his fastball so much." Or, after a second baseman had gone far to his left to scoop up a ground ball and throw out a runner, earning a round of applause from the crowd, "He made that play look a lot harder than it should have been. He was playing too close to second base with a lefthanded batter up. It should have been just a routine grounder."

After the first game of the doubleheader Mr. Rittenhouse left, and we moved from the third-base line to seats behind home plate. We had a game that we played, in which we took turns calling the pitches. Before each pitch one of us would have to predict what the pitcher was going to throw. "Curveball inside," the one whose turn it was would say, and if the pitcher then threw an inside curveball he received a point. We kept totals for each inning, and when the game was over the one with the fewest points had to buy a root beer for the other at the Hampton Park Pharmacy across the street.

Tommy won more often than I did. He almost always predicted that the pitcher would throw a fastball outside, and usually he was right. I liked to call for curveballs and changeups, hoping that the pitcher would try one, even though I knew he would probably come in with his fastball.

After the second game was done we went over to the Hampton Park Pharmacy. It was crowded, but we found a place with a couple of boys we knew from the playground, at a table over near the soda fountain. We ordered root beers, the waitress brought them, and I paid her. We began talking about the game. A little later Paul Munro and Fred Ellison, another boy on the school newspaper staff, came in, in company with two of the players on the high school team. I was chagrined to have them see me there with the other two boys at our table, both of whom were several years younger than I.

Paul and Fred waved at me. "You all set for Columbia?" Paul asked. I nodded.

"How come you're going to Columbia?" Tommy Rittenhouse asked me. I told him I was going to the press convention.

"You can get some good nookie up there," Tommy said. Tommy always spoke as if he were an experienced seducer of women, but it was only talk that he picked up from some of the older cadets at Palmer Military Academy. To my knowledge he had, like myself, never actually gone out on a date, except once when he had taken my sister to a Christmas carol concert at his church. He talked about sex all the time, however, and once when his parents were out had even taken me into their bedroom, pulled out the drawer of a table by the bed, and shown me a large box of condoms. "What do your parents use?" he asked me. I told him that I did not know; the thought embarrassed me.

We walked toward home down Grove Street and then cut across the fields, over a wooden bridge that spanned a marsh creek near an old peanut mill, and through the area known as Devereaux Woods, where I had my tree perch. The road was often used as a lover's lane at night, and Tommy liked to look for evidence in the form of discarded condoms. On our way home he pointed out several of them. "They must have been really getting it out here last night," he declared.

It was Tommy's belief that you could go into any hotel in Charleston, inquire of any bellboy, and at once be conducted into the room of a whore. He also claimed reliable knowledge of the practices on West Street, the red-light district downtown, saying that he had once gone into one of the houses with two older cadets and had waited in a parlor while they had taken two girls upstairs. I did not believe him.

When I went to Columbia for the convention I would not be staying at a hotel, but with my father's cousins, the Schwartzmanns. I hoped that when I grew older and went on trips by myself I could stay in one. By then I might be old enough to ask a bellhop to send a woman to my room.

3.

We left for the press convention early Thursday morning. There were three carloads of us going. It was a drive of about three hours. We crossed a bridge over the muddy river at the western edge of Columbia, and drove up a long hill toward the green dome of the state capitol, and I thought of how my Uncle Ben had come here to work as a reporter, more than twenty years before. Now I was here myself—not as a reporter, to be sure, but at least at a press convention, as an apprentice newspaperman, in my own right.

After we had registered and eaten lunch I found a taxicab and went to my cousins' apartment. I talked with them for a while, was given a key to their apartment, and then returned to the convention. The program that afternoon, after an opening session, consisted of a tour of the plant of the Columbia newspapers, and in company with several hundred delegates, male and female, from other high schools in South Carolina, we walked down Sumter Street toward the plant. We trooped along past the Capitol and saw markers on the walls showing where Union army shells had landed during Sherman's march northward in 1865, and past the business district to the newspaper offices, where we were divided into smaller groups and taken into the building.

The newsrooms were much like those of the Charleston newspapers, though larger and more modern. Most of the staff of the afternoon paper, the *Record*, had departed for the day, but as we walked through the *Record* newsroom I thought of how my Uncle Ben had worked there, and wondered which of the desks had been his. In the *State* newsroom, reporters were busy at their typewriters, desk men wearing green eyeshades were editing copy and checking strips of proof, and there was the same air of controlled bustle and energy that I found so appealing in the newsrooms at home.

The composing room seemed larger than that in Charleston. Tiers of linotype machines were noisily clinking and thumping, casting the news into hot type. Makeup men were arranging columns of type in chases atop iron turtles. I liked the odors of burning metal, proof ink, engravers' zinc, and newsprint. The smell seemed metallic and crisp. As we filed by, one linotype operator set each of our names in type and handed us the slugs. I read my name, spelled in raised characters: nʜoЯ ɹɒmO. The lead slug was warm to the touch. Perhaps the day might come, I thought, when that very same machine might often set slugs bearing my name, but preceded by the word ʏᗺ.

From there we went into the pressroom. There was a thunderous din as the immense Goss rotary press, double-tiered and dwarfing both in size and complexity the cylinder press at the shop where our school newspaper was printed, was producing a late run of the afternoon edition. Printed, sectioned, and folded, a stream of newspapers emerged in a flowing procession along a sliding belt, with every twenty-fifth copy tucked a few inches off center.

All this was the real thing. I felt that I should desire no fate better than some day to be part of so imposing an operation, to have a desk and a typewriter of my own in the busy newsroom, to go out into the city, into the State Capitol and the office buildings and the university, and to bring in news and type it into story form, have it set into columned format, and printed under black headlines in those multi-paged newspapers that were flowing steadily out of the web press. I was, I thought, destined for it; the ink of printing presses was in my bloodstream.

At the convention the next morning there was a business session, at which officers were elected, and then more seminars. Instead of attending any of them I decided to go out for a walk. I set off toward the business district, passed by the capitol, and turned westward onto Gervais Street. I walked past several small hotels. I wondered whether what Tommy Rittenhouse had said, about there being prostitutes in them, was true. I followed along down the slope of Gervais Street to an area filled with open-air produce stalls and counters, with what seemed to be hundreds of vendors selling vegetables, poultry, and other farm goods. Pickup trucks were parked all about, and numerous wagons with horses and mules were tied up at curbsides. Farther to the west I heard a freight train passing through, and I walked in that direction for several blocks, until I came to the Seaboard Air Line railroad station, with a gray-painted wooden waiting room and a long roofed shed stretched out alongside the tracks. People were standing about the platform, evidently waiting for a passenger train to arrive, for they had suitcases and parcels. Across the way a yard engine was shunting freight cars, sending up clouds of black smoke into the warm morning sky.

Presently porters moved out along the tracks, and from the south I heard a locomotive whistle, and then the faint ringing of crossing bells, and soon I could see, down the tracks, a train moving toward the station. The locomotive was large, jet black, with high drive wheels, and it came bearing down along the tracks where I stood, then past me, towing behind it a string of day coaches, a dining car, and a half-dozen Pullman cars. The forward motion ceased, and I watched the vestibule doors open and the debarking travelers step out onto the platform. The outbound passengers climbed aboard. They were headed north for Richmond, Washington, the cities of the Northeast. Some were obviously businessmen, going away on business trips as my father had done before he took sick. Looking up at the Pullman windows I could see passengers gazing idly out at the station during the momentary delay in their journey. After several minutes the porters swung aboard, and the train began to move out of the station, slowly and then picking up speed, leaving me behind to watch it disappear up the tracks.

I walked up the long hill on Gervais Street toward the State Capitol, and back to the convention, where I joined Paul Munro and Fred Ellison for lunch. Fred was a senior and our news editor. We ate at the university cafeteria, and I watched the convention delegates and the university students as they sat at tables talking and laughing. Paul and Fred had attended a seminar on sports page editing, and they were arguing about some of the ideas they had heard advanced. Our table had places for others, and soon a group of convention delegates, several girls and a boy, came along bearing trays of food, and asked whether they might join us. They were from Greenville High School, and we soon fell into conversation, mostly about people whom they knew in Charleston, and then about sports and other matters. They spoke in the nasal drawls of the Up-country. The boy was tall and thin, with high cheekbones like a good-looking Indian, and was very witty. Soon we were all exchanging names and addresses on the convention souvenir books, and we decided, since there was no activity scheduled for that afternoon, to go and watch the University of South Carolina baseball game.

We crowded ourselves into Fred's car, and drove to the baseball stadium. We found seats in the grandstand and watched the two teams take infield practice and then begin to play. The University team was playing Furman University, which was located in Greenville, and the girls from there began rooting for Furman. One of their players was a Charleston High School graduate, and when Fred Ellison called to him he came up from the bench to say hello. I had known him from Hampton Park Playground. "You still writing them up, Scoop?" he asked me, using the nickname that I was called on the playground. I was gratified that a college baseball player recognized me, especially since he played on the team from our companions' hometown.

It was a bright, hot day, and it was pleasant to be sitting there in the grandstand in Columbia, watching the game, which Furman was winning, and talking with the delegates from Greenville. After an hour or so the boy and one of the girls from Greenville departed, leaving the three of us with the two other girls. We stayed on for several innings—the game was one-sided—and then went back to Fred's car and drove toward the convention center.

It was still only mid-afternoon, and the evening banquet would not begin until six. "What do you say we take in a movie?" Fred suggested. The two girls were agreeable, so we continued on to the business district past the Capitol and the Hotel Columbia. The girls from Greenville were nice. They were both dark-haired, one was a little taller than the other, and they were both in their junior year at Greenville High School. Although I felt a little nervous at first, they were so friendly that I was soon at my ease. It occurred to me that I was actually out on a date—a double-date to be sure, or rather a double-triple date, but nonetheless I was going to the movies with girls.

We parked on Sumter Street and then walked along until we came to a theater. Farther up the street there was another movie marquee in sight, but one of the girls declared that she had read the story on which the movie at the first theater was based, and that it was very good, and the others at once agreed to go in and see it. As for myself, it was not the movie itself that mattered but the fact that I would be watching it in the company of the girls from Greenville.

We pooled our money, bought tickets for ourselves and for the two girls and went inside the theater. Fred led the way to our seats, and after him filed one of the girls, then Paul and the other girl, and myself. In the row ahead of us there was a couple seated in the darkened theater, with the man's arm about the girl's shoulder, her head resting against his. That was what couples did on dates at the movies, though of course it would be out of the question on an occasion like this, if only because there were three of us and only two girls. All the same, I was here at last.

Soon, however, as the story progressed, I forgot about the occasion, and who I was with, and became caught up in what was taking place on the screen. For what I had begun watching was the movie about the student nurses and the insane patient in the black nightgown, and the nurse trapped in the submerged railroad coach.

✶

Afterwards as we walked back toward Fred Ellison's car, the others noticed my silence, the fact that I was withdrawn in my thoughts. "What's the matter, Scoop?" one of the girls asked, using the nickname she had heard the baseball player use. "Did the movie upset you?"

"No," I said, "I was just thinking."

I tried to put from my imagination what I had seen. We got into Fred's car and drove toward the convention center, and gradually the pleasure of the occasion restored itself.

The two girls left to go to the home where they were staying, to change for the banquet and dance, promising to rejoin us soon. We sat around the convention headquarters talking, until finally the girls returned. They wore long dresses now, and looked several years older. In light blue and maroon gowns, their hair gathered in bunches, they were very pretty. We found our way to the banquet hall, and were soon having a good time, waving at friends, making jokes, and talking. After the banquet there was to be the dance, and I would go along to that as well, even though I did not know how to dance. One of the girls would certainly show me how. And besides, it did not especially matter whether I actually did any dancing. I would be going to a dance.

The interior of the gymnasium was emblazoned with crepe paper and decorations, mostly in the garnet and black of the University colors. There were chairs all around the sides, and a sign, WELCOME S.C. SCHOLASTIC PRESS. On the stage the University band was setting up. Everyone was standing around the edge of the dance floor talking, and the resonance of the hall bounced the concentrated murmur back and forth so that there was a continuous, low-voiced intonation.

After a while there was an announcement over the public address system at the stage. I could not make out the words, but everyone seemed to know what was being said, for they began heading for the dance floor. Paul Munro and Fred Ellison and the two girls from Greenville walked out to join the others, and I followed. They joined hands and began forming a circle, so I moved to step into the ring with them.

Quickly Paul said, "No, you can't be in this."

I stepped back, and in an instant the band began playing, the circle of boys and girls broke off into pairs, and the dance was under way.

My face burning, I moved out of the way of the dancers and back to where we had been standing. I took a seat against the wall and watched them dancing. I had revealed, to Paul and to Fred Ellison and to the girls from Greenville as well, my entire ignorance of how to act at a dance. I had gone clumsily out onto the floor without realizing what was happening. It was plain that I was a complete novice. What was more, they had obviously assumed, all four of them, that they would be the ones who would be dancing, and had not given so much as a thought to me or my presence. They were having a double date at the press convention, Paul and Fred and the two girls. In their minds I was only tagging along.

After several numbers they came back off the floor to where I was sitting. Taking chairs, they talked among themselves, a little flushed from the exertion, clearly without any sense of there having been anything awkward or untoward. I said nothing.

A little later Fred rose to his feet and extended his hand to the girl who had danced with Paul. She stood up to join him. Paul too stood up, but then he turned to me.

"You go ahead," he said.

"No, I can't dance," I told him. "You go on."

Paul gave his hand to the girl, and I watched them walk off toward the music.

I stayed for a while, observing the dancing, and then excused myself. "Oh, come on, stick around," Paul said.

"No, I've got to be going," I answered. "I'll see you in the morning." The two girls from Greenville said goodbye.

35

That night in a dream I was standing in a narrow room, or a compartment. I could see nothing; it was pitch black. There were clothes, or curtains, or fabric of some sort all about me on the walls. I kept reaching out and touching them. I felt helpless, deserted; I could not see my way, was closed in from every direction, and did not know why I was there or how I came to be there. I stood by myself, paralyzed. I knew that I was small and weak, imprisoned in a closed place, without any idea of who I was, and I could do nothing except wait helplessly in my cell. It seemed to me that long stretches of time went by, while I remained alone and without hope, weighted down with despair.

After a while I began to realize that I was no longer asleep, and that the fabrics were garments, and I was standing inside a closet somewhere in my cousins' apartment. I turned around and located the door to the closet and pushed it ajar. Was I in someone else's bedroom? I could not tell. What would my cousins think if they awoke and found me standing here? I kept very quiet.

At last I realized that I was still in the room I had been sleeping in. With relief I groped my way back to the bed, and climbed into it. Still half asleep I lay there, trying to figure out what had happened. Never before, so far as I knew, had I walked in my sleep. The thought that I might well have left the room I was sleeping in and gone into someone else's bedroom was dreadful to contemplate.

I started to drift back into sleep, but then I remembered the woman in the movie, the wild insane eyes, the full face, the black gown. Alarmed, I forced myself into full awakeness. The room was dark, but through the window I could see the dim light of predawn. I shuddered, and turned my face toward the ceiling, staring steadily and without feeling at it, until at length fatigue overcame me and I fell back into sleep.

When I returned home late Saturday afternoon, I said nothing to my parents about having walked in my sleep in Columbia. I told them about visiting the newspaper plant, and going to the baseball game and to the dance with the girls from Greenville, though of course I made no mention of my blunder in walking out onto the dance floor when the circle was being formed.

I was afraid that I might go sleep-walking again, and also I could not drive out of my mind the image of the insane woman in the movie. Merely to think of her and her black nightgown made me shiver. On the night that we got back from the convention I decided that when I went to sleep I would leave my bed light burning and the radio playing low, so that if I were to have a nightmare and walk in my sleep again I would be awakened by the light and the music. My father, however, was a restless sleeper and must have heard the radio playing, for not long after I had fallen asleep a noise awoke me and I opened my eyes to see my father turning out the bed light. "You fell asleep with your radio playing and the light on." I turned away, and went back to sleep.

4.

On the Monday morning following the convention I encountered the principal of the high school, Mr. Strohmeier, in the hallway in front of his office, and was reminded of what I had been willing to forget: that my story about the centennial celebration was due that week. I had put it out of my mind, and not thought once about it during all the time I was in Columbia.

"How are you, my boy?" the principal asked in his deep, reverberating voice. "And how is your good father?" And, when I replied that my father was all right, he said, "If you can be the man your father was, my boy, you'll do all right!"

I asked whether I might get the information about the program from him, and was told that he had a full schedule of appointments today and Tuesday, but that I might come by his office Wednesday morning. If I interviewed him Wednesday, I told myself, I could turn in the story on Thursday morning, which was the day it was due. When I saw the faculty adviser, Mr. Legaré, I promised again that the story would be in his hands on time.

That afternoon I thought about my encounter with Mr. Strohmeier. He always spoke to me about what my father *was*, as if he were no longer alive. It was true that he was retired and no longer active in the Rotary Club and other civic organizations, but he was only in his mid-forties, and might go back into business again some day soon. If he could no longer be president of the Retail Merchants Association and head fund drives, he was hardly unknown in the city. His rose garden and his fruit trees were sometimes mentioned in the newspapers, and he wrote letters to the editor about various things that concerned him, such as trash collection, the postal service, and John L. Lewis.

I tried to remember my father as he had been before his illness and the operations on his brain. Before he took sick he had been very energetic, had frequently gone away on business trips, and several times took me along with him. There was the time when we had gone on the train to Savannah, where we had stayed in a hotel and watched ships out in the muddy river, and he had presented me with a set of toy soldiers, including a white horse with a rider who could be taken off the horse. Another time we went to a farm up near Monck's Corner, which his firm was wiring for electricity, and we brought back a box containing four baby pigeons, which we kept in the backyard in a pen until finally they grew up and flew away.

The memory that was strongest, however, was something he once did. It was the summer of 1929, when I was not yet six, and we were staying in a beach house over on Sullivan's Island. My father went in to work each day on the Mount Pleasant ferry. Once, though, he went to New York City on a business trip, and instead of returning on the train he came by ship, aboard one of the Clyde Line vessels that traveled between New York City, Charleston, and Jacksonville. The ship was due to arrive in port early in the morning. My mother awoke my sister and me while it was still gray outside, and we walked down to the beach in front of our house to watch the ship pass by on its way to the downtown harbor. Everything was hazy and the water was green-gray, with a light mist over the surface of the ocean. We watched the ship as she sailed through the opening in the harbor jetties, and seemed to be headed straight for us, and then swung westward on a course parallel with the shore. The ship channel lay only a few hundred yards off the beach, and soon the ship, the *Algonquin*, drew opposite our house.

At that moment a very bright light began blinking aboard the ship. "That's Daddy!" I announced.

"It's just a signal light of some kind," my mother said.

"No it's not," I insisted. "It's Daddy." And I was quite certain that it was my father, for the light was blinking to the rhythm of "Shave and a Haircut, Two Bits!" which was a song he sometimes sang to me. That evening when he arrived home from the office he told us that he had arranged with a member of the ship's crew to let him use the searchlight to send the signal.

Thereafter, of the various Clyde liners that called at Charleston several times each week, the *Algonquin* was always my favorite. From time to time, too, I thought about that light, blinking to me across the water in the early morning mist and grayness, sending a signal from my father aboard the ship, to where I stood on the shore overlooking the ocean:

Shave and a hair cut, two bits!
Who's going to pay for it? Tom Mix!

39

Who did he marry? Marie.
Why did he marry? For money.

That was before he took sick, when he sang songs and took me on trips and played golf every Saturday afternoon and Sunday morning, sometimes taking me along to hit the ball with a cut-down set of real golf clubs he had bought for me.

He kept several large scrapbooks with newspaper clippings, photographs, letters, and other mementos, dating all the way to when he had first started in the electrical business, back before the World War. There were photographs of him taken during the war, showing him in his Marine Corps uniform, and pictures of the prize-winning displays that he had set up in his store window, articles about his store and his contracting business and his work as head of the retail merchants, and letters from mayors and business executives and other well-known people congratulating him on his achievements. There were also news stories about his having been taken sick, and how he was rapidly recuperating, and would soon be back on the job, along with numerous letters from business people and others wishing him a speedy recovery. Then one story, under a small headline, reported the sale of his store. After that the clippings all had to do with his garden, and letters to the editor about various things.

He was sick for two years, and we lived for much of the time in Richmond. I could not remember him very well from that time. My mother was away at the hospital every day. Once he was supposed to be getting better, and was in bed at home, and he promised that when he was completely well we would take an automobile trip all the way out west to Chicago. But he soon became very ill again, and I was not allowed to go into his bedroom at all, though I could hear him groaning. Then he was taken back to the hospital, and was away for a long time. My aunts and uncles had come to visit us, my Uncle Ben flying all the way from the West Coast. I found out several years later that my father had been near death. But gradually he recovered and finally he was well enough so that we could move back to Charleston, though for a long time he had to wear a bandage around his head, and his business was sold. After two years of living downtown in a second-story flat, we built our own house on Versailles Street, across from Mr. Herbert Simons' house, on an acre of land overlooking the river. He grew fruit trees and worked in his rose garden, which was located inside and around a horseshoe driveway. He had hundreds of rosebushes, on trellises and along the ground, and in the spring and summer, motorists would come up Versailles Street on Sunday afternoon and drive around the horseshoe to view the roses in bloom.

★

Tuesday afternoon our newspaper staff held its weekly meeting. Instead of riding the bus all the way home for afternoon dinner and then having to go back downtown I went to eat with my Aunt Ellen. She was a secretary at a legal firm on Broad Street, and as with all the offices on Broad Street and many others in the city, it was the custom to go home in the early afternoon for dinner. My aunt was unmarried and lived in an apartment at the Warwick, on Colonial Lake. It was said that she knew everyone on Broad Street. When she was late for the Belt Line bus in the morning, the driver would often wait for her at the corner outside the Warwick.

Sometimes it was necessary to clear off a stack of newspapers in order to sit down at the dinette table, for my aunt saved the local papers to read at her leisure, and they tended to accumulate. She always read "Little Miss Muffit," a comic strip in the *Evening Post*, but whenever Miss Muffit's adventures grew too menacing, my aunt would save the newspapers and ask her friend Mrs. Bready, who owned the Warwick, to let her know when the particular adventure was safely concluded, so that she could go back and read all the strips through to the happy conclusion.

"I saw your friend Mr. Legaré on Broad Street yesterday afternoon," she informed me when I arrived at her apartment. "He thinks very highly of you. He says you're a fine writer and you've always been the most dependable member of the staff ever since you were a freshman."

"That's nice." I thought of the centennial story, due in two days and still unwritten.

"He said you had a fine time at the press convention, and that you and some of the others on the staff went to a dance. Now sit down and tell me all about it."

I was in agony. Mr. Legaré had not been at the convention, so someone must have told him about the dance, and probably about the two girls from Greenville. That could only have been Paul Munro and Fred Ellison.

"I stayed with Cousin Sophie," I said, hoping to get my aunt onto the subject of the family. I asked questions about the days when my aunt and my father and my uncles and my other aunt, Marian, had grown up in Charleston along with the Schwartzmanns. I had asked such questions before and had seldom got much actual information. My Aunt Ellen was the eldest in the family, older than my uncles and my other aunt and my father. It was not so much that she was reluctant to talk about the past, as that her mind ran to current generalities, and apparently she did not recall much about the earlier days. She had no memory for incidents or for details.

I knew that my grandparents on my father's side had died long before I was born. I knew that they had been poor and that they had been ill for some time before they died, and that none of the boys and only the younger sister had gone to school beyond the seventh grade. All the others had been forced to go to work.

Sometimes I tried to imagine my father as he was at that time, as a boy my age. I knew how he looked when he was a little older; there were snapshots. But I could not conceive of him or of my uncles as ever having been young, in the way that I was. It seemed to me that there must have been a severity to their early lives that left no room for that.

"Were you-all very poor?" I asked my Aunt Ellen.

"Oh yes," she said, "But we had a good time."

At the newspaper staff meeting Charles Minot Legaré remarked, in reference to the press convention, "I understand Munro and Kohn made a big social occasion out of it." He had a long, sallow face and blue eyes, and a way of looking mockingly grave when amused.

Everyone laughed.

"Who told you about that?" Paul Munro asked, grinning.

"I have my sources," Mr. Legaré said. "Tsss-tsss-tsss!" His way of laughing resembled hissing.

"Ellison too!" one of the other staff members said.

"Is that right, Ellison?" Mr. Legaré asked, continuing to look preternaturally grave.

"No comment," Fred Ellison replied. Everyone laughed; Fred had a reputation as a ladies' man.

"Let's get down to business," Mr. Legaré declared after a moment. "Tsss-tsss-tsss!"

The staff meeting proceeded in routine fashion, the agenda consisting mostly of late developments with the centennial edition. But then, in reference to something involving distribution of the edition after it was printed, someone remarked that he would talk with the principal about the matter later in the week, whereupon Mr. Legaré replied, "You'll have to wait till Monday. He went off to Atlanta this morning for the rest of the week."

I was stunned. Mr. Strohmeier had told me to come by on Wednesday. Now he had gone out of town and would not be back until five days after my story was due! I had been betrayed.

I sat through the rest of the meeting wondering whether I dared go up to Mr. Legaré afterward and reveal my failure. When the meeting concluded I went over to his desk. He was talking with the two senior editors, and I waited, but the conversation continued, and after a few minutes I lost my resolve and left. I went out the front gate, crossed Rutledge Avenue, and waited for a bus to come along. After a little while I saw Mr. Legaré come out of the gate himself, and walk off downtown. "The most reliable member of the staff"—I had betrayed his confidence in me.

A grey-black Packard pulled to a stop, and the driver beckoned to me. It was our neighbor, Mr. Cartwright. I climbed in and we drove off.

"You're running late today," he said. "Did you get kept in after school?"

"No, sir. I was at a newspaper staff meeting."

"Are you all ready for the centennial program?" he asked.

"Yes, sir." Mr. Cartwright was a member of the city school board.

"We've got a very impressive program lined up," he declared. "Have you heard about it?"

I explained that I had been waiting to get the program from the principal, who was out of town.

"I might be able to help you with that," Mr. Cartwright declared.

When we arrived at his home on Peachtree Street, he took me inside, searched through some papers on a desk, and handed me a sheet of paper. Typed out on Charleston High School stationery was a carbon list of the events scheduled for the centennial observance, and underneath it Mr. Strohmeier's signature.

My father was on jury duty that week. It was unusual not to see him in the yard, because ordinarily he was always about in the afternoons. He went downtown only on Friday mornings, and returned in time to take his afternoon nap. A few minutes after I arrived home he drove up and came in dressed in hat, coat, and tie, after a day of activity downtown.

At supper he told about the case that the jury had been hearing, and why it had reached the verdict it did. He was more than ordinarily talkative. He had served as foreman of the jury. The attorney for the winning side was Mr. J. H. Short, a former state senator and a prominent realtor and developer, who was the son-in-law of one of my father's friends.

I went upstairs to my room after supper and began writing my story. I saw that I could have gotten it much earlier if I had been willing to keep after Mr. Strohmeier, because the letter that Mr. Cartwright had lent to me was dated over a month ago. I had had a narrow escape.

Our telephone was in the hallway at the foot of the stairs, and a little later as I came down the steps I saw my father in conversation. "Oh, yes," he was saying, "that was what we were worried about." And after a pause, "Yes, that was it. I just thought you would like to know," and again, "Yes, that was the point that we were worried about. I thought you'd like to know that."

I walked past him and went into the kitchen. He was obviously talking to Mr. J. H. Short. He must have telephoned Mr. Short, since I had not heard the phone ring. I made a sandwich and went into the living room, where my mother was reading a magazine. After a minute my father came in.

"Are you supposed to tell Mr. Short what went on in the jury room?" I asked.

"There's nothing wrong with it," my father said. "He was very interested to find out what we were concerned with." He had not been able to let the matter rest. He could not resist calling Mr. Short about what had happened. "I just thought you would like to know," and "I thought you'd like to know that."

I finished writing the story. It seemed wooden and unimaginative, but I could not think of anything that would make it more interesting. At least it gave the facts.

When my sister and I left for school in the morning, my father was once again in his old gardening clothes. His brief spate of jury duty was done.

★

After my first class of the morning was over, I hurried to Mr. Legaré's classroom and handed in my story about the centennial celebration. "I was worried about you, Kohn," he told me. "This is about the first time I can remember that you've ever been late with a story."

"I'm not late," I said. "It's not due till tomorrow."

"That's late for you," he insisted. "You always get them in early." In any event the story was now in his hands, and I had, however narrowly, averted disaster.

Shortly before the lunch recess, while I was in my homeroom session, the interoffice telephone rang, and my homeroom teacher, Mr. Gene Teaberry, went over to the wall to answer it. "Kohn, Mr. Legaré wants to see you during recess," he reported.

When the bell rang I hurried down the first-floor corridor to Mr. Legaré's classroom. His own homeroom students were trooping out, and when the doorway was cleared I entered.

"Sit down," Mr Legaré said, motioning me to a desk. "When did you get the information for this story?"

"Yesterday."

"Yesterday? Did Mr. Strohmeier give it to you?"

"No, sir. He's out of town. What's wrong?"

"Then who'd you get it from?" he demanded, ignoring my question.

"Mr. William Cartwright. He had a letter from Mr. Strohmeier with all the information in it. What's wrong?" I asked again.

"Its *all* wrong, that's what. It was changed over three weeks ago."

"Oh."

"Why didn't you get it from Mr. Strohmeier?"

"I tried to see him several times," I said, "but he wouldn't talk to me."

45

"What do you mean, you *tried*?" Mr. Legaré was very angry. "What do you think your uncle would do if he told one of his reporters to get an important story, and the reporter came back and said he tried to get it but couldn't?"

"I don't know. I—guess he wouldn't like it."

"Wouldn't *like it*?" Mr. Legaré declared. "I'll tell you what he'd do. He'd fire the reporter right there on the spot. That's what. Which is what I ought to do with you."

"I'm sorry."

"What in the name of the Lord is wrong with you?" he asked.

"I don't know, sir." I was doing my best to keep from crying.

"Well, I don't know, either. But I'll tell you this. You go upstairs to the office, and you see Miss Campbell and tell her you've got to have the revised program. And you copy it down, accurately, and go home after school and rewrite this story until it's correct, and turn it in the first thing in the morning, without fail."

"Yes, sir."

"Is that clear?"

"Yes, sir."

I raced up the second-floor stairway to the principal's office, thoroughly frightened, and accosted Miss Campbell. At first she was reluctant to give me the information I wanted, but when I told her that Mr. Legaré had instructed me to ask for it, she produced a copy of the centennial program. I wrote down all the information. Several of the speakers had been changed from those listed in the letter Mr. Cartwright had loaned to me, and there were other changes.

When school was done I went straight home on the bus and, after barely picking at my meal, hurried upstairs to my typewriter and rewrote the story completely. I went over it again and again, made adjustments and revisions in phraseology, then copied it once more. Then I went downstairs, telephoned Mr. Legaré at his home, told him the story was ready, and offered to bring it down to him without delay. "No," he said, "just let me have it first thing tomorrow."

For want of anything else to do, I walked out of the house, past my father, who was at work on a rose trellis, and past the Rittenhouses' and the Cartwrights' on out to the woods. I made my way to the edge of the bank and climbed up into my perch in the oak tree. For a while I watched the marshland. Just up the way were several long-legged herons poking about along the shoreline. The tide was out, and the gray-black mud, with its little streaks and curls of rainbow-hued oil, gave off a sporadic popping and cracking as the decaying organic matter under the mud surface emitted gases. It was hot and still in the afternoon sun. On the stalks of reed grass I could see tiny white snails climbing, ever so slowly. At a snail's pace, I thought. Just like the Boll Weevil.

When I turned in the revised story to Mr. Legaré at school the next morning, he read through it. "That's more like it," he said. "Why didn't you do this the first time?"

"I don't know, sir."

"What *do* you know?"

"Not very much, sir."

"All right, then, get on out of here, and try to behave yourself. Tsss-tsss-tsss!"

He seemed to think it was funny.

5.

It turned out that, after all the preparation, there was no centennial celebration. Two weeks before it was to have taken place and after the special edition of the newspaper had been printed and distributed, there was an outbreak of polio in the city. The school term was cut short, only a brief graduation ceremony was held, and all public gatherings of persons under eighteen were prohibited.

Even though I was only a junior I was supposed to attend the graduation ceremony, because special 100th-Anniversary pins were being awarded to all those who had worked on the centennial edition. I did not go to it. I felt that I had not earned my pin. The next day Mr. Legaré telephoned and wanted to know why I had not been there. I gave him an excuse about having had to do something else. Whether he suspected the real reason I did not know, but he said he would keep the pin for me and I could get it in the fall. "Have a good summer," he told me, "and try to stay out of mischief."

The morning following the last day of classes I went out to my perch and contemplated the long stretch of time that lay ahead. The epidemic of polio had ended all talk of my getting a job as an usher at the movies. Teen-agers were prohibited from attending theaters for the next three weeks. My mother grumbled at the prospect of my lying about the house all summer long without doing anything to earn money, but that was all.

It was fortunate that I had no job, for I seemed to be without any energy, and not so much physically tired as overcome by a vast lassitude. It seemed an effort to do anything, even to think. I slept until the middle of the morning every day, and sometimes took a nap in the late afternoon as well. I lounged about the house, in my room, on the porch, sometimes out in the woods in the oak tree, and did little except read. At our baseball practices I went through the motions, but that was all. Time seemed of no consequence. After dinner sometimes—during the summer months we had lunch during the day and dinner in the evening—Tommy Rittenhouse and I walked down to the Hampton Park Pharmacy and sat around talking with some of our baseball friends. Usually I stayed up late to hear a sports broadcast over Station WHAS in Louisville, Kentucky, called "George Walsh Looks Them Over," which was followed by an hour of classical music. The theme music for the concert was the overture to "The Marriage of Figaro," and I liked to lie on my bed in the darkness, with the windows open and the wind blowing lightly through the water oaks on Mr. Simons' property, and listen to the opening notes fill the room.

At some time in the early morning hours, too, usually about one o'clock, a Seaboard freight train would drift into the city from the west. I could hear the whistle sounding far off across the river and then follow its progress as it came nearer, until the wheels set up a droning reverberation as it rolled onto the trestle and came rumbling into the city, past The Citadel campus and Hampton Park, clanking across the grade crossing at Rutledge and Grove a mile away, and then disappearing, its separate sounds gradually dying out. Or I might hear the faint thumping of the make-and-break engine of a launch that came down the river each night, taking a long time to pass on downstream. For the most part the trees effectively screened off any view of the river, but sometimes if I watched patiently I could catch a brief glimpse of the pinprick of light that marked the launch's presence out in the darkness. Usually I fell asleep before it drew out of earshot.

During all this time my mother seemed to be more anxious than ever before. If I failed to pick up my room to her satisfaction, or if my sister was tardy in any of her assigned duties, she became angry, and persisted in her anger long after she had made her point. Our maid of many years had quit the previous fall, and had been followed by a succession of replacements, none of whom had lasted very long. My father urged my mother to ease up in her supervision, and let the maids perform the household chores in their own way. "What's the point of paying a maid if you have to do everything yourself?" he asked. My mother agreed but did not change her ways. "They're so unreliable," she said. "You have to watch them every minute." For the last several months we had had no maid at all.

Several times when I did something to my mother's dissatisfaction, or else failed to do something right away that she wanted done, she became furious, and rebuked me at length for my laziness.

"You're a drone," she said one day when I came home a little late

49

from baseball practice. "You play around all day, not doing a thing useful."

"I don't have anything to do."

"You don't *want* anything to do! You're lazy. Every time I see you, you're either sleeping or reading or playing baseball. You're not good for a thing."

"Just as soon as I finish high school," I said, "I'll get a job. I'll leave town, too, and you won't see me again!" I would go to Savannah or Richmond or somewhere—anywhere would do, to get away from the constant scolding.

"Some job you'll get!" she replied. "You'd be back in two weeks once you had to work for a living. You don't know what real work is."

"I don't care," I said. "I'll get something I can do."

The argument disturbed me. It was vacation time. What was wrong with playing baseball? Why did I always have to be showing initiative? I toyed with the idea of leaving home now, riding the Boll Weevil down to Savannah and finding a job. Although she seemed more anxious than ever before, she had long been critical of my failure to be thrifty and to earn money. Once when I was twelve years old I had gone downtown with my father on a Friday morning during the summer, and on the way home we had stopped at a hardware store, which also sold sporting goods. On display in the window was a left-handed baseball glove, to be worn on the right hand. For several years I had wanted a real left-handed glove. The gloves on sale at the five-and-ten-cent stores, the only ones I could afford, were made for right-handed players only. The glove in the store window was priced at $1.25, far cheaper than any other I had ever seen. I only had a quarter, but I persuaded my father to advance me the additional dollar.

I was thrilled with the glove. "Now you better not show it to your mother until you've paid for it," my father advised me. But I could not resist. At lunchtime, I brought it to the table in its box and placed it under my chair, and a little later, unable to restrain myself, I took it out and looked at it.

My mother was furious. She confiscated it at once, hid it away, and would not let me have it until I had done some work around the yard to pay back the dollar my father had advanced me.

This summer promised to be much worse than ever in the past. I wondered whether every time I came home from baseball practice or a game I was going to be reminded of my wickedness in playing baseball instead of finding a job. It seemed to me that the very notion of my baseball activity made her angry. My first-base mitt must have exemplified for her everything that was unsatisfactory with me, which was a great deal.

After lunch my father came up to my room. "I want you to stop getting your mother upset," he declared. "She has a hard enough time as it is with no maid, without you adding to it."

"I didn't do anything to upset her," I insisted. "She keeps getting on me because she says I'm lazy. What am I supposed to do, go out and run around the block?"

"Don't be a smart aleck. You have no right to argue with her. Your mother's got a lot of work to do around the house, and she can't get decent help. Now show some consideration, and don't make trouble for her."

"But I haven't been making trouble."

"Yes you have. Now I want you to stop it."

There was no use attempting to present my side, because my father would not countenance any dissent from my mother's opinion, whatever it was. He and my mother never disputed between themselves, never seemed to become vexed with one another. It was my father's frequent boast that they had "been married seventeen years, and never a quarrel."

We never did things together as a family, never went on trips or vacations together like the Rittenhouses and other families did. Sometimes in the summer my sister and I might go off to spend a week or two with our cousins in Richmond or Atlanta, but my parents never came along. Indeed, at such times my father would declare pointedly that having us away constituted his and my mother's vacation. Nor did he and I ever do anything together. When occasionally he played golf now, I was not invited to go along. Once I suggested that he play golf with me, but he dismissed the notion as if it were unthinkable.

Not that he ever did anything such as play golf except on rare occasions. What concerned him most of the time, occupied almost his entire waking attention, was the yard. He was at work on it every morning and, after his nap, for the balance of the afternoon. My mother had her flower garden along the front of the porch, and throughout the day they often consulted with one another and exchanged views on their joint enterprise. Neither my sister nor I was encouraged to become involved. It was their project.

The girl that I had seen with Paul Munro on the bus, Janice Bryan, lived two blocks up the street from us. She was in my sister's class in high school, and I had known her for several years. She was small, dark-haired, attractive, and a good tennis player who sometimes competed in tournaments. One afternoon, several weeks after school had closed, my sister proposed that Tommy Rittenhouse and I go over to the public tennis courts at Johnson Hagood Stadium with her and Janice and play tennis. I knew that what my sister wanted was to be with Tommy, but I wanted to see Janice Bryan again, too. So I telephoned Tommy and a little later we rode our bicycles over to the courts. I was paired with Janice, and we played several sets of doubles. I was not very good at tennis, but Janice more than made up for my deficiencies; she had a good backhand and a steady forehand, and much to Tommy's exasperation we won both sets.

She was dressed in a tennis outfit, with a white skirt and a green blouse, and as she scampered about the court stroking low returns across the net I admired her firm, suntanned legs and arms. Underneath her blouse her breasts, though not large, were clearly visible. She was a lively conversationalist, and she laughed a lot. Afterwards we stopped in at her house for lemonade and cookies. At one point, when I was deprecating my lack of expertise with a tennis racket, she offered to work with me on my game. That night I lay in my bed and thought of how pleasant it would be to go out to the courts with her, and afterwards to stop by the drugstore for a coke.

The next afternoon, after much trepidation, I telephoned her and asked her to play tennis. She had an engagement to play downtown that afternoon, she said, but would be happy to go the next day. So the following afternoon we bicycled over to the stadium. We rallied for a while, and she told me that I was positioning my feet so that I could not get my weight behind the swing. She made me take up a position with my right foot forward, and stood behind me and guided my left arm as I swung through the stroke. Having her lean against my back as she directed my arm was disconcerting. Next we worked on my backhand, which was very awkward. I found it difficult to pivot with my left leg across my body toward the ball, and then bring my swing through while keeping my arm extended. Watching Janice perform the move so smoothly and expertly—she was right-handed—was impressive; she seemed very competent and sure of herself.

While we were working on my serve, Fred Ellison and another boy I knew at school came onto the courts. Janice seemed to know Fred. As they stood watching us I felt self-conscious, not so much because I was so awkward as that I was out on the court with Janice. At length Fred proposed that we play some doubles. Janice turned to me. "Do you want to take them on?" she asked.

"Sure," I said, "but I won't be much help."

Not only did I enjoy the competition, but I felt privileged to be teamed up with Janice. Seeing her there at my side, in her tennis outfit, her slim, firm legs and arms braced for action, her small round breasts contoured by her blouse, her somewhat sharp features intent as she waited for the serve to come, and with a few beads of perspiration lightly visible on her forehead under her ribboned black hair, she seemed clean and attractive.

We played two sets, and on the way home Janice and I stopped in at the Hampton Park Pharmacy for something to drink. As we sat at a table, watching the frosted glass mugs of root beer make rings on the shiny table top each time we moved them, I thought proudly that this was actually a date that I was on, with a girl I liked, even though it was daytime and not evening, and we had gone to the tennis courts and not to a movie.

In the course of our conversation I manged to mention Paul Munro. "We saw you on the bus the other night," Janice said. "When was it, about a month ago? You got on at Calhoun Street, didn't you?"

I was surprised that she remembered. "Yes, I was coming home from my uncle's."

"You seemed very preoccupied, and wouldn't talk to us," she said. "We wondered why you didn't get off at Versailles Street and walk home with us."

Embarrassed, I said I almost always got off at Peachtree Street instead of Versailles, though since her home faced Versailles she must often have seen me walking past. If she noticed my discomfort, however, she gave no sign, and we talked for a while.

The fact that it was I who usually compiled and wrote the gossip column in the school newspaper appeared to impress her. I suspected that, because that column consisted of rumors and allusions about the social exploits of the older members of the student body, she thought of me as being considerably more of an authority on such matters than I actually was. It occurred to me, with some pleasure, that if school were now in session and I were compiling a column, Fred Ellison, as a member of the staff, would doubtless suggest an item to the effect that "Omar Kohn has been taking some tennis lessons lately. Nothing like some close instruction from Coach J. B., eh Scoop?"

Later, I thought about the way she had referred to my encounter with her and Paul on the bus. She had remembered precisely where I got on the bus and how I had acted. She had also expressed surprise, both her own and Paul's, that I had not walked home with them, or talked with them on the way uptown. And I had been so afraid of intruding! Still, I rather liked the image of myself as aloof, too wrapped up in my own profound meditation to have the time or the wish to talk with others.

Then I recollected my clumsy blunder with Paul and Fred Ellison and the two girls from Greenville at the dance in Columbia, just a couple of days after that encounter. Whatever Paul may have thought at the time, he had since found out that it was timidity and inexperience, not impenetrable aloofness, that explained my behavior.

Or was Janice only being flattering? Wasn't it more likely that instead of wondering why I had refused to walk home with them she and Paul had been amused at my shyness and made merry over my precipitous flight from the bus? Indeed, hadn't Paul probably long since told her about what happened at the dance in Columbia, and they had both had a fine time laughing about it?

The thought was so acutely painful that I kicked my tennis racket, which lay on the floor in our living room. The racket shot across the rug, slammed into the coffee table, and the impact sent a china ashtray flying to the floor, where it smashed. Just as I hastily got up to retrieve the pieces, my mother, who had been preparing dinner in the kitchen, came into the room to see what was happening.

"I broke it," I declared. "I'm sorry."

"You ought to know better than to swing your tennis racket around in the living room!" she declared.

"I wasn't swinging it. I kicked it accidentally with my foot, and it hit the table."

"I don't care what you were doing. You had no right doing it in the living room!"

"I'm sorry," I said again.

"You're always sorry. You do all sorts of terrible things and then you're sorry. Now get all the pieces picked up and throw them in the trash basket, and take your tennis racket out of the living room."

I collected all the fragments that I could find, deposited them in the waste basket, and went upstairs. As I was leaving my mother said, "You're the most irresponsible child I've ever known."

By the next day I had decided that my gloomy suspicions of the day before were unjustified. I knew perfectly well that Paul Munro wasn't the kind of friend who would laugh at me behind my back. It was a way I had of always going over everything in my mind and coming up with the worst possible interpretation. Other people could simply do things and go out with friends and enjoy themselves, without having to dwell upon them over and over. Why couldn't I do the same?

Friday afternoon our team played its first Neighborhood League game. Tommy Rittenhouse pitched. His curveball was working all right, and though he gave up quite a few hits, we hung on to win. I got one single and scored a run, but I did not play particularly well. On one occasion, with a runner at second base and two out, our shortstop, Dave Gregg, made a throw to me at first base that was a little wild, and I let it get through me. It went all the way to the bench, and the runner scored from second. Although it was not a good throw, I should have had it. Mr. Rittenhouse said nothing about it.

When Tommy was pitching, Mr. Rittenhouse stood alongside the end of our bench closest to home plate, and whenever the umpire called a ball on a close pitch he complained. Most of the time he did not address the umpire directly; instead he called out to Tommy,

"Don't worry about it, Tommy, just keep throwing them exactly like that." The umpire knew what Mr. Rittenhouse meant.

Actually Tommy was not our best pitcher. Junie Fox, a tall right-hander, was sometimes a little wild, but he could throw a fastball that rose, and he had a fine curve. Usually Mr. Rittenhouse played Junie in left field, however, saying that he needed Junie's swiftness out there. Junie was in fact a very good outfielder; there was no doubt of that. He was our best hitter, and batted cleanup.

Occasionally some of the boys on the team complained to me about things that Mr. Rittenhouse did. They seemed to feel that since I was still nominally the team captain and had been the one who had proposed that we let him serve as our coach, I was responsible for him. There was nothing I could do, for now that Mr. Rittenhouse had taken over he never consulted with me or treated me any differently from the others on the team. My sole duty as captain was to go over the ground rules before the game.

After the game Mr. Rittenhouse took us over to Hampton Park Pharmacy and bought root beer for everyone. While we were seated at the tables drinking them, the two umpires came in.

"Come have a root beer with us!" Mr. Rittenhouse called to them.

"No, thanks," one of the umpires replied.

"It's going to take more than a nickel root beer, Coach," Johnny Harriman remarked under his breath.

6.

The Saturday night poker game, in which my father and my Uncle Edward and Mr. Rittenhouse played, was held in a basement room of our house, which my father had built principally for that purpose. Long before time to begin, on Saturday afternoon, my father prepared the room for the occasion, counting out the chips and setting them in orderly stacks, arranging ashtrays, drawing up chairs around the circular table, and placing several electric fans so that they would function to maximum advantage. He kept detailed records of each week's play, noting the winnings and losings of each player in a notebook, keeping the individual totals, how often each player had won and lost, what his average performance was for the year, and so on. Before the game he typed his statistics on a sheet of paper and circulated it around the table. Most of the others only glanced through it, but it was very important to my father. I felt that the records were more important to him than the game itself. He was not really much of a gambler. He had a pair of dice in his bureau, but I had never known him to use them.

Mr. Rittenhouse was apparently a consistent winner, and on Sundays after the game, once my father had totaled the previous evening's figures and made his deductions, he would sometimes telephone some of the others and deplore the regularity with which Mr. Rittenhouse took money home. Unlike the other players, he declared, Mr. Rittenhouse played poker only to win, and was willing to sit by and turn over hand after hand until he drew good betting cards. Not a great deal of money was involved, since the game had an arrangement whereby nobody could lose more than four dollars in one evening, but Mr. Rittenhouse's frequent winning irked my father. Several times I heard him talking with Mr. Simons and my Uncle Edward about it. I had the feeling that neither of them thought it was important, for they merely nodded.

The game had been going on each Saturday night for many years—since before the World War, my father said. The participants began arriving shortly before eight o'clock. My Uncle Edward usually came with Mr. Joe Lehman, in his car. Mr. Edgar Fleishman usually brought Mr. Rudy Moose and Mr. Ray Lowell, the editor of the *Evening Post*. Mr. Lowell was a rotund, jolly man who was fond of my sister, and on St. Valentine's Day and at Christmas brought her boxes of Whitman's Sampler candy, which she hoarded for weeks. Mr. Rittenhouse walked over from his house, bringing the new decks of Bicycle playing cards.

One night I watched them playing for a while. It was a hot night, and the room was soon filled with smoke from the cigars, cigarettes, and pipes. The players had odd mannerisms. Mr. Lowell always announced his actions in Indian talk: "Me checkum," he would say. Mr. Simons kept his chips in front of him, and whenever he took a pot he would pick up two chips edgewise and tap them on two others in imitation of a horse's hoofbeats, calling out "Last Card Simons rides again!" Mr. Rittenhouse was very affable and friendly before the play started, but after that he watched the board intently, and seldom indulged in jokes or conversation of any kind.

The games they played were strange. I had persuaded my father to teach me the basic poker hands and could recognize five-card and seven-card stud and draw poker, but they almost never played these. Instead they preferred such games as "baseball," "lowball," "spit-in-the-ocean," "scarlet fever," "Barbara Hutton," and "Dr. Pepper" (tens, twos and fours were wild). The seriousness with which Mr. Rittenhouse in particular took the game reminded me a little of Paul Munro covering a sports event—how, unlike myself, he observed everything intently, professionally, with his entire attention focused upon the play, as if it were the only thing of any importance going on in the world. My father, by contrast, was constantly looking here and there, jumping up between hands to see whether the windows were open in the back of the basement, emptying ashtrays, adjusting the direction of fans, and making conversation. My Uncle Edward seemed detached and lost in thought, but he was always quick to make his bets and his calls, and occasionally had amusing comments to make, usually to Mr. Simons, who played the game with high glee and a running string of commentary.

After a while I went on up to the living room, where my mother was reading. It occurred to me that the Saturday night poker game was one of the very few of my father's activities in which she did not participate. I asked her why it was that my father went to so much trouble to keep records of winnings and losses by everybody.

"He likes to do it," she said.

"Does Daddy want Mr. Rittenhouse to get out of the game because he always wins?"

"Why do you ask that?"

"He keeps talking about it all the time. I heard him telling Mr. Simons about it again this morning."

"You shouldn't eavesdrop on your father," she declared. "And besides, it's none of your business. Just don't worry about it." But since Mr. Rittenhouse was our baseball coach, and Tommy was my friend, in a way it was my business.

Sunday evening I was listening to my radio when Tommy came walking into my room to see whether I wanted to play jar-top baseball out under the streetlight.

We had a game in which we used jar-tops and sawed-off broom handles. Once the jar-tops had been hit a few times and had acquired dents and tucks, they could be made to curve and dip in very irregular fashion, which made them difficult to hit. The trick was not to swing hard from the shoulders as with a baseball bat, but to punch at them with the wrists. What we did was to play nine-inning games, using the rosters of the various major league teams. I had the Giants, Indians, and Cardinals, and Tommy took the Dodgers, Yankees, and Red Sox.

We went down to the basement, collected a supply of jar-tops, and walked out to Versailles Street. There was almost no traffic at the foot of the street, which was unpaved. As we played, occasionally I looked up toward Janice Bryan's house, several blocks away, and wondered whether she was out on a date. When cars came along I watched to see whether they would stop at her house. But it was already well after nine, and if she were out on a date she would have left much earlier.

After we finished our game and were sitting down on the curb talking, Tommy proposed that we go out to Devereaux Woods. What Tommy liked to do was to walk out in the woods in the darkness, creep up close to a parked car, and try to hear what was going on. The previous summer we had gone out there at night quite a few times.

We walked past his house and through the Cartwrights' yard, and followed along the road through the fields. The woods loomed

ahead, the shapes of trees faintly discernible in the darkness. Fire-
flies were blinking here and there. We talked in low voices.

"I don't see any cars," I said as we entered the woods.

"There's one parked up ahead," Tommy whispered.

I looked, but could see nothing in the dark. Then the orange
sparks of a cigarette, discarded from an automobile, struck the
ground up ahead, and I could now make out the silhouette of a Ford
automobile.

"Come on," Tommy whispered. We stepped off the road into the
thicket, and, moving carefully, circled around toward the car. When
we drew closer to it we dropped to our hands and knees and crawled,
until at length we were no more than twenty feet away.

I could hear the sound of a radio playing faintly, and the occasional
low murmur of conversation, and then the radio switched off, and all
was silent. Off in the woods crickets were singing. An automobile
horn sounded, far off toward town.

I wanted to leave. I felt that I was an intruder, that it was demean-
ing and wrong to be doing what we were doing. In the past I had felt
no such thing, but now I was uncomfortable being where we were.

"Come on, let's go," I whispered.

"Shhhh!" Tommy said. "Wait."

We heard more murmuring, a man's voice, then a girl's. After a
minute, the girl's voice said, "No." Tommy nudged me with his
elbow. I listened, the pit of my stomach constricted. I could feel my
scrotum tightening. There came a low moan from the car. Then silence for a long time. Then the radio cut on again.

I had heard more than enough. I crept away through the underbrush, and when I was some distance from the car, I got to my feet. I
picked my way back through the thicket toward the road. When I
regained it, I waited, and after a minute I heard the bushes rustling
as Tommy made his way out. He emerged from the thicket.

"Why are you going back?" he asked.

"It's getting late," I said. "I don't want to stay any more."

"It's not much after ten. There'll be other cars coming out here
before very long. Let's hang around."

"I don't want to," I said. "I'm going. You can stay if you want."

"All right, then, let's go." We set out toward home.

"That was something," Tommy said. "Did you hear them?"

"Yeah." I felt angry with myself for having heard.

"He must have been giving it to her good," Tommy said.

I left Tommy at his house and went on into our yard, and up the front steps into the house. The lights were off in the living room. My parents had gone to bed. I walked upstairs to my room and lay in the darkness, thinking of the moan I had heard, and feeling both sick in my chest and thrilled at the same time.

7.

When I awoke on Monday morning it was after eleven. I had stayed up long past midnight listening to a concert on a Chicago radio station, and then read for a while before I fell asleep. I went downstairs and fixed some breakfast. Instead of dressing right away, I decided to go back to my room and play my baseball game. I worked it with dice, and kept box scores in a ledger that I had bought from Woolworth's. Each summer I played a 154-game season and kept batting and pitching records for all the players. While I was playing, my mother came into the room. "You haven't made your bed," she said.

"I just got up a little while ago," I told her. "I'll do it in a few minutes, as soon as I finish this inning."

"All you do is sleep and lounge around. You haven't done a bit of work since school ended."

"There isn't anything that I have to do."

"Then you ought to get a job."

She had not brought the subject up for over a week. I did not want to get involved in another argument, so I said nothing, and resumed my game.

"The least you could do is make up your bed in the morning," she said after a moment.

"I'll do it in a little while. I've just got one more out."

"A little while!" my mother began shouting. "A little while! That's all you ever say! A little while!"

Startled, I turned around. My mother was waving her hands, and her face was flushed.

"What's the matter?" I asked.

"A little while! A little while!" She began trying to hit me. "You're awful! A little while!"

She was shrieking at me. I grabbed at her arms. She kept trying to kick me and hit me.

I shouted for my father. "Daddy!" My mother was wailing, in a low moan like a little girl's, and trying to kick and hit at me. Her eyes were wide open and blazing. "Daddy!" I shouted. "Come quick!"

The front screen door slammed and my father came racing up the steps. He ran into the room, pulled my mother away from me, and held her. "There, now!" he said. "Take it easy, Jim, just take it easy."

I ran into the bathroom and locked the door. I was frightened. I could hear my mother, wailing in a low monotone. What had happened? What had I done? My heart was pounding in my throat, my teeth were chattering, I was sobbing. My mother was going insane.

Beyond the locked door, in my room, I could hear my mother, and my father attempting to calm her down. "There, there!" He kept repeating. "It's all right."

Now my sister came up the stairs. "What's wrong?" she asked.

"Your mother's just upset at Omar," my father told her. "Now go on back downstairs."

He continued to talk in low tones to my mother. I did not know what to do. The inside of my chest felt tight and constricted, and waves of cold tremors ran through me. Something I had said had caused my mother to turn on me like a madwoman. I had driven her insane. I stood behind the locked door, trembling.

My father kept talking to my mother in a low voice, and I could hear mother murmuring something, but I could not make out the words. She had stopped wailing.

After a while my father called to me. "Come on out now," he said. I started to unlock the door, then drew my hand back. It was shaking. I was afraid that if I went out and she saw me she would begin shrieking once again.

"Come out!" my father ordered.

Fumbling at the lock, I opened the door and stepped hesitantly out. My mother was seated on the bed, with my father next to her, his arm around her shoulders. She looked very small and weak. When she had been trying to hit and kick at me, her blows had had almost no force at all. Now she had my father's handkerchief in one hand, and was sitting upright and still, almost like a statue.

"I'm sorry." It was all I could think to say. "I didn't do anything."

"It was your fault," my father said. "Now come kiss your mother and ask her pardon."

I came up very uneasily and kissed her on the forehead. "I'm sorry,' I said again. "I didn't mean to upset you."

She nodded.

"Your mother's been working too hard, and her nerves are on edge," my father said. He turned to her. "Come on now, let's go downstairs and rest."

They left the room, my father with his arm still around my mother's shoulder. I listened to them go down the stairs. I made my bed and dressed, and tried to figure out what had happened. After a few minutes my sister came upstairs. "What did you say to her?" she asked. "What happened?"

I described what happened. "I guess she was mad because I didn't get up right that instant and make the bed."

"She got mad at me this morning," my sister said, "just because I put off doing the breakfast dishes for a few minutes to talk to Libbie McKinley on the phone."

"What's wrong with her?" I asked. "Is she having a nervous breakdown?"

"I think maybe she is," my sister replied.

I wondered whether she would have to be sent to a hospital.

My sister went back downstairs. If only I had made my bed, the whole thing would not have happened. At least my mother had stopped the wailing noise after my father had calmed her down. It was my doing. But how was I to know that it would upset her so much? Frequently I waited for an hour or more after breakfast to make my bed. But today it had upset her. My mother was having a nervous breakdown, and it was my doing, my fault.

I went downstairs. The door to my parents' bedroom was closed. I went out onto the front porch and sat down on the chaise lounge. It was a bright, hot day. Out in the river, beyond the marsh, a small boat was making its way upstream. I could hear the faint drone of an outboard motor. I watched it move slowly along, until it disappeared behind Mr. Simons' house.

My father had said it was my fault. I could not figure out what I had done. Whatever it was, it had been enough to cause a nervous breakdown.

That night my father drove my mother up to North Charleston and put her aboard a train for Richmond. She needed a rest, and was going to spend three weeks or more with my Uncle Charles and Aunt Maggie. Our family doctor had advised it, and my father had called Richmond and made the arrangements. In two days my Aunt

64

Marian, my father's youngest sister, would come from Augusta, Georgia, to stay with us while my mother was away.

I did not go up to the station with my parents. My father said it would be best if my sister and I stayed home, so as to cause the minimum of confusion. I kissed my mother goodbye before she left. Although she appeared tired and listless, she seemed to have recovered her equilibrium.

After they left for the station I went upstairs and began a baseball game, but could not keep my mind on it. Finally, I wrote "game called on account of rain" across the page on the ledger, and went back down to the living room. My sister had gone to a movie with some girl friends, and I was alone in the house. I looked at the newspaper, tried reading a book, and waited for my father to return.

He arrived home about 10:30. "Was the train on time?" I asked.

He nodded.

"Did she have a nervous breakdown?"

"Not exactly that."

"Is she going to be all right?"

"Yes, when she gets rested up," he said.

We sat in the living room for a while, my father reading the newspaper. I read an article in *Collier's*. He said nothing more about what had happened. A little later he went to bed. "Make sure the door's locked when Jean comes in," he told me. "I didn't get my nap today," he added.

I waited until my sister arrived, then locked the front door and went up to my room. I realized, as I lay in my bed reading a little later, that I was very tired, too. The day had been exhausting for me, even though I had slept till eleven. My eyelids were so heavy that I could not keep them open. I was too tired to change into my pajamas or even turn out the overhead light. I fell asleep without knowing that I was no longer awake, with my mind going off in a pattern that seemed to make sense and be logical.

Then I was dreaming that I got up and went downstairs to see whether the front door was properly locked, and I looked in to see why the light was on in my father's room. My father was sound asleep in his bed, turned away from where I stood looking. To my astonishment I saw that my mother had not gone away to Richmond after all, but was asleep in her bed, with her back toward me. I stepped back to leave the room, so as not to awaken her, but at that instant she began to turn over, and as the sheet that was covering her shifted, and her face, flushed, was turning toward me, and her eyes began to open very wide, I saw that she was wearing a kind of black gown. Suddenly I heard the telephone ringing, and I leaped back.

I was standing alongside my bed in my room, the overhead light was on, and I was still dressed in my clothes. It was long past midnight. I realized that I had fallen asleep. It was very hot, and I was perspiring profusely.

Had the telephone actually been ringing downstairs? I went down to listen. All was quiet. The door to my parents' bedroom was open, and it was dark inside. I could hear my father breathing steadily as he slept alone.

PART
TWO

It occurred to me once, when I was fifteen or sixteen, that all life might be afterlife—that we might all be dead. I recall that I mentioned it at a session of our Confirmation class at the Temple, to the bewilderment of Jack Marcussohn and Celia Furchgott. Dr. Raskin only smiled, however, and said, "I'm afraid you're not the first person ever to think of that." I have wondered sometimes whether the same idea might have occurred to inmates in the Nazi death camps during the second world war, as the only conceivable explanation for what life had turned out to be. Although of course there is no place for the concept of hell in Jewish theology.

It is the period between dream and awakening that I find most fascinating. In medieval times men were held responsible for sins they committed when awake, but not those in their dreams. What most terrified the righteous, therefore, was the time between dream and awakening, when the situation of the dream seemed still to exist, even while the mind was becoming conscious that it was only a dream. Under such circumstances a blasphemous or sinful thought or desire might be part of one's awakened consciousness, and thus accountable to God.

Consider that in the dream, or nightmare, that I have just described as having happened to me the night after my mother had gone away, I had not been certain whether the ringing of the telephone had been part of my dream, or had instead come from the outside and ended it, so that I went downstairs to make sure that the telephone was not actually ringing. When I did so, was I awake, or still dreaming?

I find myself unable to recall any instance during the first fifteen years of my life, which is to say, up to the spring and summer I have been describing, when the ringing of a telephone late at night ever occurred. We think of such ringing as typically bringing bad news. So far as I know, I had no reason to think so. It seems to me, therefore, that the proper analogy, the source of the dream event, must have been an alarm bell—perhaps a firedrill at school when the fire alarm went off, suddenly and shrill. The ringing of the telephone in the dream must have been in the nature of a warning that I must not dream any further, that what I was dreaming was forbidden: a taboo.

A difficulty in the interpretation of dreams is that there is almost always an inversion, a substitution involved. Pharoah's dream, as reported by the author of the Pentateuch, was of kine that were fatfleshed and lean, not of years that were plenteous or blasted by the east wind. It appears that even in dreams we dare not name the object directly, but must invoke its presence in disguise. Therefore an interpreter is required. There are times, too, when we dream a dream, and immediately think to ourselves that it was a dream, and set out to interpret its meaning, only to realize when we awake the next day that we cannot remember the interpretation. Clearly the interpretation was itself a dream.

Another example. The only time that my parents ever went off on a vacation together that I can remember was when I was about ten years old, several years after my father's illness while he was still recovering. They made an overnight trip to Jacksonville by sea, aboard the Clyde-Mallory liner Shawnee. My Aunt Marian, just as she would later do when my mother went away to Richmond, came to stay with my sister and me. My parents were gone no more than three days. What I remember most about the episode is that on the afternoon following my parents' departure, we went to a movie, one of the early technicolor films in which the hues and shades were rather crude and intense. The next morning my aunt was most amused when I reported that I had had a dream in technicolor. What I meant, however, was something quite specific: I had been conscious, while dreaming, that the dream was in lurid colors: reds and yellows and browns. Whatever the content of my dream, the intense coloration obviously had some bearing on its meaning. Now, when I thought to myself, "this dream I am now dreaming is in technicolor," was I asleep or awake? Or rather, even while I dreamed was not a portion of my consciousness aware that it was a dream?

In resuming my story, I caution myself—and equally anyone who might read it—that not merely the events being described, but their meaning as well, may not be what I believe them to be, but only the next room of a dream.

8.

Aunt Marian arrived two days later. She was my father's younger sister, and lived in Macon, Georgia, where her husband was in the dry goods business. They had no children. She had a very soft way of talking, and I liked her. She wanted to know all about school, and my work on the newspaper. She assured me that there was nothing seriously wrong with my mother and that she was merely overtired and needed a few weeks' rest. "It's been very hard on your mother since your father took sick," she said. "She had to take care of him every day for more than two years, and when he got better she was still worried about him, because he wasn't used to not being able to go to his office and do things. Your parents have had a very hard time. It wasn't easy for your father to have to give up his business and stay at home and rest every afternoon, when he'd always been so active. The strain was very hard on him, and your mother has had to do everything to keep his spirits up. It's just too much for her. She needs some time to herself, when she won't have to do anything except rest and get her strength back."

The evening that she arrived I was up in my room reading when I heard my father coming upstairs. He sat down on the sofa and watched me. I sensed that he was nervous, and I continued to read even after he began talking.

"I, uh, want to talk to you about what happened," he said. "I don't want you to think that you were the only reason your mother did what she did the other day. That was just the last straw. She's had to work very hard recently and she's been worried, and it just all caught up with her."

I made no reply, and continued to look at my book, though I was not actually reading. That's not what you said when it happened, I thought to myself.

When she came back home from Richmond, he went on, we would all have to be careful to make things as easy as possible for her, and not to worry her. He knew, he said, that recently my mother had been very anxious about me, and had perhaps been a little too emphatic in expressing her concern, but that had only been because she loved me and worried about my own welfare.

He spoke haltingly and was obviously ill at ease. I felt uncomfortable, too. After he had gone back downstairs I decided that it was probably as close as he could ever come to saying that my mother had been unfair in getting on me so much. Neither of them would ever admit openly that the other was wrong.

Well, I told myself, if I had been responsible, there was little or nothing I could do about it now. I *was* lazy and unenterprising, and without any talent for earning money, and I did not know how to change my personality so that I would be like my cousins in Richmond and enjoy going out and earning money and selling things and being successful.

For several days after the excitement and alarm of my mother's collapse and departure for Richmond, I did not telephone Janice. I was afraid that she might have heard what had happened. Finally I did so, however, and we went over to the tennis courts the next morning and played. When we were done we stopped at her house for some lemonade, and in the course of conversation it was decided that on the Wednesday following, we—Janice, my sister and I, Tommy Rittenhouse if he could go—would go out to Folly Beach for the day. Mrs. Bryan, who had friends staying out on the island, would take us.

I sounded out Tommy, and as I expected, he agreed at once. He came over that afternoon to play some jar-top baseball. After we had played two games and were sitting out on the curb on Versailles Street, he began questioning me. "Are you getting the hots for Janice Bryan?"

"Not me."

"She puts out, you know," he declared.

"That's what you think."

"That's what I *know*."

"Oh, sure." His know-it-all pose irked me. "How do you know?"

"Never mind how I know. I just know."

"Yeah, you know everything."

Sometimes I wondered whether Tommy's constant talk about sex was related to his father's religious piety. The Rittenhouses were Methodists, and Mr. Rittenhouse's name was frequently in the papers in connection with church activities. Before each of our baseball games he always made our team say a prayer. In their home there were several pictures of Jesus, and Tommy said that they prayed before every meal. I was sure that Mr. Rittenhouse had no idea of how dirty Tommy always talked when not with adults.

Our team won its second game. This time Junie Fox pitched and Tommy played shortstop. Junie walked a few batters, but he threw so hard that the other team, Copleston's Cleaners, could get no-where with his pitching. We won by 6–0. Tommy was a pretty good shortstop, though occasionally he booted a grounder or two. He was fast afoot, even if not especially smooth in his fielding, and he had a good arm. After the game we stopped in at the Hampton Park Pharmacy for soft drinks. Mr. Rittenhouse had to go somewhere, and Tommy left with him, but some of us stayed on for a while. We were happy over the results of the game, and with Junie's pitching performance. "I don't see why he doesn't leave Tommy at shortstop and pitch Junie whenever he can," somebody said.

"He won't do it," somebody else replied. "He wants Tommy to be the star."

"Well, I hope he pitches Junie when we play Southern Ice," Johnny Harriman declared. Southern Ice had beaten us out for the championship the previous summer, and everybody said that either our team or theirs would win the pennant this year. We were scheduled to play them twice.

We had a good team; there was no question about that. The nucleus was still the players that had been on the team when Tommy and I had first organized it to play pick-up ball, but when Mr. Rittenhouse had added Jack Marcussohn and Dave Gregg he had strengthened us considerably. There had been quite a wrangle when he had done it. This season all our players were a year older, and we had an excellent chance to win the championship if we could whip Southern Ice.

I played first base. When we had first formed the team and played pick-up ball I had been one of the best hitters, and I remained the first baseman when we went into the Neighborhood League. I was not especially talented at first base, but I could play it adequately. My hitting was not as good as it had been, but neither was I among the weakest hitters. Usually I batted sixth.

What I really would have liked to be was a pitcher. I could throw the ball fairly hard, and make it curve some, but I was so little able to control where it went that there was no chance of my becoming a pitcher anytime soon. What I hoped was that when I grew older I would learn how to get the ball over the plate and become a star left-handed pitcher.

My mother's departure for Richmond seemed to jar my father out of the normal routine of his life. Although he continued to work in the garden, he spent less time outdoors. He was inside the house more often, reading the newspaper and magazines, listening to the radio. He made frequent trips to Mr. Simons' house across the way to talk with him. He was, indeed, more talkative than usual at home, conversing with my Aunt Marian and with my sister and me more than he ordinarily did. He even asked me a few questions about our baseball team. Several evenings he took us all downtown to the movies.

With my mother away the routines of the family seemed to lack focus. Everything was spontaneous and haphazard. My Aunt Marian prepared meals, did the shopping, and took care of things, but it was not the same. Activities that formerly fitted into the daily functioning of the household without being remarked or thought about became tentative and improvised.

We talked with my mother over long-distance telephone some days after she arrived in Richmond. She seemed better. Her voice sounded faint and far off. I told her about how we were going to the beach for the day with Janice Bryan and her mother. My Aunt Marian assured her that all was going well, and that she was not to worry about how we were getting along in her absence, but instead to relax and enjoy herself.

"She seemed in good spirits," my aunt said afterward to my father. "Didn't you think so?"

He nodded.

"When will she be ready to come home?" my sister asked.

"In a couple of weeks," my father said. "Next weekend she's going to New York with Charles and Maggie."

The thought that she would actually visit New York City made me envious. She would be able to see the skyscrapers, walk down

Fifth Avenue, ride the elevator all the way to the top of the Empire State Building if she wished. The Dodgers and Giants would be playing at home, though of course she would have no interest in that. She might go to the waterfront, though, and see some of the ocean liners, and she could go to a play on Broadway. Above all, she could go shopping. I had an image of New York City as having vast five-and-ten-cent stores, many times larger than Woolworth's and Kress's in Charleston, and larger than any I had ever visited in Richmond or Atlanta. I knew that when my mother came home she would bring me a present from New York. If only she were to go to a baseball game she might buy me a souvenir Giants pennant such as Tommy Rittenhouse had. But that was most unlikely.

We drove to Folly Beach in the mid-morning of a hot day in late June. The way led across the Ashley River Bridge, through Windemere, across Wappoo Cut, then southward through island country that was low and flat. Along the roadside the fields stretched out, and thickly vined woods, and wide tracts of marsh grass. As we drew nearer to the ocean the marsh widened, and became creeks and vast swampy stretches with small islands of tangled oak and palmetto set in among the reed grass like oases in a green-matted desert. Occasionally we saw shrimp boats moored in creeks along the way. The last bridge before Folly Island was a high wooden affair that spanned a wide creek of black water, and then we drove along a road topped with crushed white shell, past cottages and stores, to the ocean. At the end of the road, beyond a row of white sand dunes, was the beach.

Mrs. Bryan pulled up alongside the bathing pavilion, and we got out. It was shortly after eleven o'clock. She would be back for us, she said, at four. Carrying our lunch baskets, and wearing our clothes over swimming suits, we walked up onto the pavilion. It was a large, open building, with railings around the area that was used for dances and, between the railings and the bannisters along the edge of the pavilion, wooden tables and benches. A soda fountain was located just inside, with a popcorn machine, various faucets and vats, a fogged case in which some frankfurters revolved on a spit, an assortment of cups, glasses, and plates, a grill, a snowball machine, and, attired in an apron and a white cap lettered "7-Up," an attendant seated behind the counter, listening to the radio. The pavilion roof was low, and the expanse of floor was dark, with a faintly sour odor of wet sand and salt. There was a raw, unpainted appearance to everything.

We walked toward the front of the pavilion. The beach was below us, leading down to the edge of the water a hundred feet away. Folly Beach was an eroding beach; each summer the strip of sand was narrower. It was said that within a few years the front row of houses would be underwater. Several groups of beachgoers, in bathing suits and with beach umbrellas, lounged about on the strand, with some little children playing at the water's edge. Just to the east, past an amusement park, was Folly Pier, a long roofed structure that led well out over the water. Along the underside of the roof was a long sign, DANCE TO THE MUSIC OF JAN GARBER—JULY 4–5.

"Let's go up past the houses," Janice suggested.

We set off up the beach. The ocean looked cool and very inviting. It was low tide, and there were gullies and pools along the edge of the water. The waves were breaking fifty feet or so offshore, coming in as low combers and tumbling into slate green and creamy froth as they crashed against the receding current. It was so bright that the white sand seemed to glitter and sparkle into dazzling forms. There were very few people on the beach. To the island side, past the irregular brown strip of dried stalks and seaweed that marked the tide's farthest encroachment, were dunes, their crests fringed with sea oats, and beyond them shingled and clapboard houses, built high on pilings. The houses were drab-looking and with weatherworn woodwork and porches screened with rusty-looking mesh. Of the local beaches Folly was the least lovely. Unlike Sullivan's Island and the Isle of Palms to the east of the city, Folly was without zoning restrictions of any kind. Relatively few local people had houses there; most of the inhabitants were people from Upstate. But it was a convenient beach to go to for the day, easier to get to from the city, and with no toll bridge. We walked on past occasional bathers, until at length we had passed beyond the built-up area and could see only low matted trees and vines beyond the dunes.

We spread beach towels onto the hot, dry sand, thrust the pole of a beach umbrella into the sand and worked it into firm terrain, and sat down to survey the view. The surf was breaking steadily. A few shore birds were picking their way along the margin of the receding water. Beyond the breakers the flat green ocean stretched out to the horizon. Bathers in the surf down in front of the built-up area were little more than small dots in the water. Over everything was the low drumming roar of the waves as they broke in continuous motion against the shelving beach.

"We've got it all to ourselves," my sister said.

"I'm going in the water," Tommy Rittenhouse said after a minute. We took off our outer garments. Even though I was wearing my swimming trunks underneath, I felt awkward as I stepped out of my trousers. Janice Bryan was wearing a blue bathing suit with a thin red-and-white stripe that ran from over one shoulder across the front down to her waist. The suit was closely contoured to her body, and in the bodice was a slight indentation where her breasts divided. Her skin was tan and smooth. She put on a white rubber bathing cap.

Tommy got up and headed for the water. My sister followed. We watched them as they strode into the surf, their feet splashing water as they went, until soon they were in deeper water and receded into it, with only their heads and upper bodies above the surface.

"I think I'd better put on some suntan lotion," Janice said. She located a blue glass jar of Noxzema in her beach bag and began applying white lotion to her arms, legs, shoulders, and face. "It'll probably wash off some in the surf," she said, "but I don't want to get burned too bad." The oil in the lotion gave a faint sheen to her tanned skin. "Put some on my back, will you?" she asked, handing the jar to me. I scooped out a dab of lotion with my fingers and applied it to her skin. My fingers trembled a little as I brushed the lotion across her shoulder blades, spreading it around until it thinned to transparency. "Thanks." I rubbed some onto my arms and shoulders and legs. "You want some on your back?" she asked.

"Yeah."

With her fingers she smoothed the cool lotion over my back.

"Ready to go?" I asked.

"Okay." We got to our feet and walked toward the ocean. I still felt awkward and uncomfortable. We strode out through the shallow water until the water was up to our waists, and we had to thrust our legs forward against the swirling flow to make progress. The water was chilly. I slipped down to my shoulders to let it envelop me, and after a moment the chill was gone. Tommy and my sister were a little farther out, just beyond the first row of breakers, their heads rising and falling in unison as the incoming swells slid past them. We made our way to them, jumping and sidestepping to avoid the combers.

"The surf's not bad," Tommy said. "Must be slack tide."

From just above the surface of the water, immersed up to my shoulders, I gazed around at the beach and the dunes. It was as if the ocean were a vast bowl, and the shore its rim, curving away in either direction, with the houses, pavilion, and the pier marking the eastern extremity, and a receding, seemingly infinite line of white beach, dunes and a low foliage of trees at the other. To seaward there was visible only the tossing crests of waves, and above that the sky, gleaming blue and with a few white cumulus clouds. Ebbing and flowing, the current tugged lightly at my body as I shifted my feet aboout on the cool sandy bottom to keep my balance. Occasionally a wave a little steeper than most moved in upon us, and it was necessary to bend my knees under the water and propel myself upward to let the wave surge harmlessly landward, around and by me, to where it might lift and form a crest and then tumble over with a roar close in to the shore.

Janice stayed nearby, looking about, with her shoulders just out of the water, and with tiny droplets of ocean visible on her skin where the suntan lotion had congealed the water. "Isn't it nice and calm today?" she called. I nodded.

Tommy Rittenhouse spied a steep wave coming, turned toward it, and dove under the surface, to emerge moments later a dozen feet beyond. He swam back, his head turning from side to side and his arms churning the water. Janice began swimming too, not seaward but parallel to the shore, and then turned on her back and floated along the surface. My sister swam toward her.

I did not know how to swim. I had never been able to learn, not even when I had been sent to a YMCA swimming class at the age of ten. As long as we had held onto the side of the pool and practiced kicking movements, I was all right, but when it came time to turn loose and move out unassisted into the water, I could not do it. The moment my head went under the surface I had lost all control over myself and broken for the side of the pool. The instructor, a man named Fudge, had worked with me for a long time, holding me up in the water by the waist and letting me work my arms and legs, and as long as I could feel his hands about me I was able to do what he showed me. But the instant he let me go and I felt myself unsupported, I would panic and attempt to climb up onto his shoulders. Nothing could make me lose my fear; I was helpless. Finally Mr. Fudge gave up and informed my parents that there was no way to teach me how to swim. And yet I was not afraid of the water; I liked to go on boats very much.

So I stood there, balancing in the water as the waves moved gently around me, my feet barely touching the sand bottom, and watched the others as they swam.

After a while we went back to the beach. The light wind off the water was chilly, but the sun was hot and soon dried us. We lay down on the beach towels, and soon the sun was baking down on us. Janice took up the jar of lotion and applied it in turn to each of our backs, and then handed it to me and I put some more on hers. We lay there for a long time, talking a little, but mostly just listening to the surf and letting the breeze from off the water brush mildly against our bodies.

I felt very much at peace. Thoughts moved idly about in my consciousness, in no coherent sequence. It was like sitting out on my tree perch in the woods earlier in the spring, except that now I had no sense of needing to divert my thoughts to keep from fretting over things I had failed to do. Moreover, I was not alone.

Eventually Tommy said, "Let's eat!" We dusted the beach sand from off our hands and arms, and Janice and my sister passed around ham and cheese sandwiches, pieces of fried chicken, and deviled eggs. From a thermos jug Janice poured lemonade into paper cups. It was icy cold and had a sharp sweet taste. As we ate and drank, we looked out at the ocean.

"I can see a ship," my sister declared. We looked in the direction she was pointing, and made out the outline of a freighter far across the water. The bridge, the main cabin, and the masts were visible, and a smudge of smoke drifted from the stack, but the hull was below the horizon, so that the superstructure seemed to be floating by itself like a ghost in the green sea.

"There's some boats down there too," Tommy declared, pointing westward. Some shrimp trawlers were in sight, working offshore, one of them with nets extended aloft on either side of its hull so that it resembled a brown-and-white butterfly on the water.

"I'd like to go out on one of them sometime," Tommy said.

"Think of the awful smell, though," my sister objected.

"I think I'd rather be on a sailboat," Janice said.

"They're too slow," Tommy said.

We finished eating. "Let's go look for shells," Janice suggested.

"Not me," said Tommy. "I'm going back in the surf."

"I've had enough surf for a while, I'll go with you," I told Janice, trying to sound casual.

"I think I'll swim more, too," my sister said, as I knew she would.

Tommy threw a glance at me that was also a smirk. "Don't go too far," he said. He and my sister headed back to the surf.

Janice took a scarf to carry shells in, and we started up the beach. We walked close to the edge of the water, which came flooding toward us in thin sheets of tide and then receded, leaving clusters of bubbly foam that winked and popped as they evaporated in the air. Along the very edge, when the water had just drained off, the sand was so dark and wet that it reflected the sky, and we could see little sand urchins, swept in momentarily by the tide, burrowing frantically in the sand to disappear from sight. The tide was coming in now, and small shore birds, sandpipers and plovers, skittered along the edge in brisk, stiff-legged bursts of motion, foraging for food. Offshore, up ahead, the shrimp boats were working back and forth.

Occasionally Janice stopped to pick up a shell. She seemed to know the names of all of them. The long blue ones were mussels, and were inlaid with white and purple. There were moon shells, shaped like spinning tops with apertures to the side, and little slipper shells that resembled tiny, semirounded footware. She found several sand dollars, dried bone white in the sun and with cloverlike filigrees emanating from the center. I picked up a long, yellow, bladelike shell, so thin it was almost translucent. "That's a jackknife clamshell," she said. We searched for conch shells and finally found one half-buried in the sand, about seven inches long, white with a spiral top and a wide body that tapered to a point like an elephant's trunk. I carried it out into somewhat deeper water and sloshed it about until the sand was all gone from the opening. The inside of the shell was pink and lemon-colored.

We walked on, retrieving new shells from time to time. We were far up the beach now. The shrimp boats working offshore seemed measurably nearer. After a few minutes more we stopped. "We've come quite a way," I said.

I looked back up the beach. All I could see was sand, dunes and surf. My sister and Tommy were too far off to be made out. The beach was deserted. Behind the line of dunes were palmetto trees and thickets.

If we were to make love here, no one could see us, I thought, and at once put the thought out of my mind.

"I wonder what Fred Ellison's doing this summer?" I said.

"I don't know," Janice answered. "What made you think of him?"

"I just happened to."

"I guess we'd better turn back," she said after a minute. "It must be gettin on to three o'clock."

We walked down the beach. The tide was now rolling in over the footsteps we had made earlier. It was a long way back. Eventually we could make out the shape of the beach umbrella, and as we drew nearer we saw that Tommy and my sister were sitting under it. We walked on toward them and finally came up to where they waited.

"Where'd you go?" my sister asked. "To Savannah?"

Janice laughed. "We were almost down to those shrimp boats. What time is it?"

My sister opened a straw beach bag and drew out a watch. "It's 3:15," she said.

"Let's take a quick dip and then go back to the pavilion." Janice picked up her white bathing cap from the towel and drew it over her hair. We went out into the surf until we were in water that came up above our waists. I had been out on the shore for so long that the water chilled me again for a moment. The surf was rougher now, as the tide moved in. Tommy dove into the incoming breakers and the others followed. I drifted about for a while, enjoying the water, until one by one the others came back through the surf, first my sister, then Tommy, and finally Janice. We went back up onto the shore. There was some lemonade left in the thermos jug and we finished it up.

We took down the beach umbrella, shook sand out of the towels, packed our belongings in the beach bags and baskets. I pulled my shirt over my shoulders; despite the lotion I had applied earlier, I was burned some. My woolen trunks were still too wet for me to put my trousers over them, so I slung my trousers over my shoulder. We walked down the beach, past the cottages, toward the pavilion.

Under the pavilion roof it was cool and humid. Janice and my sister went off to the bathhouse to change back into their clothes. As we stood around waiting for them we saw Mrs. Bryan drive up in her car.

My trunks were itching me, now that they were half-dry. I pulled my trousers up over them and fastened my belt. I had better put a towel on the car seat, I thought, or the seat would get wet.

"Boy, I'm tired," I said. "We went a long way up the beach."

Tommy Rittenhouse snickered. "Did you get any?" he asked.

"Shut up, you fool," I replied as Janice and my sister came up to join us. We went down the steps together toward Mrs. Bryan's waiting car.

9.

When we arrived home, my father told me that Benny Smith, the director of the playground department, had telephoned, and wanted me to call him back. I did, and was informed by his secretary that he had left the office for the day and would see me at our team's Neighborhood League game at Hampton Park Playground tomorrow. I wondered what Benny Smith wanted with me, now that Mr. Rittenhouse had taken charge of our team.

It turned out that I had gotten a good deal more sun out at the beach than I realized. My arms and shoulders were red, and very hot, and they hurt when anything touched them. I should have worn my shirt when we had gone for the walk up the beach looking for the shells. "You're as red as a beet," Aunt Marian said. I coated my upper body with burn lotion after I took my shower, and that helped some, but it was still painful.

The next morning the sunburn was better, but it still hurt when I moved my arms. I could only hope that nobody would run into me during the game. I telephoned Tommy. He had been burned, too. "The old man's mad as hell at me," he said. "Says I should have remembered about the game today."

Shortly after we arrived at Hampton Park for the game, I found out what Benny Smith wanted. Just before we were to begin batting practice he showed up, and asked me to go over to the playground office with him. The man who was the scorekeeper for the nightly softball games at Moultrie Park, down by the Colonial Lake, was entering the hospital for some minor surgery. Would I be interested in taking over his scorekeeping duties for the next three weeks? The salary would be seven dollars a week for five nights of scorekeeping, Monday through Friday, three games each evening. The scorekeeper at Hampton Park would come by when his games were done to get the line scores and the batteries, and take them to the newspaper office. The likelihood was that I could get a ride back uptown with him if I wished.

At last I had a job—one I knew I could do. Although it would last only for three weeks, it was a job, and proof that I was capable of earning money. Moreover, if I showed that I could handle the work, Benny Smith said, it was quite possible that next summer I could have one of the two scorekeeper's jobs for the entire season.

"By the way," he said as I got up to leave. "How did Rittenhouse come to coach your team?"

"He offered to do it," I replied, "and we let him. Is there something wrong about it?"

"No, it's all right," Benny Smith said. "None of the other teams have adults in charge. I wish he wouldn't argue so much with the umpires, though. I don't think it sets a very good example for the boys."

I said nothing. There was no way that I could tell Mr. Rittenhouse not to argue with umpires.

"Anyway," he added, "as far as the league's concerned, you're in charge of the team. When he started coaching last season I made it clear that we don't recognize adult coaches in this league. Is that understood?"

"Yes, sir."

I went back out to the ball field. Junie Fox was pitching batting practice, which meant that Tommy would be the starting pitcher in the game. I was surprised, because I had assumed that if Tommy had gotten himself as sunburned as he said he had, Mr. Rittenhouse would go ahead and pitch Junie, since the team we were to play, the Cremo Cardinals, was a good club. Their catcher, Red Manning, who played on the high school team in the spring, was a dangerous hitter.

Tommy ran into trouble from the outset. Red Manning hit a triple to score in the first inning to move two runs. Unfortunately for the Cremo Cardinals, however, they had no pitching, and we soon tied the score. After that both teams scored runs, but we pulled ahead and had a two-run lead going into the bottom of the seventh and last inning. But then Tommy walked two batters in a row, and Mr. Rittenhouse began arguing with the umpire, and before long the umpire was telling him either to go back to the bench or he would throw him out of the game. Finally Mr. Rittenhouse summoned Junie Fox to pitch, and Junie struck out three batters in a row and we won. Mr. Rittenhouse had some more words with the umpire after it was over.

On the way home, Tommy told me that he had urged his father to let Junie start the game, and again in the fourth inning had suggested that Junie be brought in to pitch. It had not been a very good day for

Tommy—or for myself, either, for that matter. My shoulders and arms were so sore that it hurt every time I swung a bat. I had been unable to get around on the pitch, and had twice grounded out with runners on base.

Tommy and I had ridden to the game with Mr. Rittenhouse instead of bicycling, and we had to walk home. We had not gone two blocks, however, before a car pulled up alongside us. It was Fred Ellison. "Give you a lift?" he asked. We got into his car. It was a blue Ford V-8 coupe, with white trimmings, a radio, and leather seats. Tommy was very impressed with it. Fred let us out at the corner of Peachtree Street, and as we walked home, Tommy kept talking about the car. "Maybe the Old Man'll give me one like it when I go off to college," he declared.

"Not if you get sunburned like that before any more ball games," I said.

I left Tommy at his front gate and walked across Pendleton Street into our yard. My father was spraying his orange trees. I told him the good news about the scorekeeping job. He told me to write my mother about it, and to make sure to mention what Benny Smith had told me about next summer. After dinner I wrote the letter. I described the trip to the beach and the ball game. I wanted to ask her, when she went to New York, to try to find a Giants pennant for me, but I decided against it. It was wiser not to mention spending money to her just yet. My letter would probably not arrive in Richmond before she left for New York with my uncle and aunt.

My father always went downtown on Friday morning. He had various errands to run and usually stopped in to see friends at their offices. He was very chary about staying very long when he did. When he had been in business, he said, an old man named Mr. David, who had been a prominent merchant, used to come by his office and keep him away from his work for long periods of time talking. "When you're busy you don't have time to sit around and talk," he said. So he always kept his visits brief, but he always made them, too. I felt that having to go to the bank and on his other errands was an excuse he used to take the trip downtown to see everybody.

85

I went along with him the day after the baseball game. We drove first to the newspaper office. My father knew all the reporters and usually stopped in for a brief chat with Mr. Ray Lowell and an exchange of greetings with my Uncle Edward. As for myself, I borrowed a pair of shears and began looking through the stack of exchange newspapers for baseball pictures. The table was located just outside the door to Mr. Lowell's office, and I heard my father talking to Mr. Lowell about the current statistics for the Saturday night poker game, and how Mr. Rittenhouse was the biggest winner by far. Mr. Lowell seemed to be no more perturbed about it than my Uncle Edward or Mr. Simons had been. After a few minutes my father went over to my uncle, told him that my mother would be returning home the following weekend, then disappeared down the hall toward the *News and Courier* offices. I finished going through the newspapers, and while I waited for him I told my uncle about my job.

We left the newspaper office and drove down to Broad Street, where my father found a parking place near the Chamber of Commerce. Broad Street was the city's legal and financial district. I liked walking on Broad Street with my father. We encountered various persons he knew, some of them among the better-known businessmen and attorneys in the community. They always inquired about his health.

In front of Bowman and Israel he stopped to talk with Mr. Meier Bowman, a friend of our family's who was very prominent in civic affairs and was on the city council. "Come on and I'll buy you a dope," my father offered. Mr. Bowman said he was due down the street that instant.

"Why do you call them dopes?" I asked my father as we walked on.

"Back when Coca-Cola first came out, they used to say that it had a narcotic in it," he explained.

A little farther on, I saw Mr. Strohmeier, the principal of the high school, coming along. He was tall and bulky, with a sizable paunch. He and my father exchanged greetings. "This is a fine young man you've got here," Mr. Strohmeier told him, putting his hand on my shoulder. The sunburn hurt, but I could not say anything. After a minute Mr. Strohmeier said goodbye and left us.

"Did you know him when you were a boy?" I asked.

"Yes, they lived across the street from us."

"Where was that?"

"On St. Phillip's Street."

When we reached the corner of State Street, in front of the People's Bank, someone called to my father from behind. It was Mr. Cartwright, who lived on Peachtree Street, just beyond the Rittenhouses' from us. Mr. Cartwright was a certified public accountant, and his office was in the People's Building.

My father talked with him for a minute. "Come on and I'll buy you a dope," he said.

"Good enough," Mr. Cartwright agreed.

We crossed over to the south side of Broad Street, went into Robinson's, and found a table. The waiter served the cokes to us. The place was crowded with people talking. Everyone on Broad Street always wore coats and ties in the summer, no matter how hot it was. Overhead several large wooden-bladed ceiling fans revolved tirelessly.

While we were seated at the table, Mayor Lockwood came in with Mr. J. Waties Waring and someone else. The mayor waved at my father and Mr. Cartwright, and stopped to chat for a moment. The Lockwoods had been our next-door neighbors before we moved up to Versailles Street. He looked at me. "Boy, you've grown up since the last time I saw you!" he told me.

After the mayor left, Mr. Cartwright said that he wanted to talk to my father about the possibility of doing something about Devereaux Woods. Their house was at the foot of Peachtree Street, just where the road turned in to the woods, and Mr. Cartwright said he was getting tired of cars parking out there and the headlights shining into his bedroom window at all hours of the night and morning. "Somebody was blowing a horn out there about two A.M. the other night," he declared.

My father said that the proper course of action would be to call Chief Ortmann and ask that patrol cars make regular trips through there at night. "Let them hand out a few tickets and the word will get around fast enough," he said.

"I thought of that," Mr. Cartwright said, "and they're supposed to come through there anyway. But you can't arrest them for just parking, you've got to catch them in the act, you know," he laughed.

My father did not laugh—probably, I thought, because I was present. "Maybe so," he said, "but I bet if they know a patrol car's going to be coming through there every so often, they'll find somewhere else to park."

"That's true. Maybe we ought to get up a petition." Mr. Cartwright shoved back his chair. "Well, I got to run. Let me know if you get any more ideas about it."

"All right," my father told him.

We rose to leave. My father glanced around the room and spied Mayor Lockwood seated over near the counter talking with several people. "You go on out," he told me. "I'll be along in a minute." He went toward the mayor.

I walked outside, not looking back, and waited for him on the street.

When we emerged from Robinson's my father consulted his watch. It was five after eleven, and he had to go by the Carolina Savings Bank on the corner, and then he had an appointment at the Power Company on Meeting Street at 11:30. He would pick me up at one o'clock on the corner of East Bay and Broad, outside Demos' Restaurant, he told me.

I walked past Walker, Evans, and Cogswell, where the school newspaper had been printed my first year in high school, and then turned up the iron staircase to the office of the law firm where my Aunt Ellen was employed. She was at work at her typewriter, by the window overlooking East Bay Street. I told her about my job, and talked with her and her coworker Miss Shaeffer, for a few minutes. Then I went back down the iron steps to the street, past the bank, crossed over to the Pirate House, and walked down the narrow passageway of Exchange Street toward the harbor two blocks distant.

There was no ship tied up at the Clyde Line docks that day. The tide was halfway at ebb. Black pluff mud stretched out twenty yards or more from the shore. Just downstream was Thelning's Marine Railway and the twin piers of Adger's Wharf. I walked along the shore, next to the rusty railroad tracks, past the remains of an old wooden boat. Only the curved prow and a few beams and ribs still projected through the mud and the marsh grass. I went past Thelning's, and onto Adger's Wharf. Under a rusty tin shed black women were packing shrimp into large gold-colored tin pails and icing them down. Others were sorting shrimp into large heaps, according to size. In among the shrimp were occasional small fish, and the women tossed these off the dock into the harbor water as they worked. Dozens of seagulls, attracted by this largesse, hovered about in the air, dipping, wheeling, turning, and lifting as they maneuvered for position. There was a strong smell of shrimp everywhere. I remembered what my sister had said when Tommy remarked that he would like to go out on one of the trawlers we had seen at the beach.

I strolled through the shed and out onto the open area of the north wharf. Alongside the wharf were tied an assortment of small craft, most of them rigged for shrimping. Their crews, for the most part black, were at work drying out nets, hosing down decks and holds, repairing nets and lines, or else lounging about talking. The boats were of various shapes and sizes, painted in all manner of colors, or else without any paint at all. Old automobile tires lined their gunwales. There were also two larger trawlers, in much better condition, broad-beamed and with high sides, painted white. They had nameplates along their cabins: "Finisterre" and "Three Brothers."

I went all the way out to the point of the wharf. Just across the way, on the downstream side alongside the south wharf, were the three White Stack tugboats, the *Cecilia*, the *Robert H. Lockwood*, and the *James P. Congdon*. They were painted a handsome brick red, with white trimming, tall white stacks, and jet-black hulls. The boilers of all three were kept fired for immediate service, as was evident from the wisps of light smoke that trailed from the tops of the stacks.

The White Stack fleet was one of two in the city. The other was farther upstream; its boats were the *Hinton* and the *Waban*. I was a partisan of the White Stack craft. They were owned by the three Lockwood brothers, one of whom was the mayor. I remembered how, when I had been ten or eleven and we had lived next to the Lockwoods downtown, I had regarded the two Lockwood boys, who were several years older than I, as among the more fortunate of the earth for being in line eventually to captain the tugboats. At the time, Mr. Lockwood had been an alderman; now he was mayor.

I had been proud when he stopped by our table in Robinson's to say hello to my father. If only my father had been willing to let it go at that, instead of going back over to him again when we were about to leave. It was like his calling up Mr. J. H. Short on the telephone the night after he had been on the jury duty.

I wondered why he did not try to go back into business, now that he had largely recovered his health. He had not even had any of the nervous spells recently, so far as I could recall. In the years immediately following his illness he would refer sometimes to the time when he would open his electrical store again. Once I had asked him whether, when he did, he would get his old store back. It was a large building, remodeled from a movie theater, on King Street, and though it had several times changed ownership in the years since he had given it up, there was a narrow strip of metal, with the words *Kohn Electrical Company*, still in place along the top of the show windows. His reply had been that if he went back into business it would be on a much smaller scale.

Out in the harbor the water was shimmering in the sunlight. There was not a ship in sight, or even a smudge of smoke out beyond the low silhouette of Fort Sumter that would indicate the coming or the departure of an oceangoing vessel. A little upstream from where I stood, on an island just beyond the ship channel, was the rounded brick structure of Castle Pinckney, in colonial days a fort and now a cable station. To the south was the low green shoreline of James Island, beyond the mouth of the Ashley River. The High Battery was out of sight beyond the Yacht Club. Upstream, to the north, the faded green wharves of the Clyde Line blocked the view of the waterfront, but to the right of that I could see the immense steel arches of the Cooper River Bridge, joining the city to Mount Pleasant on the east side.

In 1929, when the bridge had been close to completion, we had spent the summer on Sullivan's Island, and we would walk down the beach to the end of the island and see the still-unjoined span of the bridge in the distance, the two ends reaching out toward each other, and, over the course of the summer, drawing closer together. To get to and from the city then, it was necessary to ride the ferry. I remembered the two ferryboats, the angular *Lawrence*, with its tall twin stacks that belched forth clouds of black smoke, and the *Palmetto*, newer and wider of beam and powered by gasoline engines. They were large ferries, capable of transporting dozens of automobiles at a time. When we drove aboard, with much thumping and rattling of chains, we got out of the car, went up onto the upper deck, and watched for the other ferry to pass by as we crossed the harbor.

The bridge had put the *Lawrence* and the *Palmetto* out of business. Where were they now?

Out beyond Castle Pinckney, emerging into the open where it had been screened from my view, was a squat, low shape, halfway across the harbor. It was the little ferryboat operated by Captain Baitery, tediously making its way toward Sullivan's Island. It was all that was left of ferryboat service now. I had ridden over there and back aboard it once, on a bicycle trip to the Isle of Palms with my Uncle Edward. It was a small craft, capable of carrying no more than a half-dozen automobiles each trip, and required almost an hour to traverse the harbor, its gasoline engine throbbing monotonously as it crept along the water. It was a far cry from the *Lawrence* and *Palmetto*, with their powerful engines, long cabins, and dozens of automobiles under covered decks.

Even so, it was a ferryboat. And if one wanted to get across the harbor on a ferryboat, a small one was better than no ferryboat at all.

It was getting time for me to meet my father. I left Adger's Wharf and headed back to Broad Street.

IO.

Saturday night, I went down to my Uncle Edward's apartment to listen to music. My uncle was reading when I arrived. "When do you begin your job?" he asked. "Monday night," I told him. I talked with him for a little while. He was difficult to converse with, for he usually responded in monosyllables, and I always felt that I ought to think of something more to say, and found myself searching for items of conversation. He was a quiet man.

He kept to an almost unvarying routine. Each afternoon when he returned from work, he took a nap, and then went riding on his bicycle along Gadsden Street and nearby areas, stopping here and there to talk with children. All the little children in the part of Charleston from Bennett Street to Colonial Lake and Murray Boulevard along the river knew him and waited for him. He played little games with them, brought them chewing gum and candy, and liked to listen to them talking and singing. He had a cook come in late each afternoon to tidy up and prepare a simple dinner for him, and in the evenings he read and listened to his phonograph or the radio. On Saturday nights he played poker. Sundays he either went out on his sailboat or else for a bicycle ride. Each August he took a two-week vacation, during which he either went sailing or made bicycle trips of several days' duration, to towns within a radius of fifty miles or so from the city.

He had little social life, so far as I knew, and never traveled anywhere. My father said that except for his bicycle jaunts the only trip my uncle had ever taken over the past fifteen years or so was the time he came to Richmond when my father was critically ill in the hospital and expected to die.

After my uncle departed for the poker game, I played a phonograph album that I found on his table. It was a piano work by Mozart, the "Sonata in A Major." It opened with a grave little melody that was developed in all sorts of ways. It was incredibly lovely. At the close it had a wild kind of dance, ending in utter abandonment. When it was over I played it all the way through again.

Next I selected a Mozart symphony, and while I listened to it I read an article in a magazine. I put on another Mozart symphony after that. There was nothing else around that I wanted to read, so I got out a photograph album that I had found earlier in the summer, and went through it again. There were numerous photos of my uncle and my father in their late teens and early twenties. When my Uncle Edward had been young, he had been extremely good-looking, much more so than my father, with a square face and very clean features. My father's face was considerably thinner, and except for the fact that in the old photographs his face was not lined and had no wrinkles on its brow, he looked now much as he did then.

All the photographs of my father in the album, I noticed again, were taken when he was a grown young man, or else in his very late teens. I should have liked to have seen him, and my uncle, when they had been boys, or no older than I was now. It was strange that there were absolutely no such pictures at all, neither in my uncle's album, nor in one that I had seen at my Aunt Ellen's, nor in any of the several family photograph albums at our house.

I replaced the photograph album in the bookcase. Before I left for home, I went to the bathroom, and while there I noticed, under the washstand, a slip of paper. I picked it up. There was some penciled writing on it, in my uncle's hand. He must have dropped it from his pocket. Apparently it consisted of some notes to remind him of things: "Pick up shirts." (There was a package of shirts in laundry wrapping paper on his bureau.) "Send check to Heb. H." "Cigarettes." (I had noticed three new cartons of the Turkish cigarettes he smoked on top of his book case.) "Leave A Maj out for O."

The "A Maj" must have referred to the piano sonata that I had found lying out on his table. He must have taken it from the rack in order to lend it to someone who would call for it. I wondered who "O" might be.

Omar.

Had my uncle placed the Mozart album there with the specific idea that I would notice it and play it?

I placed the piece of paper back under the washbasin, just where I had found it, and left the apartment.

93

The softball games at Moultrie Playground began at 7:30 P.M. and continued until after 10:30 each evening. There were three games for me to score each night. The opening game was always between two of the teams in the No. 3 league, which was made up largely of unskilled players, men in their twenties, thirties, and even forties. The games were always high-scoring affairs, with scores like 17–14 and 15–10, and though they were supposed to last seven innings, they seldom did, because there was a rule that no inning of a game was to be started later than one hour after the game's commencement. What usually happened, with all the hits and errors, was that the No. 3 league teams seldom got in more than four or five innings before the hour time limit expired. The difficulty was that once an inning was begun, it had to be completed, so that if another inning were to start within four or five minutes before the one-hour limit, the rest of the inning had to be played out—which meant that the next game sometimes was late a half hour or more getting under way.

Play in the No. 2 league was of markedly better caliber. But it was the games of the No. 1 league, always the third of the evening when scheduled, that most people came out to watch. Many of the No. 1 league players also played baseball in the Municipal League. The pitching was fast and accurate, the fielding expert, and the pace of the games very swift, and the scores almost always low.

During the three games each evening I sat in a little wooden hut behind the home plate screen and kept the score in a book. Occasionally Paul Munro stopped by to see a game, and joined me. When the last game was over, I waited for the scorekeeper from Hampton Park to arrive. He was a man in his thirties who lived in our part of town, east of Rutledge Avenue, so instead of writing out the line scores and batteries for him, I went along with him to the *News and Courier* office, typed out the information on the games I had scored, waited while he finished preparing his summaries, and then got a ride back uptown. I was sorry that the newspaper did not publish accounts of the games as well as the line scores, because I would have enjoyed writing stories about the No. 1 league games.

Finding myself in the newspaper city room late in the evening and using a typewriter there made me realize that since the end of the school term I had to all intents and purposes stopped thinking about newspaper work and writing.

In the newsroom, however, with the reporters at work on their stories and the desk men editing copy and writing headlines and checking proofs, I felt again my ambition to be a newspaper man. The managing editor of the morning paper, Mr. Witte, was a friend of my father's, as was the state editor, Mr. Wish. I talked a little with both of them. But I did not converse with Billy Ball, the sports editor. He gave me no more than his usual distant nod. I was certain that he did not like me and held no very high opinion of my abilities, which I presumed he judged from my stories that had been published in the afternoon paper. I felt that if ever the time came when I would want a job as a reporter, this man, if he had anything to say about it, would be almost the last person in the world to give me one.

When I was done typing out the line scores, and was waiting for the Hampton Park scorekeeper, who was a slow worker, I walked over into the telegraph room, a glass-enclosed space located between the city rooms of the morning and afternoon papers, and looked at what was coming in over the teletypes. The major league scores were all in. The Giants had lost again. On the news there was an account of a speech that Hitler had given, in which he blamed the existence of the Polish Corridor on a Bolshevik-Jewish conspiracy that separated the German peoples from their true union. My father had said that there was likely to be a war in Europe within a year's time, and that the British and French would have to stop the Nazis soon.

If there were to be a war, I thought, it was possible that a German ship caught out on the high seas might seek refuge in Charleston harbor, as the *Liebenfels* had done in the last war. I remembered the photos of my Uncle Edward when he had gone out to interview the captain. Perhaps if the war were delayed long enough until I graduated from college and became a reporter, I might be assigned to go out into the harbor and write a similar story. But of course in the last war the Germans had not been Nazis, and had not persecuted Jews and put them in concentration camps, whereas now a German ship might very well be captained by a Nazi, which would make it difficult for me to interview him.

The Hampton Park scorekeeper finished typing out his scores, and we left the newspaper office and drove up King Street toward our part of town. It was almost twelve o'clock, and the city seemed deserted. Everyone had gone to bed. At the intersection at Grove Street where the Seaboard Air Line tracks crossed King Street, however, the warning lights were flashing and we had to wait behind several other automobiles while a freight train crossed, heading west. It was a long train. Finally the caboose came into view and clattered along the tracks across the intersection. Then the crossing lights ceased to blink red and the warning bells were silent, the guard rails were raised, and the automobile traffic could move again. Already far down the tracks, as we moved on, I saw the green and red lamps on the rear of the caboose receding into the darkness.

Our baseball game with the Southern Ice team on Tuesday afternoon was for first place in the league standings. Neither team had lost thus far. I got to the Hampton Park playground a little late, to find our batting practice already underway. Out on the mound, throwing to the hitters, was someone I did not know and had never seen before. He was close to six feet tall, stockily built, and blond-haired with a sallow face. He was lefthanded.

"Who's that?" I asked Jack Marcussohn, who was waiting to bat next.

"Somebody named Jessen. Mr. Rittenhouse says he's spending the summer on the Terrace with his aunt. I've never seen him around before."

"Is he going to play for us?"

"I don't know."

I went on out to first base and began taking throws when the ball was hit to the infield. If the new boy was going to join our team, it was odd that Mr. Rittenhouse had said nothing whatever about him before.

After a while it was my turn to hit. The new boy threw me some medium fastballs, and I laid down a bunt and then hit several liners past shortstop. Then he came in with some really swift pitches, and I could not touch them, nor did I do any better on a couple of sharp-breaking curves. He was good, all right.

Jimmy Love stepped in to hit, and meanwhile Mr. Rittenhouse called out to Junie Fox, who was standing out in left field, and asked him to throw to one batter. Junie came on in, and after the new boy had finished giving Jimmy Love his swings, Mr. Rittenhouse told him to come in and hit next, and Junie went out to the mound to throw. Junie loosened up a little, then grooved a few pitches in for the new boy to hit. The new boy laid down a perfect bunt along the third-base line, then hit a pitch to deep center, and another to the area between left and center which would have gone for at least three bases in a game. I watched Junie. He put a little more on his next pitch, but that too was banged over second base for a hit. Then

Junie came in with his best fastball, and the new man fouled it off. The next one, however, he clouted far out to right field, over Billy Maxwell's head.

"How do you like him?" Mr. Rittenhouse had come up alongside me as I waited for throws at first base.

"He's good," I said. "Is he going to play for us?"

"Yeah, he wants to."

"Is he eligible?" I asked.

"Yes, he's spending the summer over on the Terrace, with his aunt," Mr. Rittenhouse replied. "That makes him eligible."

When the new boy had finished hitting and our team came in from the field, Mr. Rittenhouse introduced him to me. "Mickey, I'd like you to meet Omar Kohn," he said. "Omar's the captain and the brains of this outfit. Omar, this is Mickey Jessen."

Mickey Jessen nodded. We shook hands, and everyone went over to the bench. It was quite in character for Mr. Rittenhouse to invite a new player to join our team without telling me, I thought, and then to make a big deal of introducing me like that, in order, as he believed, to flatter me.

While the Southern Ice team was taking infield practice, Joe Dodge, their captain and pitcher, came over to our bench. "How come you got Mickey Jessen out there, Scoop?" he asked.

"Mr. Rittenhouse says he's going to play for us," I answered. "Do you know him?"

"You damn right I know him. He pitches for Summerville High School. He's not eligible."

"Mr. Rittenhouse says he is. He said he was spending the summer with his aunt on the Terrace."

"We'll protest if he plays. It's not fair to bring in somebody like that."

Joe went on back to the Southern Ice bench.

"You think they'll protest?" Mac Miller asked.

"I don't know. The whole thing's news to me."

"You didn't know about him coming?"

"The first time I ever saw or heard of him was when I got here today and he was throwing batting practice," I said.

"What's he going to play?" Mac asked.

"I don't know. Right field, I guess. Looks like he can pitch, though."

"He's got on a first-base mitt," Mac said.

I looked. He did.

So that was why Mr. Rittenhouse had said nothing about it to me. The new boy was going to take over my position, and if I played, I would have to go to right field in place of Billy Maxwell.

When it was time for us to take infield practice, Mr. Rittenhouse called me over. "I'd like to try Mickey at first, just to see how he looks," he said. "You mind going to right field for today?"

I do mind, I wanted to say. Mr. Rittenhouse had a way of putting questions in a form so that any objection would seem to be self-serving on my part. I merely nodded and headed out to right field. Billy Maxwell was already out there. "What you coming out here for?" he asked.

"Mr. Rittenhouse told me to. He wants to play Mickey Jessen at first."

"Well, shit," Billy Maxwell said. "I ain't going to ride the bench for somebody like that."

"Looks like we don't have any choice," I said.

"Well, I'll quit first, goddamn it. Who in the hell does he think he is, anyway? It's our team, ain't it?"

"He's the coach," was all I could think to say.

When I went out with the lineup to go over the ground rules with the umpires and Joe Dodge, Joe asked to see our lineup card, glanced at it, and told Flash Gordon, the home plate umpire, that he was playing the game under protest.

Flash waved to Mr. Rittenhouse to come out. "They're protesting the game because you're using that boy on first base," he told Mr. Rittenhouse.

"I checked out his eligibility with Benny Smith last Tuesday," Mr. Rittenhouse declared. "He's spending the summer on the Terrace. He's perfectly legal."

"Well, I don't care, we're protesting," Joe Dodge said. "It's not fair to bring in guys from outside like that."

"Suit yourself," Mr. Rittenhouse told him.

Joe Dodge was tall and bony, and he always wore a dilapidated felt hat—not a baseball cap, but a regular man's hat with a brim—when he pitched. He was very fast, had a good curve, and was a strong competitor. But in the second inning Junie Fox got a double off him, and Mickey Jessen knocked him home with a long triple, and then stole home himself on the very next pitch. From that point on it was no contest. The final score was 13−5, and Mickey Jessen had hit a home run.

Despite our success, however, nobody seemed particularly happy. Johnny Harriman sounded off at Mr. Rittenhouse's decision to pitch Tommy instead of Junie, and the use of Mickey Jessen made him furious. Billy Maxwell, of course, joined in, and so did Dave Gregg. Junie Fox and Mac Miller did not say anything, but I could tell they were not pleased, either. "It's our team, not his," Johnny kept saying.

When the game was over, Mr. Rittenhouse invited everyone over to the Hampton Park Pharmacy for drinks, as usual. Because of my scorekeeping job, I could not go; the game lasted much longer than our games usually did. As I rode off on my bicycle, however, I noticed that Johnny Harriman, Dave Gregg and Billy Maxwell were not walking toward the pharmacy with the others, but were leaving for home.

The whole business was upsetting. I thought about it during the softball games that evening, especially during the first game, a No. 3 league affair between two very poor teams. At one juncture I lost track of who was at bat, and my scorebook showed only two outs when the teams began changing sides. I had to go over to the bench of the team now in the field and ask questions in order to figure out where I had gone wrong.

What had happened to our team, I felt, was, finally, my fault. I should not have accepted Mr. Rittenhouse's offer to be our coach, or else, when I had, then I should have made it clear from the start that as the legal captain of the team I intended to keep charge of the line-ups. Knowing him as I did, I should have foreseen that he would not have merely tried to help us play better, but would have begun looking for better players. He coached baseball the way he played in the Saturday night poker game, interested only in winning, not in the companionship or the fun. My father was right.

The third softball game was more than a half-hour late in getting started, and the Hampton Park scorekeeper had to wait a long time for me to get done so I could go with him to the *News and Courier* and report the scores. While I was seated at a typewriter in the newsroom, deciphering my scribblings, the sports editor, Billy Ball, surprised me. "Do you know anything about the Neighborhood League?" he asked.

"Yes, sir, I play in it."

"What's this about some team protesting a game because the other team brought in a player from Summerville and gave him a job so he'd play for them?"

A job? "I don't know anything about that," I told him. I described what had happened.

"The way I heard it, the kid was actually given a job so that he'd stay in town to play," Billy Ball said. "I'll call Benny Smith in the morning and find out the story." He turned back to his work.

I could not believe Mr. Rittenhouse had really given Mickey Jessen a job at his drugstore to play for us. Whoever had told Billy Ball about it had probably got the facts all exaggerated and distorted.

When I got home I lay in bed with the light out, and kept thinking about Mr. Rittenhouse and the team. I would not be surprised if Johnny Harriman, Dave Gregg, and Billy Maxwell were to quit now. And perhaps several of the others might follow suit. Or they might go and complain to Benny Smith. I remembered what Benny had told me, that in the eyes of the league I was still the captain. It was entirely likely that I would be dragged right into the center of the dispute. In order to avoid that confrontation, I would quit at once, the first thing tomorrow morning.

A little after nine o'clock in the morning my father woke me up and told me that Benny Smith wanted to speak to me on the telephone. I went downstairs, groggily, and picked up the receiver. Benny asked me to tell him everything I knew about how Mickey Jessen had come to play in the game. At first, when I said that it had been Mr. Rittenhouse's doing, he insisted that as far as the Playground Department was concerned Mr. Rittenhouse had no official capacity and that it was up to me, as team captain, to explain the matter. But after I convinced him of how little I had to do with running the team, and how thoroughly I had been in the dark about Mickey Jessen, he relented and said that he would speak with Mr. Rittenhouse.

Later that morning I called Janice Bryan and asked her to play tennis with me in the afternoon. It was not so much that I wanted to play tennis, or even to be with Janice, as that I was afraid Tommy

Rittenhouse might come by and want to play jar-top baseball. I did not want to talk with Tommy any more than necessary while the business about Mickey Jessen was going on.

Janice and I rode over to Johnson Hagood Stadium on our bicycles and played a couple of sets of singles. Afterwards we went to her house for lemonade. I asked her how it was that she knew the names of so many beach shells. She told me that she collected them, and took me into her room to see her collection. I felt self-conscious to be in a girl's bedroom. She had a large glass-front cabinet with more than a hundred seashells of various kinds. On the wall of the room, next to her bed, was a framed chart showing the geological evolution of various kinds of shells. She also had several loving cups on her bureau, which she had won playing tennis, and a glass case on the wall with some ribbons and medals in it.

My Aunt Marian and I were due down at my Aunt Ellen's apartment for dinner a little after six. From there I could walk around Colonial Park and be at Moultrie Park in time for the softball games at 7:30. My aunt would be leaving for Macon tomorrow, after taking care of us for almost three weeks. Sunday my mother would return, and although my father was grateful to my aunt for having come to help, he was impatient for my mother's arrival. He missed her company. His routine had been disrupted, he had had to do things at times when he did not expect to have to do them, and efficient as my aunt was, her ways of keeping house were different from my mother's.

Aunt Ellen came home from her job on Broad Street a few minutes after we arrived at her apartment. She and Aunt Marian proceeded to prepare dinner—or rather, Aunt Ellen worked at getting dinner ready, while Aunt Marian worked at straightening up things.

While they were in the kitchen I read the newspaper and then located an album of old photographs from the closet and looked at the pictures. There were very few of my Aunt Ellen herself, but numerous photos of the family in all its branches, for my aunt, by virtue of age and attitude, was generally considered the custodian of my father's family's identity. Such few items of furniture and decoration as had belonged to my grandparents, now long since dead, remained in Aunt Ellen's possession. She also "saved things"—clippings, magazines, souvenirs; her closet was crowded with them. On the walls of her apartment were family photographs, a framed scroll showing an American doughboy kneeling at the feet of the maiden Columbia and awarded to my Uncle Ben for having been wounded in action during the Meuse-Argonne offensive in 1918, and various other items, almost all of which had some family significance.

While dinner was underway, and I kept an eye on the clock so that I would not be late for my job, my Aunt Marian mentioned to Aunt Ellen about having gone on a trip with her husband, my Uncle David, whom I did not know very well, up to the mountains of North Carolina, near Brevard.

"I went there once," Aunt Ellen said.

"When was that?" Aunt Marian asked. "I don't remember that."

"Oh, it was long ago. Don't you remember when Pauline Lehman and I spent a week at a farm?"

"No, I don't."

I recalled a photograph in the album. "Is that when you rode the horse?" I asked. My Aunt Ellen began to laugh.

"Oh, no, Ellen," Aunt Marian said. "You know you never rode a horse in your life."

"Well, she got up on a horse," I said. "Didn't you?"

Aunt Ellen was laughing so hard she could scarcely sit straight in her chair.

"I'll show it to you," I told Aunt Marian. Aunt Ellen continued laughing. I got the photograph album and turned through it until I found what I wanted. It was a snapshot of Aunt Ellen, much younger, seated atop a rather large horse. In the background was a mountainside. "See?" I said, handing it to Aunt Marian.

My aunt looked at it. "Well, I never thought you'd ever been on a horse," she said.

Aunt Ellen looked at the photograph, and burst out laughing again. She was laughing so hard that the tears ran down her cheeks.

"When was this taken?" I asked, but she only continued to laugh. To judge from the photo, she must have been in her late twenties— during the World War. At that time my father would have been in his very late teens or early twenties.

"Why aren't there any pictures of the family when they were children?" I asked.

"But there are," Aunt Marian said. "I've seen snapshots of your father and Edward at the beach, and things like that."

"Those are all later. I'm talking about when they were ten or twelve."

"Oh, that's when they were in Atlanta," she replied.

"Atlanta?" I had never heard of that before. "When were they in Atlanta?"

My aunt did not reply.

"What were they doing in Atlanta?" I asked.

"Don't you know about that?" Aunt Marian asked. Aunt Ellen had stopped laughing and was looking at me.

"No. What is it?"

She was silent for a moment. "I thought you did, or I wouldn't have mentioned it," she said. "You see, Mama and Papa were very ill for a long while before they died. There was no one to take care of the boys, so they were sent to the Hebrew Home in Atlanta until they got a little older."

The Hebrew Home? "You mean that Daddy was in an orphan asylum?"

Aunt Marian nodded. "Yes, with Edward and Ben. Until they were old enough to come home and work."

"For how long?"

She thought about it. "From about 1904 until 1907. Ben came home a year earlier; he was older, you know."

So that was why, whenever anyone died my father always sent a gift to the Hebrew Home instead of flowers. That was what the words "Send check to Heb. H." had meant on the note I had found under the washbasin at my uncle's.

I looked up at the clock over the kitchen range. It was within a couple of minutes of 7:30 P.M. I had forgotten all about the time. Shouting goodby as I ran, I grabbed up the scorebook from the living room table where I had left it and raced out the door, down the hall, down the circular staircase, and on outside. Sprinting, I crossed Beaufain Street, circled the upper half of Colonial Lake, dashed across Ashley Avenue and, panting for breath, half-walked, half-trotted across the outfield toward the diamond. Somehow I managed to get the lineups into the scrapbook as each player came to bat for the first time, and recorded the progress of the game from the scorer's hut.

I thought about what I had discovered, seeking to fit the information about the orphan home into what I knew. What I found most astonishing was not that my father and uncles had once been forced to live in an orphan home, but that such a thing could actually have happened in my own family, to my own father and my uncles. And yet, it had happened, and they had then continued to live their lives, resumed their identities, and gone on to become what they were now. My Uncle Ben living out on the West Coast, writing scripts for the movies; my Uncle Edward in his apartment reading and listening to Mozart and Beethoven on his Capehart phonograph; my father married, in his garden, tending his orange trees—how far they now were from what must have been a calamitous event, the breaking up of their very home and family.

I thought of how it must have affected them. Surely they must remember it even now, if only in dreams. There must be times when they woke up from a nightmare, having dreamed that they were back in the orphanage in Atlanta and that all that had happened since had been only a temporary condition, and been impelled to turn on the light and look around them at the rooms they now inhabited, to reassure themselves that it was indeed *now*, not *then*, and that they were grown men and not orphan boys any more.

✳

The evening wore on. Midway during the No. 2 league game, Junie Fox and Mac Miller showed up. They had come down to watch the Gulf Oil–Lemoco No. 1 league game, which would pit the two best softball teams in the city against each other. I opened the door to the scorer's hut and made room for them on the bench. I asked Junie whether he was ready to pitch tomorrow—though perhaps, I thought, Mr. Rittenhouse might pitch Mickey Jessen instead. "I'm ready if you need me," Junie replied, as he always did.

"He'll probably use you," I said. "He pitched Tommy Tuesday."

"What do you mean 'He'?" Mac Miller asked.

"Mr. Rittenhouse."

"Man, haven't you heard?" Mac asked. "Benny Smith awarded the game to Southern Ice, and kicked him out of the league."

I was stunned. "I don't believe it!"

"That's what Bub Deas says," Mac insisted. Bub Deas was the playground supervisor at Hampton Park.

"So we're back where we started," Mac said. "Only now we're a game behind in the standings."

A little later in the evening Benny Smith himself arrived at Moultrie Park. He asked Junie and Mac to leave the hut so he could talk privately with me, and then he told me what had happened. He had made inquiries in Summerville and around town, and found out that Mr. Rittenhouse had indeed given Mickey Jessen a five-day-a-week job in the stockroom at his pharmacy. Jessen had not already been visiting with his aunt on the Terrace for the summer; rather, he had moved in with them during the week so that he could take the job. Southern Ice's protest had been upheld, and Mr. Rittenhouse had been told that he was no longer to be involved in the operation of our team. From now on, Benny Smith said, adult coaches were not going to be permitted in the Neighborhood League under any circumstances.

So that was that.

The next morning's *News and Courier* contained only a small item, under a one-line headline:

PROTEST ALLOWED

A protest by the Southern Ice team of the Neighborhood League, claiming that the Rose Garden Rebels used an ineligible player in Tuesday's game, which Rose Garden won by $11-5$, has been upheld by Playground Commissioner Benny Smith, and the victory awarded instead to Southern Ice.

Nothing whatever about Mr. Rittenhouse. I asked my father about it, telling him what had happened. "He wouldn't want that to get in the paper," my father said. "My guess is, they just decided to hush it up. If he didn't have any official status as coach, they didn't have to announce that he can't be coach any more."

"But how about the business of offering Mickey Jessen a job?"

"They probably figured there wasn't any point in making it public," he said. "The less said, the better, I suppose."

When I suggested that Mr. Rittenhouse's actions resembled the way he played poker in the Saturday night game, however, my father made no comment. Obviously that was not something he intended to discuss with me.

I was worried about what to say to Tommy. But the question was taken out of my hands later that morning when Tommy came over to the house. "The old man's quitting," he announced. "He got mad because they wouldn't let him use Mickey Jessen, and he told Benny Smith to shove the Neighborhood League all the way up!" He had more to say about Benny Smith, none of it complimentary.

So that was how it had been presented to him. Apparently he did not know that his father's decision to retire as our coach was anything but voluntary. Or did he? I was not sure. His belligerence struck me as a kind of bravado. If he really believed his father had quit voluntarily, then why did he add, "The old man's got friends on City Countil that would fire Benny Smith tomorrow if he told them to, but he said it wasn't worth it"?

I also had the feeling that Tommy attributed, in part, at least, his father's departure as coach to me—and was going to some pains to show me that he was not angry at it. He knew that Benny Smith had given me the job as scorekeeper, and he may have concluded that Benny had consulted with me before making his ruling, and that I resented being pushed out of my first-base position.

"Look, Tommy," I said after a while, "if your father's quitting, I can't help it. I didn't have anything to do with it."

"I never said you did."

Tommy left for home. My father had gone downtown and taken Aunt Marian to the train station. Ordinarily I would have gone along, and then accompanied him on his Friday morning rounds, but he was not going either to the newspaper office or Broad Street, because he had an appointment at the Power Company that would take all morning, he said, and might run into the afternoon as well.

Everything had happened so rapidly lately. Here it was July, and the Neighborhood League season was more than half over. Scarcely a few weeks more, and those miserable Back-To-School advertisements would begin appearing in the store windows on King Street. It was turning out to be the shortest, most confusing summer I had ever known. It was like Tommy's joke about the swearing parrot. The parrot cursed and swore from the time his curtain was removed from his cage in the morning until it was replaced at night. One day the lady who owned the parrot had just removed the curtain for the day, when she spied the preacher coming up the front walk. So she hastily replaced the curtain, then went to the front door and let the preacher into the living room. And then, from under the curtain, the parrot said, "Jeezus Christ, what a short day!" It was something like the way I felt.

In another five months, I would be sixteen and could get a driver's license. My father had promised to teach me how to drive when the time came. But even if he did, it was doubtful that he would ever let me use our car very much. In fact, he had talked several times about selling the car, saying that we had no need of it. In good weather we could ride the bus, and in bad weather take a taxicab. My sister and I had argued vigorously against it, but I knew that if and when he and my mother decided that we did not require an automobile, what we thought about it would carry no weight whatever. If my father ever went back into business, however, he would surely need to have a car.

I thought about the orphanage again. I wanted to ask my father about it, but I was afraid to do so. It seemed to me that it ought to be something to be proud about, having had to live in an orphan home and then becoming a prominent and successful businessman. But it might be painful for him to have to reveal that his father had been unable to take decent care of his family. It must have been a terrible thing to endure.

Also, I still felt uncomfortable about what had happened with Mr. Rittenhouse. It was not that I was not glad that he was no longer our coach. I knew that the other players on the team would all be happy at the turn of events, and I was sure that it would be much more fun playing on the team now that it was our own again. Yet I could not get rid of the feeling that somehow it had been my fault that Benny Smith had put him out. I felt guilty about it because I had *wanted* him to be removed, even though what I wanted had in no way affected Benny Smith's actions. And I had wanted it for the wrong reason: not because he had violated the rules by bringing in an ineligible player, but because the ineligible player was a better first baseman than I was. And it was no good telling myself that it didn't matter what I had privately felt, since it had nothing to do with what had happened and nobody else even knew I felt that way. I felt ashamed of myself—ashamed because I didn't feel sorry.

Our game that afternoon was with the Condon Tigers, who operated out of Marion Playground. They were a tough bunch of boys, and they had remarks to make about Mr. Rittenhouse no longer being our coach. When we bicycled over for the ball game at Hampton Park, Tommy was already in a bad mood. In the first inning he came up as our leadoff batter, and some boy yelled from the Condon bench, "How come they still let you lead off when your old man's not coach any more?" Tommy hit the first pitch into deep center-field, and wound up on third base. "That's how come, you bastard!" he yelled back. He scored a few moments later on Mac Miller's sacrifice fly, and as he trotted in he thumbed his nose at the Condon bench. Then Junie hit a double, and Johnny Harriman drew a walk, and I got hold of a low outside pitch and dumped it into right field to score them both, and Jack Marcussohn singled me across, and from then on it was no contest. We scored in every inning but one, while Junie Fox pitched a two-hitter.

Tommy kept letting the Condon players know how thoroughly they were being beaten. I tried to get him to let up, but to no avail. At one point the opposing pitcher got so angry that he began throwing at Tommy, and Flash Gordon had to stop the game and inform both sides that there was to be no more harassment, on penalty of forfeiting the game. When it was all over, Tommy began jawing with a couple of the Condon players, and I was afraid there was going to be a fight. But Junie Fox stepped in between them and broke it up, telling Tommy to shut up and the Condon players to clear out or he would personally break a bat over both their heads. Junie was six feet tall and he weighed 190 pounds, and did not often get angry. The Condon players knew better than to debate the point. One of them did say something about Tommy calling him a bastard, but Junie replied, "Yeah, you-all started it the first time he came to bat, with that business about his old man. Now get the hell away from here!" They did.

12.

My mother came home from Richmond on the afternoon Coast Line train. We were waiting when she stepped down from the coach at North Charleston. She had been gone for over three weeks. She looked smaller, somehow, and more frail, but she seemed in good spirits and happy to be home. On the drive back to town she told about her trip to New York. She and my aunt and uncle had stayed at the Hotel New Yorker. They had gone to the Roxy Theater, Radio City, a musical comedy on Broadway, and one afternoon she and my Aunt Maggie took the subway all the way down to the tip of Manhattan Island and rode the Staten Island Ferry across the harbor and back. They passed close to the Statue of Liberty, and had seen the *S.S. Normandie* steam by, en route to France.

When we arrived home she opened her suitcase and handed me a package. Inside were sixteen felt pennants, one for each of the major league baseball teams.

I took them upstairs and laid them all out on my bed. They were the same size, except for the Giants', which was twice as large as the others, orange with grey and black lettering.

I got some tacks from the workbench in the basement and arranged them around the fiberboard walls of my room, spacing them carefully, the American League teams on one side of the room, the National League teams on the other, and the Giants pennant directly above my bed. Then I lay down on my bed and surveyed them. I was so happy that I felt almost like crying.

Late that afternoon Tommy Rittenhouse came over. He was clearly envious. Although the pennants he had up in his room were larger and more elaborate than any of mine, they were only for the four teams he had seen play. "When we go to New York in August," he said, "I'll get the old man to buy me the ones for the other teams, too."

That night, through the open window next to my bed, I could hear my mother and father talking in their room, which was directly underneath mine. I could not hear what was being said, but they talked for a long while. It was good to have my mother back home. There were no more people in the house than when my aunt had been staying with us, but now the house seemed full again.

The next morning my father had business downtown, which was unusual for a Monday, and my mother went down with him to catch up on the grocery shopping. Before they left I showed her my first salary check. My father told me to endorse it and he gave me a five dollar bill and two ones for it. "Now don't spend it all now," my mother advised. "You'll want it for Richmond." Uncle Charles and Aunt Maggie had invited us to come up and visit them for a week. I handed her the five to keep for me.

After they left I decided to go out for a walk. Instead of heading for Devereaux Woods and the fields beyond there, I set out in the opposite direction, along what was now Riverside Drive. When we had first moved up to Versailles Street four years earlier, there had been only thickets, vines, and trees to the north of our house, except back at the very end, close to where the marsh cut in, where there had been a narrow rutted road leading in from Mount Pleasant Street to a few acres of plowed ground and a wooden shack that some black people lived in. The farm was gone now, along with the shack, and a street had been cut through from Versailles northward, with several houses already under construction along it.

I had not walked out that way for some time. I went along the dirt street, past the houses to where it came to an end at the point of the old road from the east. I saw now, however, that the road had been widened into a street itself, and had also been extended westward, down toward the river, through a field near where the old shack had once stood, and on beyond that to a stand of trees. I walked on down the road to the trees, and then along some automobile ruts that skirted them. Just past the trees there was an open space that fronted directly upon the river. A straight line of sewer pipe led over the marsh, supported by concrete foundations placed every twenty feet or so, to a white sandbank a hundred yards distant. I knew the sandbank was there, from where the river channel had been dredged two autumns before, but I had not realized that a sewer line now led out to it.

The pipe was a foot or more in diameter. I looked around in the trees nearby and found a fallen limb, broke off its branches, snapped the tip off down to where I now had a balancing pole some eight feet long. Then I took off my shoes and socks, tied the laces together and slung them over my shoulder, and using the pole I stepped out along the pipe. It was a walk of a hundred yards or so, and I proceeded carefully, pausing at the support foundations. I reached the sandbank and stepped down off the pipe into white, firm sand. It lay along the edge of the marsh, with a fringe of reed grass already beginning to grow into it in places. I crossed the sandbank and in a couple of minutes was standing at the river's edge.

Downstream I could see along the marsh all the way to the low black line of the Seaboard trestle more than a mile distant. Upstream there was a clear view of the docks at the fertilizer and wood-preserving plants, and I could see a ship tied up at one dock. The river was several hundred feet wide in front of me, and beyond that more salt marsh and, in the distance, a line of trees on the western shore. I had been out to the river's edge a few times in the past, back when Tommy and I had built the little boxlike skiff and paddled it along the marsh creeks. But this was the first time I had actually been able to walk right out to the river. I stepped out into the water up to my ankles, and let it flow around me. It was cool and pleasant. The footing was uncertain, however, and my feet soon began to sink into the sand, so I stepped back to where it was dry and firm.

The sandbank seemed to lead upstream for some distance, and I set off to explore it. Little hills appeared here and there, and I discovered they were piles of shells and small rocks and pebbles worn smooth by water action. The rocks, however, were not hollow and light like the ones at the beach, and not one-sided but concave. They were shaped alike but of different sizes. The dredge must have sucked them up from the river bottom and dropped them in heaps. At another mound I found literally hundreds and hundreds of shark's teeth, most of them small, but some that were several inches long. I had seen such teeth before, but never in anything like the quantity that lay before me.

I loaded my pockets full of shark's teeth and some of the rocklike shells, thinking that Janice Bryan might like them for her collection. Then I went on to look around the bank. After several hundred yards I reached a stream that cut through from the river to the marsh, barring further progress. To the east, toward the land, I could see where the marsh spread much farther inshore than where I had crossed, seemingly as much as a mile wide before there was solid ground. I could make out the low, faded red wooden building of the Etiwan Fertilizer Company at the foot of Herriott Street where the bus turned, and next to it some white buildings that I realized must be the Carolina Rifle Club. Out in the marsh, halfway to the shore, I could see some raised areas, which I thought must be the target pits for the rifle club. This would be no place to be caught when target practice was going on. At one place up by the next sandbank there was a line of shrubs and little trees stretching all the way from the sandbank to the shore, as if there had once been a road or an embankment leading out to a now-vanished wharf along the channel.

The stream that blocked access to the next sandbank could probably be waded across without much trouble, but I decided to forego it for the present. Instead I walked back over to the river's edge, sat down on an old wooden box of some sort that had probably washed ashore from a boat, and looked around. I felt absolutely alone, even more than in the tree perch in Devereaux Woods, for there it was a matter of being screened from sight by the foliage of the trees, while here I was out in the open, in full view, and yet there could be no one closer than a half-mile from where I sat. Everything was quiet except for the lapping of the river current against the edge of the sand, and, far away to the southeast, the faint, irregular thumping of hammers from one of the houses being built on Riverside Drive.

After a few minutes I stretched out on my back in the sand, my hands linked to cradle my head, and gazed for a while at the light blue sky above, with a few clouds spotted here and there. I closed my eyes. It was too bad I did not have a pillow or beach towel to keep my head up out of the sand, I thought, for then I could take a nap out here, all by myself, with no one to disturb me. When at length my hands began to grow tired under my head, I turned around and, resting my chin on my arm, lay on my stomach facing the river. I felt like Robinson Crusoe.

A plank of some kind floated into view out in the river, a dozen yards from the edge, and I watched it drift slowly by, carried by the current. It was black, as if creosoted, and probably came from the Century Wood Preserving Company about a mile upstream. When I had been a small child, my father had once taken me there, and had said that his company was doing the electrical work on the project. I also recalled him saying that he had personally installed a complicated switch box, involving thousands of amperes, even though he had no training in such work and had never installed one before. I had asked him whether he was not afraid of being electrocuted, and he replied that there was no danger if you knew what you were doing.

The plank was headed seaward toward the mouth of the harbor. How long would it take before it got there? Some days at the very least, even if its progress were not interrupted and the incoming tide did not hold it back. More likely it would drift into the marsh somewhere on its way downstream and be trapped there until the next full-moon tide bore it off on its way again.

I lay watching the river current for a long time, and then at last climbed to my feet and headed home.

After breakfast the next morning I went outside to find my father. At the softball game I had met a man who said he used to work for him, and I wanted to tell him about it. He was not in the garden, however. My mother told me that he had gone downtown again. "Is he on jury duty again?" I asked.

"No," she said, "he had some business."

"What kind of business?"

"Just some business, that's all." Something in her answer puzzled me. A little later I was sitting out on the porch reading the morning paper, and my sister came out.

"Do you know where Daddy went this morning?" I asked her.

"No."

"Mother said he had to go downtown on business again. That's two days in a row."

My sister nodded. "I think something is going on," she said. "Last night they stayed up talking for a long time."

"What were they talking about?"

"I couldn't hear." My sister's room was on the same floor as my parents', but separated from it by a hall and a bathroom.

Shortly before one o'clock my father drove into the yard, parked the car in the garage under the house, and came up the cellar stairs. He was carrying a kraft folder with the initials SCPCO on it.

What kind of business, I wondered, did he have with the Power Company that was requiring so many trips downtown? And I wondered what was in that kraft folder.

We had a baseball game that afternoon, against the Cremo Cardinals again. The schedule had been revised because of the polio epidemic, and the games were more closely spaced. When Tommy Rittenhouse and I rode over to Hampton Park on our bicycles, he was in a sour mood. He got into such moods sometimes and was quarrelsome and talked everything down. He had uncomplimentary things to say about several of the players on our team. The league umpires were against us, he said, and were determined not to give us the benefit of any close calls. When Tommy got that way there was nothing much to do except let him talk and try not to pay any attention.

Junie Fox pitched for us, and he was wilder than usual. In the fourth inning he walked two batters in a row, and then the next batter sacrificed them along to second and third. I called time and went out to the mound. Tommy and Johnny Harriman joined us, and Mac Miller came out. The question was whether to pass the next batter intentionally, loading the bases but setting up a possible double play, or let Junie pitch to him and hope he would not hit a fly ball and enable the runner on third to tag up after the catch and score. The difficulty was compounded by the fact that the batter was the Cremo Cardinals' best hitter, Red Manning. Junie and Mac wanted to take their chances pitching to him, while Tommy argued vehemently in favor of walking Red and hoping for a double-play ball.

We decided in favor of pitching to him. Red hit a shot to Tommy's right, between shortstop and third. Tommy made a backhand stab and scooped it up, looked to third to hold the runner, then threw to me at first.

He had to hurry his throw, and it was high and off the base. I lunged after it, but it glanced off the tip of my mitt, went bounding toward the fence, and both runners scored.

"I told you we should have put him on," Tommy declared as he came in to the bench after the third out.

The remark irked me, because it was Tommy's throw, not the strategy, that had done the damage. "It would have worked if you'd made a good throw," I replied.

"Mickey Jessen would have had it for us," Tommy retorted.

"Go to hell," I said.

Eventually we scored three more runs and won the game, but the episode left a bad taste in my mouth. When the game was over I got on my bicycle and pedaled off toward home without waiting for Tommy. If he wanted to be friends with me, he would have to apologize. As I turned into Peachtree I glanced back over my shoulder along Rutledge and saw him coming on his bicycle, two blocks away. He was making no effort to catch up with me, and I did not wait for him.

What caused him to get into his ugly moods, I did not know. He liked to grouse about things almost any time, and usually it meant nothing at all. It was more or less his way of being sociable. But when he was in one of his sullen fits, he seemed determined to run down and foul everything in the world.

As I lay in bed that night, I continued to wonder what my father's business was with the Power Company? Obviously they were involved, but if he were advising them about electrical matters, why would he say nothing about it? Could it be that my father was thinking of going back into business? Did the Power Company want him to come to work for them? I could scarcely believe it. He had had to give up his store and his contracting business because the doctors had told him that he could not stand the strain of business any more. But it had been almost eight years since then. He was much better now, strong enough to work out in the yard all the time, digging and pruning trees and pushing dirt around in a wheelbarrow, setting up trellises and moving concrete blocks, even in the hottest weather.

I tried to imagine how it would be if once again, as it had been when I was a little boy, he would go downtown each morning to his store, or office or whatever, and come home in the evening. It would be nice, when I was downtown, to be able to stop by my father's office, the way that Tommy could go by the Rittenhouse's pharmacy. I could not believe it. Besides, what difference did it make to me whether my father went into business again or did not? What did I care?

The following morning, when I went down to breakfast, I asked my mother where my father was.

"Out in the yard, I guess," she said. "Why?"

"I thought he might be going downtown again."

"He didn't have any business downtown today."

"Is Daddy ever going to go back into business?" I asked.

She looked at me. "Why do you ask that?"

"I was just wondering."

"He may, sometime, if the doctor says it's all right," she said.

"When do you think that will be?"

"I don't know. It all depends. It might not ever be."

From the way she talked, it seemed unlikely that there could be anything to my conjectures. Still, her reply had not ruled out all possibility. "Sometime" could be several years from now, or it could be next week or next month.

I went back upstairs to get dressed, and as I looked out the front window I saw my father standing at the concrete birdbath, using a garden hose to scour it free of accumulated algae. He was dressed as usual in an old pair of pants and a dirty undershirt with a hole in the back. He looked more natural, dressed that way, than in the business suit with coat and tie that he wore when he had to go downtown. He also looked older. He was only in his mid-forties, but he looked like an elderly man.

Tommy Rittenhouse came over in the afternoon. I was in my room playing my baseball game when he walked in.

"Want to play some jar-top baseball?" he asked.

I was still irked with him. "Why don't you ask Mickey Jessen to play with you?"

"What do you mean?"

"You said you'd rather have him on first base, so why don't you go play jar-top with him?"

"I didn't say that. Anyway, I didn't mean anything by it. I was just shooting off my mouth."

"Let me finish this game," I said, "and we'll go play."

I threw the dice for the last inning and recorded what each batter did in the scorebook. Actually, Tommy and I had begun playing the dice game together, several years earlier, and though he had since lost interest, some of the names of the players on the team in my imaginary league were those he had chosen for them. One thing I always liked about Tommy was that he enjoyed playing games almost as much as I did. We had a basketball game that we played in the winter, out in my yard, pretending we were college teams, and he owned an elaborate football game called "Tom Hamilton's Pigskin" that we played in the fall.

We went downstairs to the basement, got the collection of jartops and the sawed-off broomstick we used for a bat, and went on out through the front yard to Pendleton Street, where we set up operations. We finished our game and made out the lineups for a second.

"When are you going to Richmond?" Tommy asked.

"In two weeks. After I finish the last week of my job."

"How long you going to be there?"

"About a week, I guess."

"Too bad you can't go up to Washington and see the Senators play while you're up there."

"I wish I could." I had never seen a major league game. "When are you-all going to New York?"

"I don't know," Tommy said. "We might not be going."

"How come?"

"Oh, a lot of things are going on," he said, "and they might not be able to get away."

By "they" I gathered that he meant his parents. "That's too bad," I said.

We played another game. Tommy won, as he did more often than not. Afterward we went back up to my room. While we were sitting around talking, my mother came up with some towels for the bathroom. "Hello, Tommy," she said. She had not seen him since her return. "How are you?"

"Hello, Mrs. Kohn," Tommy replied. "I'm all right."

"How are your mother and father?"

"They're all right too."

After she went downstairs, Tommy asked, "Do your parents ever fight?"

"No, they never even argue."

"You're lucky," Tommy said.

"Do yours?"

"Sometimes."

"You mean, really *fight*?"

"No, they just get mad and yell at each other a lot."

"Mine never do," I said. I tried to picture Mr. and Mrs. Rittenhouse yelling at each other. Mrs. Rittenhouse was a small woman with a very soft voice, and it was difficult for me to envision her shouting at Mr. Rittenhouse.

Tommy said nothing more about it, and after a while he went home. I wondered whether there was any connection between his parents arguing and the fact that the trip to New York might not come off. If so, it might also explain why Tommy sometimes got into such black moods, as he had done yesterday.

My father did not go downtown the next morning, either, so I decided that whatever his business with the Power Company had involved, it had nothing to do with his going to work for them. There was, after all, no reason why he should. Of course it would be nice to be really well off, like the Rittenhouses, and be able to take trips to New York and go on vacations together and buy all sorts of things and have two automobiles, one of them new each year. Our own car was six years old.

13

I had never gotten around to showing Janice Bryan the shells and the shark's teeth I had found out on the sandbank, so I went over to her house early that afternoon. She was delighted with the shells, which were not actually shells, she said, but ancient fossils, formed by the sand inside the shells hardening into rock. Her Uncle Kenneth, who was a professor at the College of Charleston, had told her about them. We matched them up with the pictures on the chart in her bedroom. Most of those I had found were called Pelecypods. According to the chart they could well be millions of years old. She did not know anything about the shark's teeth, but we decided that from their weight and hardness they were probably fossils, too. She said she would ask her uncle about them.

She wanted to know whether she could go out to the sandbanks with me and look for others. I explained that to get there it was necessary to cross over on the sewer pipe, but she seemed to think nothing of that.

"When do you want to go?" I asked her.

"Any time."

"How about tomorrow afternoon?"

She could not go then, she said, because she was scheduled to play tennis down at East Bay Playground. "Friday afternoon?" she said. That would not do, either, because our baseball team had a game on Friday. We decided to go out on Saturday morning.

It rained all day Thursday. I could hear it beating on the roof before I went down for breakfast. From the sound, I feared it would be a day-long rain, which would mean the softball game would be canceled. Janice Bryan's tennis match at East Bay was certainly off. After breakfast I went out onto the front porch and watched the rain. It was coming down hard, blowing, and the oak trees on Mr. Simons' property were swaying in the wind. My father's orange trees were being pelted, and the rose bushes were bowing and tossing in the downpour. The gutter pipes along the roof were singing as the water rushed through them.

My father was always restless on a rainy day, when he could not be outside. He busied himself at his desk for a while, made a few telephone calls, then went down into the basement, where I heard him hammering and sawing at his workbench. Eventually, I knew, he would put on his raincoat and go outside anyway, having discovered some reason to do something that could not be postponed until after the rain ceased. Unlike my Uncle Edward, he never read books, only the newspaper or an occasional magazine, and when he finished with that, there was nothing else left to divert him.

I went back upstairs and set up my baseball game. I was behind with my league—I had planned to play a minimum of fifteen games each week, but the softball scoring job had thrown me behind my schedule—and I arranged the scorebook. The dice, however, were missing. I searched my desk for them, but could not locate them. I wondered whether I had knocked them off into my wastebasket by mistake, and they had been thrown away.

My father had a pair of translucent green dice, which he kept in his top bureau drawer. I had never known him to use them, and on several occasions had asked to borrow them, but he had always refused to let me take them. I decided to try again, and I went down to the basement and asked whether I might use them.

"All right," he said, "but bring them back when you're finished." He went up and got them and handed them to me. "Be sure you return them, " he said again.

I completed two games, and was in the middle of another one when I heard a ship's whistle, down toward the city. It was probably a freighter, en route to the docks upstream. If I went out to the sandbanks right away, I thought, I might get there in time to watch it pass by. But I dismissed the idea. It would be too tricky trying to keep my balance on the slippery pipe.

A short time later I heard another whistle, this time from a tugboat, and fairly close by. I put on my raincoat and sprinted out the front yard, through the gate in the picket fence, and across Mr. Simons' property toward the marsh. I found a place under a huge water oak where dense branches shielded me from the downpour. My glasses were fogged up from running through the rain, and I took them off and cleaned them. The tugboat, which I recognized as the *Cecilia*, was coming from a quarter-mile or so downstream, and several hundred yards behind it was a large freighter, with a gray hull, yellow superstructure, and a white stack with a red stripe around it.

I liked to watch ships in the rain; the falling water seemed to soften their outlines and make them look like paintings. Watching these reminded me of the time we had gone down to the beach to see the ship bringing my father home from New York, and he had flashed the light to the rhythm of "Shave and a haircut, two bits." I watched as they came along, first the tugboat, then the freighter, moving past me and on upstream. The freighter was riding low in the water, probably laden with Chilean nitrate. As she made her way upstream I could see white lettering of a name along her stern, but through the rain and haze I could not make out what it said.

After a while I went back to our house, running from tree to tree for shelter. As I ran up the steps to the porch, I saw that my father was out in the rose garden, in his raincoat.

That afternoon, while my father was taking his nap, I again approached my mother about the Power Company business. "Is something going on with Daddy and the Power Company?" I asked.

"What are you talking about?" she countered.

"Is Daddy going to do something for the Power Company, like go to work for them, or something?"

"What makes you ask that?" She was pretending not to understand.

"You know what I mean," I said. "What's going on? Everything's a secret around here."

"Nothing is going on," my mother replied. "Nothing that's of any concern to you."

"Nothing's ever any concern to us," I objected. "Why can't we ever be told what's going on?"

"Have you written to Aunt Maggie yet?" she asked. She had told me to write to my aunt in Richmond and tell them how much I welcomed the invitation for my sister and me to come for a visit.

"Not yet. I'll do it tonight."

"Make sure that you do, now. It's very nice of her to want to have you and Jean there."

"You're changing the subject," I told her.

She smiled. "I don't know what you're talking about."

Friday morning my father had another appointment downtown. "With the Power Company?" I asked. "Don't worry about it," he told me. "It's none of your concern." My mother went along to do the shopping, and I rode as far as the Free Library on Rutledge at Montague. I returned several books I had borrowed and went upstairs to find some new ones to read. There was a biography of Robert E. Lee in four thick red volumes, which I had looked at before. Since I would be going to Richmond in a couple of weeks, and Robert E. Lee had been the city's defender, I thought that now would be a good time to begin them. They had great numbers of footnotes and looked very scholarly and technical, but I took the first two volumes down to the check-out desk.

As I was leaving the library, Mr. Legaré came up the steps from Rutledge Avenue. He examined the books I had borrowed. "Is that your idea of light summer reading?" he asked. I talked with him for a little while, and he said that sometime before school began in September he wanted me to stop by his house and talk about the newspaper staff for the year ahead.

"What got into you last spring, anyway?" he asked.

"I don't know," I told him.

I went on out to the corner and waited for the uptown bus. The day was clear, with a brisk breeze from the northeast. After rain the day before, the air was not nearly as hot as it had been. There would be no trouble getting in our baseball game in the afternoon, even though the infield might be a little muddy. I rode uptown and got off at Versailles. When I walked past the Bryans, Janice was at work with her mother in the flower bed in front of the house, and I stopped to talk. She reported that she had shown the fossil shells and the shark's teeth to her uncle, and he had been very interested and even wanted to know whether there was any way that he might get out to the sandbanks and look around for himself. "The only way I know is to walk the pipe," I said.

Mrs. Bryan laughed. "I don't think Kenny would care to try that," she said. "Maybe sometime he can find somebody with a motorboat."

My sister had gone out and the house was locked. I got the front door key from under the chaise longue cushion and let myself in. I was about to go up to my room and begin reading the biography of Robert E. Lee when I had an idea. I went into the dining room, to my father's desk. It was a tall cabinet, with doors that opened out. I reached around to the back where the key was hidden, and opened the cabinet. Taking care not to disturb anything, I looked for the folder with SCPCO on it. I could not find it; he must have taken it with him. Then, just as I was about to close the door, I saw that underneath the file box was a document of some sort. I lifted the file box off of it.

What I saw was a printed form, with the words MEDICAL EXAMINATION REPORT—SOUTH CAROLINA POWER COMPANY at the top. Clipped to the form was a note that read "Quin—just have your MD complete this at your convenience. It'll be grand to have you with us." It was signed "Pete." Carefully I replaced the file box atop the paper. I closed the doors and returned the key to its hiding place.

So it was true. He was going back into business, with the Power Company.

I realized how I had longed for the day when he could at last return to being a businessman. No longer, when I had friends come to our house and they saw him working out in the garden in his undershirt, would I feel compelled to explain to them that my father was "retired." He would be Important, he would be Somebody. And no doubt he would rejoin the Rotary Club, and begin playing a part in civic activities again.

I began to remember how it had been, back before he took sick. How he would take me on trips with him; and take the family out driving in the country on Sunday afternoons and on the way home stop by Creticos Fruit Store and buy apples, grapes, sickle pears, bananas, and all kinds of delicious things to eat; and bring home a fox-terrier puppy in a crate; and when we stayed out on the island in the summer and there was a water shortage, arrange for an army water-tank to be placed in the backyard; and have Santa Claus send us a personal phonograph record before Christmas, in which Santa's voice sounded oddly like his, and reminded my sister and myself of our shortcomings and promised to arrive on schedule Christmas night if we mended our ways; and when I had to go to the dentist's for the first time, take me there himself and present me with an enormous green pencil box with little drawers in it containing colored crayons and pencils and a sharpener and a ruler; and when we went driving one Sunday afternoon and happened upon a place where an old black man's cabin had just burned to the ground, arrange to send him lumber and roofing material and other things to rebuild it; and when I was afraid of firecrackers, buy me a cap pistol and show me how to shoot it and convince me that it was only a loud noise and could not harm me; and take me over to The Citadel and find a sergeant who gave me a real sword and scabbard, and then have it cut down and a rubber tip placed on it so that I would not hurt myself; and on Christmas morning take me down to his store and let me sit right in the show window and operate the electric trains myself, sending them through tunnels and around bends and past crossing signals that lowered and rose as they passed and stopping them at little stations; and many other things. Most of all, what I remembered was a feeling of well-being.

But it was difficult for me to keep that memory clear, for there kept intervening the reality of the man who was now my father—the sick man with his head swathed in bandages, his slow recovery, and his preoccupation with himself, to the exclusion of any real interest in what I did or thought or was, keeping his thoughts always to himself, working in the garden in his undershirt, not knowing or caring what I was doing just so long as it caused him no problems and did not interrupt his nap.

Our baseball game that afternoon with Copleston's Cleaners was one-sided. Not only did we win handily, with Tommy Rittenhouse pitching a strong game, but I got two good hits of my own. The final score was 8–2. Junie Fox and Mac Miller kidded me about it when we went over to the Hampton Park Pharmacy for soft drinks afterwards. "What's got into Scoop?" Mac kept saying.

"Scoop's been drinking the base-hit juice," Junie replied.

"No, that's not it," Mac declared. "Copleston's burnt a pair of his old man's britches, and he was getting back at 'em."

We now had only two games left on our schedule. On Tuesday we would play the Condon Tigers again, and on Friday came the big game with Southern Ice.

Tommy, who barely a week before had been so gloomy, was now very optimistic about our chances. As we rode home on our bicycles he declared his intention of pitching a shutout against Condon's. He was still angry at them because of what had happened last time. Their batters, he said, could not handle good curveball pitching, and he was going to give them a steady dosage of just that.

About the possible postponement of his trip to New York he had nothing more to say. I thought about what he had said about his parents sometimes getting into violent arguments. If that was what caused him to get into his bad moods, then apparently there had been no such disputes recently, for he seemed to be in excellent spirits.

"Let's go out to Devereaux tonight," he suggested. "We haven't been out there in a long time."

I reminded him that I had to work at the softball games at Moultrie Park. "Oh, that's right," he said, "I forgot. Maybe I'll just go by myself. If I see anybody you know I'll tell you."

I asked my sister whether she had heard any talk about my father planning to take a medical examination. She had not. She was still sure, she said, that something was going on, for there had been conversations, and calls in which my father had taken the telephone receiver into his bedroom and closed the door. She too had asked my mother what was happening and had received the identical response: that it was not her concern. I said nothing about having seen the medical examination form in the desk. I told her that I thought he had been offered a position with the Power Company.

"Do you think he'll take it?" she asked.

"Sure. Don't you?"

"I don't think he would," she said. "He might get his nervous spells again. Mother says the doctor doesn't know why he gets them." What she said did not make sense to me. Why would my father have nervous spells just because he went back into business? I hoped Jean was wrong.

It was Saturday morning now, and my father was out in the garden. I heard my mother upstairs, operating the vacuum cleaner in the guest room. So I went into the living room, made sure nobody was coming, and took a quick look inside the desk. The medical report was no longer under the file box.

I went by Janice Bryan's house to take her out to the sandbanks. Janice was ready to go. She was wearing tennis shorts and a man's shirt and had on a straw hat. Except for the fullness under her shirt, she looked like a boy. She had a small knapsack slung over her shoulders to bring back shells in.

"If you two don't look like something else!" her mother remarked as we prepared to leave. "Just like Tom Sawyer and Huckleberry Finn."

"We're properly dressed for the occasion," Janice said.

Her mother laughed. "Don't fall off into the mud," she advised. "And if you get mud on your feet and legs, rinse off with the garden hose before you come into the house again."

We went back up Versailles Street and then along Riverside Drive, and followed the road down to the grove of trees and to the edge of the marsh. Then, barefooted, we made our way across the pipe. I let Janice walk first, so that if she lost her balance and slipped off the pipe I could go after her, but there was no need of that. "This is fun!" she called back over her shoulder.

We hiked across the sand to the edge of the river. The breeze was breaking the water into little planes and hollows, and not too far away from us some seagulls were circling, hovering over the water, feeding on a school of fish. Every so often a gull would plunge into the water, settle for a moment, then rise aloft again with a small fish in its beak, whereupon other gulls would give chase, and there would be much dipping, calling, and crying as they dueled for possession of the catch.

"They don't cooperate very well, do they?" Janice remarked.

"No, it's every gull for himself," I agreed.

"And herself." she said. "Isn't it marvelous out here? You can see all up and down the river."

We walked upstream to a mound of rocks and shells. Janice began combing through the piles of debris, extracting various shapes and sizes of shells. "I think this kind's a rhinoid," she declared, holding up a small, columnlike shell. She picked up another small shell. "This one's a brachiopod," she said. "See where the two sides are different sized? The pelecypods all have identical sides. Uncle Kenny says the brachiopods are hundreds of millions of years older than the pelecypods."

I found a small, white tube-shaped shell about two inches long. "I wonder what this is?"

She looked at it. "You know, it looks like part of a clay pipe stem.

Maybe it's from an Indian pipe. Uncle Kenny said we might find some Indian things out here, too."

We moved on to another cache, this one with a mass of shark's teeth on one side. We selected an assortment, including one Janice found that was almost four inches wide. "Think how huge the shark that had this tooth must have been," she said. "This one must have been as big as a whale, at least."

"Maybe the sharks had bigger teeth back in prehistoric times," I said.

She laughed. "I hadn't thought of that. I'll ask Uncle Kenny."

We strolled along until we came to the place where the stream separated the sandbank from another one to the north. "We could probably wade across, if you want," I said.

"Okay."

I rolled up my pants. At its narrowest point the stream was little more than twelve feet across. The bottom was soft, but the water was no more than a foot deep at any place.

"Alea jacta est!" I announced.

"What's that mean?"

"It's what Julius Caesar said when he crossed the Rubicon. It means, the die is cast. You know, dice. Don't you take Latin?"

"I did, but I'm finished. I'm not going to take four years of it," she said. "Are you?"

"I hope so. I just barely passed this year, though."

"Fred says it's real hard in the senior year," she said.

"Who's Fred?" I asked.

"You know. Fred Ellison."

So she not only knew Fred Ellison, but knew him so well that she referred to him automatically as just Fred. No doubt she had gone out on dates with him, in his car.

"What's he doing this summer?" I asked.

"He's working for his father, I think. I haven't seen him since school's been out, except that time when we played tennis."

Was the last meant for my benefit?

There were more mounds of shells and debris to examine along the new sandbank. From each, Janice took specimens for her collection, until her knapsack was bulging. We walked almost half a mile, to the end of the sandbank. There was still another up ahead, but it was separated from us by a wide expanse of marsh.

"This is as far as we go, I guess," I said. It seemed to me that we had come almost halfway to the fertilizer and wood-preserving company docks. To the land side the marsh had widened until the shore was far away. The river itself was narrower here, and I could see sandbanks on the western side too.

We went over to the edge of the river. "Wouldn't it be nice if we could get over there?" Janice said.

"We'd have to have a boat."

"It looks almost close enough to swim."

"You're crazy," I said. "That's a long way, and the current's too strong, too."

"I was just kidding," she said. "We could go in swimming right here, though, if we wanted to."

"Not me. Besides, we don't have our bathing suits."

Janice giggled. "We don't really need bathing suits, you know. Nobody's around for miles.

I felt myself blushing. "We better not," I told her. "That's a very powerful current. Besides, I can't swim, and if you got in trouble, I couldn't help you."

She laughed. "I'll take my chances. But you're right, it wouldn't be a good idea. The water looks awfully cool and nice, though."

We sat down in the sand, and looked for a while.

"I think I'll just take me a little sunbath," she said after a few minutes. She stretched out on the sand, her head on the crown of her straw hat. "Wake me for tea!" She closed her eyes.

I sat facing the water. What had she meant about not needing bathing suits? Had she been serious? And now here she was, lying right beside me, out here at the edge of the river on a sandbank with no one within a mile of us, as she had herself remarked. Did she— was this an invitation? What if I were to lean over and kiss her ever so lightly on her lips, as she lay there? Should I? What would she do if I did?

I glanced around at her. She was lying with her eyes closed, a slight smile on her face. I felt my crotch tighten at the thought. *What would Fred Ellison do?*

"What are you thinking about?" she asked, without opening her eyes.

"Nothing in particular." *If only you knew.*

"My mother would be horrified if she knew where we were," she said.

"She knew we were coming out here."

"Yes, but not all the way up here, all by ourselves."

"Well, she won't know unless you tell her," I said after a moment.

"No, she certainly won't."

After a few minutes she sat up. "I guess we'd better go back. You never know when a tugboat might come cruising by." She giggled. I laughed too, as if it were a joke we were sharing. A joke on whom?

I put Janice's knapsack over my shoulders and we started back along the sandbank.

"I wish Uncle Kenny could get out here," Janice said. "He'd love to have a look at all these fossil shells."

"There might be a way over there," I told her. "See that line of bushes?" I pointed across the sandbank to where the line of shrubs and little trees I had noticed on my previous trip seemed to go through the marsh from the sandbank to the land near the Etiwan fertilizer plant.

We walked across to the shore side of the sandbank until we came to the spot. There did appear to be a narrow, if somewhat boggy, line of earth through the reed grass. "Shall we try to go back this way?" I asked.

"Sure."

We stepped from the sandbank onto the dark earth. There was a kind of rough path leading through the marsh, and we moved along it. Not far upstream was a creek, no doubt flowing from the gap between the sandbank we had been on and the one farther upstream, and I wondered whether at one time there had been a road leading out to a dock alongside it. Occasionally we passed what appeared to be remains of pilings in the mud. Several times we came to places where the marsh completely drowned the trail, and once it appeared that we might have to turn back, because of a stretch of mud and marsh grass too broad to jump across. But I found an old piece of planking, and by placing it so that one end rested upon a clump of marsh grass part way across, we were able to step out on it and then leap across the boggy space onto solid ground.

It was a long way, and now that we were well away from the edge of the river the breeze was so light that it served only to stir up the heat and odor of the swamp about us. We were walking along what was clearly a road, with old oil cans, refuse, and junk dumped along the sides. Several times, too, I noted discarded condoms, indicating that the road had its nighttime uses as well. If Janice saw them she gave no sign of it. Finally, we found ourselves behind the Etiwan factory, with the oak trees and white fences of the Rifle Club off to the side, and we walked through onto Herriott Street, at the end of Rutledge Avenue. We were still a long way from home.

When finally we got to Janice's, I was very thirsty, and I was glad when she offered to make lemonade. Our shoes and legs were matted with dried mud, so we went around to the back of the house where Janice turned on the hose, and washed the mud off her legs and shoes. "How about you?" she asked.

"I'll wait till I get home," I said.

I sat down in an iron chair on their patio, and she went inside. After a few minutes she came out with a tray, holding two glasses and a pitcher of lemonade. The drink was cold, tart, and very good. I drained my glass and she poured another.

"That was some trip," said Janice.

"It was a real expedition, all right."

PART THREE

Not long ago, when I was in Charleston for a visit, I drove out to the neighborhood where we had once lived, and I found a street that, so far as I could determine, went down almost directly to the point from which the pipes had once led across the marsh to the sandbanks along the river's edge. The pipes were no longer there. As for the sandbanks, it was difficult to recognize them, and only my knowledge of how they had gotten there enabled me to identify them as sandbanks, because they were now quite overgrown with shrubbery, and even some trees were visible here and there along them. I was able to make out, approximately, the path back through the marsh that I had once discovered. What struck me most forcibly about the scene, however, was the shrinkage of what I had held in my memory. I had remembered the pipes as leading out several hundred yards across the marsh; now it looked like a stone's throw from the mainland to the banks. As for the path back through the marsh, what I had remembered as involving so long and arduous a hike, was at most a quarter-mile or so in length.

It is customary to attribute such shrinkage to the difference between a child's dimensions for viewing the world and those of an adult: when one is three or four feet tall, everything must appear longer, bigger, taller. But when I had first gone out to those sandbanks I was no more than a couple of inches short of my adult height, and I had continued going out there from time to time until 1942, when my family moved away from Charleston to Richmond, and by then I was eighteen years old and as tall as I was ever to grow.

I attribute the reduced dimension of the terrain, therefore, not to any difference in the perception of actuality, but to what my imagination had accomplished as it looked back, remembered, and enlarged the significance of my experience. We have a way, I think, of expanding particular aspects of our past so that not only do they come to dwarf other memories and associations, but their own physical dimensions become enlarged.

While we were living in Richmond eight years before the events described in this narrative, and my father was still recuperating from his operation, the last great reunion of the United Confederate Veterans took place. It was a major civic occasion, and the newspapers published special editions to chronicle it, and to sell advertisements in so doing. As an eight-year-old I was especially impressed by one such advertisement, recounting how a particular Confederate soldier had come back to the ruins of Richmond after the war, having lost all he had, how he had set up a little bakery, and, as the city slowly recovered from its ordeal of defeat and fire, had prospered along with it, so that now the bakery was among the leading businesses of the community. I kept the advertisement in my memory—a full-page ad, with a drawing of the Confederate veteran and his little bakery in the still-devastated city, and under the picture an account of his change of fortunes. I had forgotten the name of the bakery, however, and was curious as to just which present-day bakery it had been. So once, during the late 1950s when I was associate editor of the afternoon newspaper and happened to be back in the file room looking up a reference, I thought to see whether I could find the advertisement in question. I took down the unwieldly bound volumes for 1932, looked through them until I found the Confederate Reunion edition, and searched for the advertisement. There it was, just as I remembered it—the line drawing of the baker in front of his store, the legend underneath.

There was, however, one difference. The advertisement in question was by no means a full page, but only a small seven- or eight-inch two-column ad tucked in among many other larger display advertisements. Why was it that the advertisement had so taken my eight-year-old fancy that I had not only remembered it but expanded it many times?

When I consider what its contents were, I believe I know.

Memory, therefore, can expand; it can also contract—to the point of not remembering at all. It can also rearrange, and group. Here is an example. Do you remember the movie I described myself as having gone to in Columbia, about the crazed woman in the hospital? Well, I was sure that I had seen that movie, at that time, and in that company. The movie was Miss Susie Slagle's. It had been, I remembered clearly, one of two movies in a double feature, the other of which was Son of Frankenstein. In the interests of economy of storytelling—I think—I omitted mention of the latter. But after I had written the scene, I asked a friend to check on the spelling of the title, and he reported it as I had remembered—but with the information that the movie in question had not been produced until seven years after I remembered myself as having seen it!

Just to be certain, I made two other checks and found that there had been no double feature but only one movie, Son of Franken-stein, *shown at that theater in Columbia that week. The evidence is unimpeachable.*

Clearly I could not have seen that movie at that time. But equally clearly the meaning of that movie for me had strongly to do with other events that did happen then or shortly afterward, and my memory had, without so much as even asking my permission, simply gone ahead and moved the movie to that time, in compliance with a truth that was more important than chronological accuracy.

Yet another, lower layer, as they say. Why was it important to have the movie title spelled correctly? After I was convinced that I had not seen the movie then, I simply removed the title from the narrative, and it made not the slightest difference either to me or to the authenticity of the narrative. But so long as I thought I was dealing with memory rather than imagination, then I could not tol-erate the notion of the movie not being properly named and spelled correctly. Why is this? If one thing is to be invented out of the whole cloth, why need something else be reproduced with scrupulous ac-curacy? Why did James Joyce write home to his aunt in Dublin, while writing Ulysses, *to find out whether a middle-sized man could climb the iron fence at No. 7 Eccles Street and lower himself to the ground without undue difficulty? Who would care whether the iron fence in the novel was of a height identical to that in real life? Why did the author who invented Leopold Bloom out of the whole cloth, so to speak, care about falsifying the dimensions of the iron fence over which Leopold Bloom climbed? But he did care.*

14.

When I went down to my uncle's that night to listen to music, I took along the first volume of the Robert E. Lee biography. He looked at it and made no comment. I asked whether he ever read books about the Civil War.

"No, it never interested me," he said.

"Did you know any Confederate veterans?"

"Yes, there were still quite a few around town some years ago."

"Did they talk any about the war?"

"I suppose they did," my uncle said. "I don't remember."

After he departed for the poker game, I put on a Brahms symphony—he had left no albums out for me—and then looked at the book he had been reading. It was the *Anabasis*, by Xenophon. I could not understand why my Uncle Edward, or anyone else for that matter, would want to read about a military campaign in ancient times and yet feel no interest in the Civil War, which was much closer to his own day. If I had grown up during the time when there were still numerous Confederate veterans around, I thought, I would certainly have made it a point to talk with them and ask about the war. Indeed, I had talked with old Major Frampton, who had died three years back, though it turned out that he had never fought in the war, but had only claimed to be a Confederate veteran. I had heard my Aunt Ellen speak of an uncle, dead long before I was born, who had fought in the Confederate Army and been wounded at Gettysburg. I would have enjoyed knowing him and asking him about the fighting. I felt that he would have told me about it, too, because my Uncle Ben, who now lived on the West Coast, had been wounded during the Argonne Forest attack in the last war, and he had shown no reluctance to talk about his military days.

My father had been in the Marines during the war. I remembered a photograph I had seen, of the victory parade down King Street after the World War was over, in which all the local soldiers, sailors, and Marines marched. My father, dressed in his Marine uniform, was in a row all by himself. He was the only Marine there, he had explained. I had seen clippings in his scrapbook telling of how he had left his electrical store in charge of someone else in order to enlist in the Marines. I had also seen snapshots of him standing guard with his rifle, taking a nap after a march, and sitting in a tent with some fellow Marines. He had been scheduled to be sent to France, but the Armistice came. I remembered wishing that the war could have lasted a little longer so that he could have gone overseas.

After he had been sick in Richmond and was still recuperating there, he had taken me to the parade of the last big Confederate reunion. I had been much impressed by the various marching units, but when the Confederate veterans themselves came along I was disappointed, for instead of soldiers in Confederate gray marching in ranks, all I could see was some very old men riding in open cars and waving their canes at the crowd. But then, as we watched, my father said aloud, "Give the old boys a hand!" and the crowd along the street burst into a tremendous roar, with everyone shouting and clapping for the old soldiers. At the time, he had been home from the hospital only for some few weeks, and his head was bandaged, so that he resembled a wounded soldier himself.

While he was in the hospital I did not see him for a long time, though I had a dim memory of being taken to the hospital once. I remembered a huge walnut door at the entrance to the building, and something about walking down a long, dark hallway. But beyond that I could recall nothing about it, though I had tried hard to bring the memory back. I did remember listening to him groaning in pain while he was still at home, in a room that I was not permitted to enter, and then the next day he had been taken to the hospital again for a long stay.

My mother said once that my father was unable to stand pain, and that when he had first come down with the head cold that had developed into mastoiditis, it had been a mistake to operate on him. If he had been able to put up with the pain, she said, the doctor would not have decided to operate.

The day he had first been taken to the hospital, I was seven years old. He had been home in bed for several days, with a severe head cold and a bad headache. Then one morning he was no longer in his bed. The door was open, and there was a blanket folded in place on the bed, which was made up and unslept in. "Where's Daddy?" I asked.

"He's gone to the hospital," my nurse said. "Your mother's gone with him."

The room looked cold and empty, and the blanket on the bed

seemed a pasty green. I remembered the dark oaken paneling of the door frame and the hall, and the stillness. What had happened after that? I could not recall any more. All I remembered was the green blanket at the foot of the bed, and the cold, and the feeling of having been left by myself, and saying to myself, *He's gone to the hospital.*

And though several times during the next two years he had returned from the hospital for stays at home, and eventually returned for good, and in the eight years since then had gradually recovered his strength until now he was thinking about going back to work, in a way my father had never come back from the hospital.

While I was down at my Uncle Edward's that Saturday night, my Uncle Ben called long distance. My mother told me about it on Sunday at breakfast. He was in New York City, on business, and would fly down to Charleston when he was finished and spend a few days with us before returning to California. He would be arriving on Wednesday afternoon.

He was my father's oldest brother and was a script writer for RKO Studios. Although I had not seen him for almost two years, I wrote to him from time to time, and he always answered. Each Christmas he sent a check for my mother to buy gifts for my sister and me. Before going out to California he had been a playwright and had several plays produced on Broadway, including two that had afterwards been made into movies. In contrast to my Uncle Edward, I recalled him as being quite willing to talk about anything. I felt that I could even ask him about the orphanage.

"Is it true," I asked my mother, "that Daddy and Uncle Ben and Uncle Edward were in an orphanage in Atlanta when they were children?"

"That's right," she said. "How did you find out about that?"

I told her that Aunt Marian had mentioned it, adding that she had thought I already knew.

"Your Daddy's parents were very ill," my mother said, "and they couldn't take care of the children. Ellen was the only one old enough to work, so the boys had to go to the Hebrew Home in Atlanta."

"Why didn't Aunt Marian go?"

"She was too little. She wasn't in school yet."

"Didn't my grandfather have any insurance?" I asked.

"No he didn't. He was very poor. That's one reason why your

Daddy was so careful to take out so much insurance when he was in business. Otherwise we wouldn't ever have been able to build this house, and live as well as we do."

There was a photograph of my grandfather on my Aunt Ellen's wall. He had a flowing moustache and looked very grave. Aunt Ellen said he should have been a scholar, not a merchant, and that his own father had been a learned man and teacher in Europe, from a family of scholars. It was interesting that of my grandfather's three sons, two were writers. My father was the only one who had gone into business.

This was the sort of thing, I thought, that I could talk to my Uncle Ben about.

I went over with Tommy Rittenhouse Sunday afternoon to see the Municipal League doubleheader at College Park. Outside the ticket booth we encountered Johnny Harriman and Joe Dodge. Joe was captain and pitcher for the Southern Ice team that we were battling for the Neighborhood League pennant. We went in and sat together about halfway up in the stands, just behind home plate. A few minutes later Junie Fox and Mac Miller came along and they joined us. Junie and Joe began informing each other about what our respective teams were going to do to one another at the big game on Friday. I liked Joe. He was a tall, thin boy who had been raised in the Up-country, and he spoke with a nasal twang to his voice.

"We're going to take you," Junie predicted. "We got the hitting now."

"Come on, man," Joe replied. "You tads couldn't bat your way out of a paper sack."

"What you talking about?" Junie countered. "We got the best hitting club in the league. Isn't that so, Mac?"

"Whatever you say, man," Mac told him. "I hear you talking."

"You know it," Junie said. "We're loaded. Even Scoop's hitting the ball now."

"Come on now," Joe Dodge objected, "where you getting all that?"

"Scoop got himself a double and a single the last game," Junie insisted. "Isn't that so, Mac?"

"Yeah, man. Scoop hit that ball all the way out to left center. Went for two bases. A fast man would have had three."

"Is that so, Scoop?" Joe Dodge asked.

I laughed.

"Scoop's not saying anything," Junie said. "He's just chalking up the RBIs."

I laughed again.

"Now Rittenhouse, when he gets a hit," Junie went on, "he lets everybody know about it."

"Well, he won't get any Friday," Joe Dodge said. "None of you boys will. Not even Scoop."

I had to laugh again. The likelihood of my being able to hit Joe better than Junie and the others was comic.

"It depends on who's pitching," Tommy declared. "If you're pitching, I'll get two doubles and a single. If it's somebody else, I might not get but two doubles."

Joe Dodge laughed. "You're going to remember that when I strike you out three times running."

The chances of Tommy, or anyone else, getting three hits off Joe Dodge during a seven-inning game were remote, and we all knew it. On the other hand, with Junie pitching for us the base hits were likely to be even rarer. When Junie got into trouble it was from bases on balls, not hits. What it took to beat him was a low-hit game by the opposing pitcher, a streak of wildness on his part, and a timely hit with runners on base.

As we sat talking and watching the game in progress, just below us in the bleachers were several men who were also doing a great deal of talking, not to each other so much as to the players on the field. I recognized one of them, a man in his late twenties or early thirties, as Joe Schott, who until the present summer had been a player in the Municipal League himself. It was he who had been captain and second baseman of the Charleston Oil team that had won the championship of the league two seasons earlier. He had always been one of my favorite players. He and his companions in the bleachers below us had obviously been drinking, and from time to time they interrupted their commentaries on the game and the players to pass a bottle back and forth. They were very loud, especially Joe Schott, and as the successive batters came to the plate they shouted remarks, mostly berating their appearance and their competence.

For a while it was amusing, but after a time the incessant haranguing began to annoy me. Some of their comments were embarrassing and even vicious. They seemed to know the domestic arrangements of all the players, and be quite willing to announce them in public. They talked about the way they looked, how much they drank, and where they worked. The first baseman of the Tru-Blu Brewers, Tom Coberly, was known as a heavy drinker. "Don't breathe on the ump, Tom, or he'll keel over and die in this heat!" Joe Schott called. To Turkey Baumholz, the windmill-windup pitcher of the Sokol Tigers who had a hawklike profile, they called out, "Hey, Turkey, you got a nose like a parrot! Curveball hit that thing, it'll be too slippery to hold!" Melvin McFarland of Tru-Blu had done time in the federal penitentiary in Atlanta for bootlegging, and Joe Schott's message to him was, "Hey, Sheep, better not get too close to them balls. One of 'em might have a chain on it!"

The players tried to pretend that they did not hear, but since home plate was no more than forty feet away, it was obvious that they could miss none of the taunts. So abusive did Joe Schott become that at length even his companions were embarrassed and urged him to tone down his remarks. But to no avail. As the game wore on, he grew only more vociferous.

When Herb Feinstein, an outfielder on the Sokol Tigers, came to bat, and when he took three straight outside pitches, Joe Schott yelled, "He don't feel comfortable until there's three balls hanging over him!" Several of the fans laughed, but I could see Herb Feinstein's neck turn red, and I was embarrassed.

"Come on, Joe, stop all that," a companion told him. "You making too much noise." But he was not to be silenced. "Hey, Feinstein, what kind of interest you charging these days?" he yelled, and "Rub some pork on it, pitcher, and he won't touch it!"

Feinstein did his best not to show that he heard. But when Joe Schott yelled, "Hey, Hitler wants you, Feinstein!" Herb Feinstein turned around and glared at him, as if he were about to come up into the stands after him.

Schott's anti-Semitic remarks make me look around for another seat where I could not hear what he was saying. I was relieved when Feinstein drew a walk and moved on down to first base.

Tommy Reilly, the Sokol shortstop, now came to bat. "Hey, Tommy, I hoped you prayed for a base hit when you went to confession this morning!" Joe Schott yelled. The pitcher came in with a fastball and Tommy Reilly missed it. "You gonna have to eat more fish next Friday! The Pope's going to be mad at you!" I glanced over at Junie Fox, who was a Catholic, and saw the muscles working in his neck.

The pitcher threw a curve, which Tommy Reilly took for a called strike two. "Better swing at that kind, Tommy!" Joe Schott yelled. "That ain't Bishop Walsh back there calling balls and strikes!"

At that point Junie Fox leaned forward, grabbed Joe Schott by the shoulder, and said, "That's enough mouth out of you, Joe."

Joe Schott swung around. "Who the hell you think you are?" he snarled, and stood up, swaying, to face Junie.

"You heard me," Junie declared.

"Come on, Joe, let's go," one of his friends said.

"Yeah, we seen enough of this game," another agreed. "Les go."

"You want me to kick the shit out of you, kid?" Joe Schott demanded of Junie.

Fortunately, two policemen who evidently knew Joe Schott came up and took him by the arm. "Let's go, Joe," one of them said. "You had all the baseball you need for today."

"Nah, lemme be!" Joe Schott argued. But the policemen were insistent, and without further ado they conducted him down from the bleachers and out of the ball park. Although the others seemed to think no more of the episode and continued to watch the game and to talk among themselves, I could not forget it. Joe Schott had been very drunk, and his remarks to Herb Feinstein had been not so much the expression of any overpowering racial hatred as of the desire to heckle the batter, so that he chose whatever weapons that came immediately to mind. Even so, the overt anti-Semitism, the public taunting of Herb Feinstein for being a Jew, was something I had never before encountered among adults, and it left me unnerved. There was an ugliness to the whole affair that was open and inescapable.

When the game was over Tommy and I headed back home, walking down Grove Street and cutting through the fields and over the creek toward our houses. "What's the matter with you?" Tommy asked after a time. "You worried about something?"

"No, that business with Joe Schott just upset me a little."

"Aw hell, he was just drunk," Tommy said. "I hope they locked the son of a bitch up."

"I hope so too," I said.

144

"I thought Junie was going to punch him for a minute, there," Tommy said. "Joe Schott was so drunk he would have fallen on his butt."

"Junie's got more guts than I have."

"Yeah, and he's a hell of a lot bigger than you are, too. I sure as hell wouldn't take on Joe Schott, not even if he was so stinking drunk he couldn't stand up."

No, I thought to myself, but you would have at least gotten angry at him. But my response had been embarrassment.

15.

After lunch on Monday I was sitting out on the front porch reading an article in *Collier's* when my mother asked me to come into the living room. My sister was also there.

"I want to tell you both about something," my mother began. She proceeded to say that my father had been asked to take charge of the South Carolina Power Company's retail store in the city.

"Is he going to do it?" my sister asked.

"No." My mother shook her head. "He wanted to, but the doctor wouldn't let him. He telephoned Mr. Godshalk this morning and turned it down."

My heart sank. I realized that I had known how it would be all the while. "Why can't he?" I asked.

"The doctor doesn't think Daddy could stand the strain. The additional income wouldn't be worth the risk."

"Why would it be such a risk?" I asked.

"Because he would have to give up his insurance and his disability pension," my mother said. "And while the salary would be more than he gets now, it wouldn't be that much more."

"But if he found that he couldn't take the strain," my sister asked, "couldn't he just go back to the insurance and the pension?"

My mother shook her head once again. "It isn't that simple. The doctor would have to certify that he's well, in order for him to take the job. And the doctor won't do it, because he knows about the history of the operation and the nervous spells. So Daddy would have to get another doctor, and then if he took the job and the nervous spells started coming back, he couldn't get the insurance again, because the medical examination would say he's not sick anymore."

"Why couldn't he just go back to the first doctor, then?" I asked.

"It isn't that easy," my mother said. "You'd have to understand about insurance companies and medical reports." She stood up. "I've told you about it, and that's all I'm going to say. The only reason we decided to tell you is that you were asking so many questions. Now I don't want either of you to say a word about this to anybody outside the family. Just keep it to yourselves."

She went out of the room. She had seemed nervous and had been reluctant to say even as much as she had. She had done her best to be patient under our questioning.

"Well, that's that," my sister said.

"I guess so." There was nothing more to be said.

I went back out to the front porch, sat down on the chaise longue, and looked out at the river. Although I felt disappointment, it was not as much as I thought it would be. I had never really believed it could happen. I had sought to persuade myself otherwise, but deep inside I knew what the outcome was going to be.

From what my mother had said, my father would have had to go against his doctor's verdict and try to find another doctor who did not know about his medical history. In other words, he would have had to lie to the new doctor, or at least minimize the seriousness of his previous illness, and tell the new doctor that the nervous spells were permanently gone, even though he had no real way of knowing that, since neither he nor his regular doctor knew what caused them in the first place.

But wouldn't the new doctor immediately call his old doctor and ask for the details of his medical history? Any good doctor would do that. So there was no real way he could have hidden the matter, without telling an outright lie and finding a doctor somewhere who would look at the ugly cavity behind his ear where the mastoid bone had been removed, and still take his word for it that there were no complications.

What I could not understand was why, if all this was so, it had taken him so long to decide to turn down the job. I counted back. It had been more than three weeks earlier that he had begun going down to the Power Company. So if he turned the job down only this morning, he must have spent the intervening time trying to figure out a way that he could get around his doctor's opposition.

He had wanted to take the job, but he could not. He had wanted to be manager of the Power Company's retail store and to be a businessman again. He had wanted to do it so badly that he had refused to accept his own doctor's verdict, had delayed saying the word until the last possible moment, hoping to think of some way to trick or cajole or convince himself into doing what he knew he could not do: go back into business. Because he couldn't risk jeopardizing his family's security.

I went upstairs to my room and lay on my bed and read some of the Lee biography. The war had come, and Lee was sent out to the mountains of western Virginia to coordinate the activities of two small Confederate forces. He was without authority to make them work together, and the result was a disaster, for which the newspapers all blamed him. "Evacuation Lee," they had called him because of the withdrawal of the Confederate forces from the area. General Lee had said nothing whatever in his own defense.

Something happened Monday night that disturbed me very much. The softball games were over early for a change, so instead of going to the newspaper with the Hampton Park scorekeeper and getting a ride uptown with him, I wrote out the line scores and the batteries, gave them to him when he arrived, and caught a ride with Flash Gordon, the umpire. He let me off across from the playground, and I decided to look inside the Hampton Park Pharmacy to see if any of my friends were there. I found Mac Miller and Johnny Harriman seated in a booth with Joe Dodge. Soon afterward the pharmacy closed for the night. We stood outside talking, then Joe said goodnight, and Mac, Johnny, and I walked up Rutledge Avenue. We were arguing about the major league pennant races, and when we got to Maple Street, where Johnny lived, we sat down on the curb outside Lohrfinck's Grocery Store and continued our discussion. We were talking away, when a small brown dog came along, which Johnny said belonged to one of his neighbors. The dog sniffed around for a time, then sat down alongside Johnny. Presently, from the shadows of a hedge next to the grocery store, a little black-and-white cat emerged.

At once the dog went into action, running at the cat and growling. The cat arched its back and hissed. We watched the confrontation in silence. After a moment I decided to rescue the cat. I rose to my feet and was about to go over and pick it up, when the cat made a bolt for the street, ran squarely into the tire of a speeding automobile, and was knocked back into the gutter. It lay there, working its legs and twitching, while the dog barked away at it. Johnny and Mac were laughing. Finally the cat stopped twitching and lay still. The dog went up to it, sniffed, and trotted away.

As soon as I could I said goodnight and walked homeward. I felt sick at my stomach. When I was safely out of sight I stopped and retched several times.

Again, as at the Municipal League game when Joe Schott had been sounding off, I felt a distance between myself and my friends. What to them had been an occasion for hilarity had only made me sick.

I remembered another game I had seen several years earlier. Two adults seated just below me had been arguing. They were obviously brothers, both in their twenties to judge from their appearance; both were fat, with thick necks and round heads. The argument had grown heated, and finally one of them turned to the other and said, "If you don't shut up I'm going to have to take you behind the stands and teach you a lesson." And the other brother had said no more.

The pain and humiliation had upset me, the willingness of the one to embarrass and hurt the other, the shame of the other in being threatened with a beating as if he were still a child. It was a level of adult behavior that I had not known existed, and yet, as I was coming to realize, it did exist, and in far worse forms than a near-fight at a baseball game. The Germans were beating and imprisoning Jews. No doubt they would soon invade Poland, trying to dominate, hurt, conquer. If I were in Germany, I would doubtless be in a concentration camp by now.

Yet Beethoven and Mozart and Schubert had been Germans. I had even read somewhere that Hitler enjoyed listening to the music of Wagner and Beethoven. How could the same person who listened to the Eroica Symphony hate people and send them to concentration camps? How could Mac Miller and Johnny Harriman, who were good persons and friends of mine, laugh at the sight of the little cat in its death agony?

Was it the fact that I was a Jew that made me so vulnerable, so unable to take pleasure in violence and pain? It was not that a Jew could not be tough; I had a cousin who had been a professional boxer. But was the way I shrank from anything that involved giving pain, and could not even feel anger at those who treated me unfairly, related in some way to being Jewish?

I thought of the little black-and-white cat twitching in the gutter, and the dog barking away, and Mac and Johnny laughing uproariously. Maybe the trick was to learn to identify with the dog, not the cat. My trouble seemed to be that I always identified with the cat.

When I arrived at Tommy Rittenhouse's the next afternoon to ride to the game with him, he was not ready to go yet, so I went in to wait for him. I noticed at once that he was in a bad mood. He finished dressing, and as we were leaving, his mother spoke to me from the living room.

"Hello there, Omar! How you doin', old pal?"

"Hello, Mrs. Rittenhouse."

"Let's go," Tommy said at once.

"You boys goin' to the game? Goin' to play ball?" Her voice seemed slurred.

"Yes, ma'am," I replied.

"Well, you be sure an' Win that game. You have to Win. Win," she repeated. "Remember that."

"Yes, ma'am."

"Because if you don' Win—" she paused, "you'll Lose, And you don't wanna—ever—Lose. Will you be sure and 'member that?"

"Yeah," Tommy said. "Let's go."

There had been a glass on the end table next to the chair. I was embarrassed for Tommy and sorry that I had gone in instead of waiting for him outside. I remembered hearing my mother, or someone, say that Mrs. Rittenhouse sometimes drank, but I had never seen her drunk before. It would have been better if I had not seen it.

Shortly before it was time for the pitchers to begin warming up, Johnny Harriman suggested that we let Junie start the game. "No," I said, "Tommy's pitching today."

While we were taking infield practice some of the players on the Condon Tigers started to make comments, and Johnny Harriman and Dave Gregg, the shortstop, began answering back. I looked over to where Tommy was throwing to Jimmy Love, along the sidelines. I saw him glancing over at the Condon bench between throws. It might have been the better part of valor, after all, to let Junie pitch, I thought, but there was no turning back now.

Because the outcome of the game meant so much to the pennant race there was a good-sized crowd in the bleachers, including many of the Southern Ice players. Southern Ice had lost one game thus far, as had our team. I knew that Joe Dodge and the others, though they were our friends, were hoping that we would lose today, so that we would be a game behind them. On the other hand, the Condon Tigers were known as the league troublemakers and were not very well liked, so there was no shortage of support for our side.

We got into difficulties in the second inning when, after walking the leadoff batter, Tommy plunked one of the Condon players on the arm with a curveball that failed to break. It was unintentional, and the pitch was not thrown hard, and it put a runner in scoring position with no outs. The Condon bench immediately began yelling at him. The next batter laid down a bunt, but it was hit too sharply, and Tommy threw out the runner at third. Although it was a force play, however, the runner went barreling into Jack Marcussohn as he fielded the ball and bowled him over. Tommy and Dave Gregg ran over, and there might have been trouble if the umpire, Flash Gordon, had not acted at once to order them back to their places, and to inform the Condon bench that the next player who tried a similar maneuver would be put out of the game. We got the side out without any runs scoring, on a couple of short fly balls.

Things were quiet then. But in the bottom of the third inning we got our first two runners on base, which brought Tommy to the plate. The first pitch was high and inside, forcing him to hit the dirt to avoid being beaned. The next pitch was also thrown well inside. Tommy began yelling at the pitcher, and Flash Gordon stopped the game and quieted things down. The third pitch came in over the plate, and Tommy knocked it into left field. Both runners scored. The play on him at second base was close, and when the second baseman put the tag on him he swung his glove at Tommy's head with a sweep considerably in excess of what was required. Tommy leaped up and went for the Condon player, and they were rolling in the dirt, while the players on both teams came running up.

I arrived just as the Condon pitcher jumped on Tommy, who had emerged on top, and I began trying to pull him away from Tommy. I grabbed him by the shoulders and was tugging at him to get him away, when there was a tremendous jolt and I was knocked sprawling. I looked up to see that one of the Condon players had run headlong into me from the side. Just as I began crawling to my feet I saw Junie Fox send him flying with two hands shoved at his chest. Then somebody dove for Junie, who caught him under his arm and flung him down, too. Johnny Harriman was clinched with the Condon pitcher. By now the umpires and some spectators from the bleachers were separating players and shouting for everyone to stop. As I got up to my feet, a little dazed, I saw Joe Dodge, wearing his felt hat, with his long arms stretched out holding apart Jack Marcussohn and a Condon player, who were trying to get at each other.

When order finally was restored, Tommy and the player who had swiped at him with his glove were put out of the game. My left arm was hurting and my ears were ringing. I told Junie to start warming up and Jimmy Love to go to right field.

Before we went back into the field we scored four more runs. Junie Fox hit a triple with two men on. When my turn came, I found that I could scarcely swing the bat without my shoulder and upper arm paining me. All I could do was to dribble a weak grounder to the pitcher for the third out. I waved Billy Maxwell to come in from left field and take over first base, and I went on out there, hoping that no balls that required a throw would be hit out to me.

The remainder of the game went quickly. Junie Fox struck out batter after batter, giving up neither runs nor hits nor bases on balls, and allowing only two ground balls to be hit to the infield. When it was over, Tommy and I rode home together. He had a cut on his cheek and his shirt was torn, but he was not otherwise any the worse for wear. My left arm and shoulder were so sore that I had to guide my bicycle with one hand. Tommy was still furious and raged and swore all the way home. He was also angry at Flash Gordon for having expelled him from the game. "The son of a bitch tried to take my head off," he declared, "and he throws both of us out the goddamm game! What kind of fair play is that?"

I went home and took a shower, letting the hot water play on my arm and shoulder. They still ached a great deal. Afterwards, when I went downstairs to eat dinner before going to work, my father asked me what had happened. I told him, and he felt my arm from my shoulder to my hand. "I think it's just a bad bruise," he said. He gave me a pill to ease the pain. "If it still hurts very much tomorrow, you'd better go down to the doctor's," he told me. The pill made me a little woozy, and it was all that I could do to keep my attention sufficiently focused on the softball games that evening to maintain track of the score.

By the time I returned home that night the effect of the pain pill had worn off, and my arm was aching again. My father heard me, and he came out into the hallway, in his pajamas and with his eyes blinking from the light. "How's your shoulder?" he asked. I told him that it still hurt. He gave me another pill, telling me that it would help me to sleep. "I'll take it if I need it," I said. I got into bed and tried to ignore the pain in my arm and shoulder. Finally I got up and went into the bathroom, ran some tap water into the glass, and swallowed the pill. I returned to my bed and lay on my right side and after a time the pill began taking effect. I lost the coherence of my thoughts, and my mind seemed to be floating about in the wind, veering from side to side in quick, sudden flights.

When I woke up I looked at the clock on my bureau. It was after twelve noon. I had slept for eleven hours. My brain felt a bit encumbered, as if there were fish nets draped over my thoughts. After a time I got up, went into the bathroom, let the tap water run until it was cold, and then splashed water all over my face. I went downstairs and read the newspaper while I ate breakfast. There was an account of our game in the sports section, with one paragraph reading

> An altercation in the third inning following a close play at second base resulted in the Rose Garden starting pitcher, Tommy Rittenhouse, and second baseman Fred Hampton of the Condon team being ejected from the game.

Although my arm and shoulder were still sore to the touch, they did not ache any more. After I finished eating, my mother rubbed some Bengué ointment into my muscles, and my arm felt better. When I lifted it, however, it hurt, and in the mirror I could see some discoloration about the shoulder.

The morning before, I had made a date with Janice Bryan to play tennis in the afternoon. Since this was now impossible, I walked down to her house to explain. We talked for a while, and the subject of the movies came up. The upshot was that we made a date to go to see the movie *Stagecoach* on Saturday night.

My sister was sitting on the front porch when I got back. I sat down in the rocking chair and after a minute, trying to make my voice sound casual, I remarked that I was going to the movies with Janice Saturday night. My sister laughed.

153

"What's so funny?" I asked.

"She said last week that she was going to make you take her to the movies."

"She didn't make me. It was my idea."

I wondered whether my sister had told Janice that she was going to make Tommy ask her for a date. If so, I thought, she would have a far more difficult time carrying out that intention.

Tommy came over in the late afternoon. He had a bandage over the cut on his cheek. "The old lady's afraid I might get it infected," he said.

He had called earlier in the afternoon, and my sister had told him I was over at Janice's. "You been up to see Janice Bryan, huh?" he remarked.

"Uh huh."

"Are you getting anywhere with her?"

"I'm not trying to get anywhere." I decided to say nothing about the forthcoming date.

"You ought to, man. She puts out, you know."

"You're always saying that," I told him. "To listen to you, you'd think every girl in town spends all her spare time getting laid."

"Not all of them, but some. I know *she* does."

"You know everything."

"Yeah? Well, remember that night we went out to Devereaux and got up close to that Ford car? That was Janice Bryan in there with Fred Ellison."

Fred Ellison. Janice did go out with him. "How could you tell?" I demanded. "It was dark, and you couldn't see any better than I could."

"I was closer than you," he insisted. "I recognized their voices."

I laughed. "Like hell you did. You don't have any more idea of who was in that car than I do."

All the same I worried about what Tommy had said. I had never mentioned anything to him about Janice being a friend of Fred's. The specific identification jarred my usual assumption that it was all just talk on Tommy's part.

I thought of something else. As we had crept up upon the parked car that night, I had seen the sparks of a cigarette, thrown from the window, as it struck the ground. At the baseball game in Columbia, when we had gone there with the girls from Greenville, Fred had

154

several times tossed cigarettes to the ground in just that way. Perhaps Tommy had indeed recognized their voices.

No, I still did not believe it. It was all in Tommy's imagination. *The Ford car.* That was it. When Fred had given us a ride home from a game that day, Tommy had been enormously impressed with his car. No doubt he later realized that it was the same car that he had seen in the woods that night. Fred's car was distinctive looking, even in the dark. So it might well have been Fred in the car. But there was no reason to believe that Janice had been with him. Tommy had added that detail for my edification. That was all. I had a date with Janice to go to the movies Saturday night. Fred Ellison was not involved, and neither was Tommy Rittenhouse, and there was no reason to believe that there was anything more to the matter than what was obvious and on the surface.

And anyway, even if there were, I had no automobile.

16.

It seemed appropriate for my Uncle Ben to come home to Charleston on an airliner. We arrived at the airport a half hour before his plane was scheduled to land. There was a yellow Taylor Cub in view out at the far end of the runway. Against the background of pine forest it appeared tiny and insignificant. I watched it as it took off down the runway and lifted into the air, its motor emitting a thin buzzing monotone in what was otherwise a still summer afternoon. Aloft, it drifted off toward the south, in the direction of the city, and passed beyond earshot.

We were standing just outside the small white-painted wooden building that comprised the waiting room and the operations office, and occasionally I could hear the crackling rasp of voices on a communications radio. I tried to make out what was being said, but the talking was in brief bursts and in terms that I could not understand. All I could do was to listen out for the sound, from somewhere up in the sky, that would herald the approach of the airliner. I kept my eyes on the northern horizon, above the line of pines, hoping to catch sight of a dot that would materialize into a plane. After a minute I did make out something and strained my vision to identify it as an oncoming airplane, then as it veered away I realized it was a crow or a pigeon or some other kind of bird, and nowhere as far away as I had supposed.

But now we could hear the drone of an airplane, deep-voiced and not as tenuous as the sound of the Taylor Cub, and from inside the operations building several quick spurts of communication that were clear and quite loud, and could only be emanating from somewhere close to the field. I peered into the sky just at the northern end of the field, but could see nothing. Then there was the *Thump!* of an airplane's tires striking a runway, and the abrupt braking roar of the motors, and I turned hastily to the west to see a white-and-blue airliner already moving along the ground, its tail settling as it slowed to taxiing speed. I realized that I should have been watching not in the direction that the plane was bound from, but that opposite the prevailing west wind, as indicated by the wind sock above the hangar.

An attendant walked through the gate onto the field, and, like the conductor of a symphony orchestra who with his outstretched arms summons forth the ensemble of the strings and the brass, he guided the plane into position just in front of the terminal. The roar of the motors subsided, the propellers swung to a stop, the attendant kicked chocks under the wheels and fastened clamps to the wing flaps, the cabin door opened, and a set of steps swung down to the concrete surface. First a steward, then a passenger, emerged, and then I saw my uncle stepping down from the cabin. My sister and I hurried out to greet him.

He was smaller than I remembered, smaller than either my father or my Uncle Edward, and quite thin. He was dressed in a gray double-breasted suit and wore dark sunglasses. As we drove toward the city he told us about his house. He had a cottage not in Hollywood but in a place called Carmel, on a cliff overlooking the Pacific Ocean. He had taken leave from his screen writing and had completed a new play, and his trip to New York had been to discuss it with a producer.

After we arrived home and he had been shown to our guest room and talked with my Aunt Ellen on the telephone, we sat in the living room. My uncle lit a cigar and began puffing on it. My sister asked him all kinds of questions about the movies and about actors and actresses, some of whom he knew quite well. My mother wanted to know whether there was any particular dish he would like for dinner tomorrow night, when my Aunt Ellen and Uncle Edward would be eating with us. Anything would be fine, he declared. But my mother insisted, and finally he said that what he would really enjoy, and could not get out on the West Coast, was some shrimp and crabmeat. The crabs in the Pacific Ocean, my uncle said, were a different variety than ours, larger and not nearly so tasty. As for the shrimp, the only place he had ever been able to get the kind of sweet little shrimp that were served locally was on the South Atlantic coast.

"We'll have them," my mother declared. My father would drive downtown to Carroll's Sea Food in the morning to buy the shrimp, and as for the crabs, she and I would catch them ourselves, from the dock behind Mr. Simons' house.

My father offered to fix a drink for my uncle. "Let me make it," my uncle said. He had a particular concoction, made of Scotch whiskey, lemon juice, and bitters, that he had invented, and had named after a friend of his who was the British consul in San Francisco. He called it "Perfidious Albion."

"Is his name Albion?" my sister asked. My uncle laughed. Perfidious Albion, he explained, meant Treacherous England, and was what the French called the British.

He mixed the drinks, pouring one for my mother and another for my father. I watched them enviously. Except for eggnog at New Year's, I could never recall having seen them take a drink before. They kept whiskey on hand in the pantry, but only for the rare occasions when they had guests. My father took a sip of the drink and put the glass down on the end table. My mother took several sips, and announced that she liked it.

"Do you want to taste it?" she asked me.

I went over and she handed me her glass. I touched it to my lips and took a tiny sip. It had a bitter taste. I handed the glass back to her.

My uncle continued talking. After a time he asked my mother whether she wanted another drink. "Oh, no," she replied, "one's enough for me." She giggled. A minute later when my uncle said something amusing, she giggled again.

"It's gone to your head," my father told her.

"Don't be silly," my mother said, and giggled again.

I thought about Tommy Rittenhouse's mother. She had been drinking the other afternoon, but her response had not been to giggle.

My mother got up a little unsteadily and left the room to begin preparing dinner. "I feel so sleepy," she said.

My father laughed. "Don't fall asleep over the stove."

"I've already got dinner cooked," she answered.

"Let me show you my orange trees," my father said to my uncle. He got up, and my uncle followed him outside.

I wanted to show my uncle some of my newspaper articles, but there would be time for that in the next couple of days. I went on up to my room to resume reading the Lee biography. I kept thinking about my uncle's stories about the movie stars and the restaurants and the cottage he had at Carmel, and of how he flew all the way across the continent, and I imagined how nice it would be to live in a cottage on a cliff overlooking the Pacific Ocean and drink cocktails with the British consul and play golf with James Cagney. My father had once said that Uncle Ben had tremendous willpower, and told of how, in order to qualify for officer's training during the war, he had set out to learn trigonometry all by himself, from a book, even though he had only a seventh-grade education, and he had done it. Whereas I had barely been able to make a passing grade in plane geometry, even with the help of a teacher. If willpower was what it took to be a successful writer, I thought, then I was in trouble.

Benny Smith, the director of playgrounds, came by Moultrie Park during the softball games that evening. "What's this I hear about you getting into a fight the other day?" he asked. I told him what had happened.

"Those kids from Marion Playground are a rough bunch," he said. "But I figured you were one person who'd have sense enough not to get involved in that kind of stuff. Just be careful at the big game Friday. That's going to be tense out there."

He informed me that my work as scorekeeper had been commended by the umpires, and that next summer I could count on something for the whole season. There was also the possibility of a basketball scoring job opening up for me in the winter if I was interested.

Later that evening Joe Dodge and Johnny Harriman showed up to watch the No. 1 league game. They sat in the scorer's hut with me, and I mentioned that Benny Smith had said to be careful about Friday's game. They laughed. "Reckon I'll have to sharpen my spikes if it's going to be like that," Johnny said.

"How you going to spike anybody," Joe asked him, "when you ain't even going to be on base all afternoon?"

"I'm going to be on base, all right, and Scoop's going to drive me in. Ain't that right, Scoop?"

"You get there first," I said, "and then we'll see." I wondered whether I would be able by then to swing a bat hard enough to get the ball out of the infield, much less drive in a run.

"Next year we ought to put a team in the Twilight League," Joe Dodge said. "Take the best players off both teams, and we'd do all right. How about that, Scoop?"

"It might be," I said. The Twilight League was made up of grown men and older boys. Although it was a cut below the Municipal League, the caliber of play was considerably better than in our league, which was restricted to players sixteen years or younger.

"Hey, that's a good idea," Johnny Harriman declared. "We ought to do that."

"We'd have to find a manager," I said.

"Rittenhouse's old man could manage," Joe Dodge said, and laughed.

"No thanks," Johnny said. "Not for me."

"We don't need no adult manager," Joe declared. "Scoop could be the manager, and I could be captain. How about that, Scoop?"

"We'll have to see about it," I told him.

"Sure, we got all winter," Joe agreed.

It was an intriguing idea. But the jump from the Neighborhood League to the Twilight League would be formidable. I ran down the lineup of our team in my mind. No more than four of them were likely to be able to play that kind of baseball: Junie Fox, Tommy—as an infielder, not a pitcher—Johnny Harriman, Mac Miller. And myself, perhaps. Though I might not be up to it, either. Besides, if we combined the two teams, Red Finkelstein, the Southern Ice first baseman, was a much better hitter than I was, and I was too slow afoot to play regularly in the outfield in the Twilight League. But if I were manager, there was no reason why I had to play at all. Merely to manage a team in the Twilight League would be quite sufficient for me.

The dock behind Mr. Simons' house was small, about eight feet long and four feet wide, fronting on the marsh. A creek led directly into it, then spread out on either side. Once the tide began coming in, crabs could be depended on to move upcreek at a steady rate. I came down first, to rig the lines. I tied a piece of old meat and a weight to one line, and tossed it out into the creek. Then I prepared two more and threw them in, and by then the first line had already moved from its position. I gave it an easy pull, felt the resistance, and began moving it toward the dock. There was a crab on it, flippers trailing in the current while it held onto the bait with one claw and worked away at the meat with the other. I lowered it back into the water a little, then slipped the dip net underneath and brought it up. He was a good crab, and I banged his body against the washtub so that he stretched out straight, and then let him drop into the tub. He scuttled across to the far side brandishing his blue-red claws. By the time my mother arrived there were four crabs in the washtub, and I had not even had time to rig up a fourth line.

My mother, in coveralls and a wide-brimmed straw hat, had brought along a campstool. I moved over and she took up her station on one side of the dock. While she tended the lines I prepared the remaining line. "I've got one," she said almost immediately. She enjoyed crabbing, but we seldom did it, because she was the only one in the family who liked crabmeat. In years past we would come down to the dock several times a summer and fill a washtub half to the brim with good-sized crabs, and then she would have to telephone all over town to find someone who wanted them. Thus she welcomed my Uncle Ben's request for a meal of crab and shrimp.

I liked to go crabbing. Once the first flurry of activity was over and most of the crabs in the vicinity had been caught, there was just enough action to keep from being bored, and plenty of time to think and to look around at the marsh and the sky and watch the wading birds. No skill was involved in taking the crabs. They were both stupid and gluttonous, and they seldom took alarm and let go the bait. Even if one did, I only had to lower the bait back to the bottom and leave it for a few moments, and the crab would return. Netting them could be more difficult. Sometimes the crab would see the net moving in the water and would begin to swim away from it, holding onto the meat, and then it was necessary to hook the net beyond and behind the crab and bring it around him before he could let go and scoot sideways to safety in the current.

Crabs were not the only inhabitants of the creek. Schools of tiny minnows would come along, swimming with the tide, spread out in ordered formation like a minute flotilla moving in unison, until, heeding an invisible signal, they would turn as one and speed off in another direction. There were also mud minnows, with a facility for picking at bait intended for crabs. Being much more wary they could never be seen unless the bait were moved up toward the dock so slowly as hardly to move at all, whereupon it was possible to see their fat little bodies, several inches long and very swift, working under the water as they tore at the fringes of the meat. There were larger fish in the creek, white perch and mullet, but I could never see them. And tiny grass shrimp, too small to be netted, sometimes broke the surface of the creek water in swift leaps.

The marsh grass, stretching out a hundred yards to the river, was home for numerous small white snails that fastened themselves to the long green reeds. There were also hordes of insects. Several years earlier, when I used to paddle along the creeks of the marsh in the little skiff we had built, there were times when, moving down a narrow passageway, I might discover myself in the midst of a swarm of tiny white insects, and would have to hold my breath and paddle my way through before I could breathe freely again. Occasionally I would be startled, upon rounding a sharp turn, by a heron rising abruptly from the marsh with a flurry of wings to seek privacy elsewhere. There were also muskrats and other animals in the marsh, which I sometimes heard but almost never saw. Sometimes I would sit in my tree perch above the marsh in Devereaux Woods, absolutely still for long periods of time, listening to the movements of some animal out in the reed grass and hoping to catch sight of it. All I could ever see was an occasional marsh rat as it skittered along the bank.

By now my mother and I had deposited so many green-backed crabs into the washtub that the bottom was completely hidden. My sister and my Uncle Ben came walking down the bluff to see how we were doing. As usual my uncle was smoking a cigar and wearing his dark sunglasses, and he had on a light gray sport shirt. He remarked on how different the Atlantic coast was from northern California, where, he said, there were almost no tidal marshes, and the ocean came right up to the shore, with narrow beaches and cliffs. While my uncle stood there we netted several more crabs and deposited them in the tub. "How many do we have?" my mother asked. I counted them, stirring them up with the handle of the dip net to dislodge those hidden from sight. "Seventeen," I said. The crabs lay still in the hot sun, the tiny mandibles along the front of their shells moving slowly, and sometimes with little clusters of bubbly froth about their mouths.

"We'll get a few more, and that will be all we need," my mother said.

My uncle and my sister went back up the hill toward home. "Why didn't Uncle Ben ever get married?" I asked.

"I don't know," she said. "He never met the right person, I suppose."

"It's funny that Daddy's the only one of the three who got married."

"Your father was always more interested in people," my mother said after a moment. "Ben and Edward like to spend their time reading books and listening to music and things like that."

"All of your brothers got married."

"They're very different," she said. "They're not like the Kohns. I've got one on the line," she added.

I took the net and waited. As she drew the crab toward the dock, the sunshine glittered on her diamond wedding ring. I reached under with the net and snared the crab. "This is a big one," I said. "He's got barnacles on his shell."

"He must be an old bachelor," said my mother.

"How do you mean about the Kohns being different?"

"They're just—different, that's all. They're not like other people. Your Daddy's the most like others."

"Do you think it was because when they were young they were so poor?"

"No, I don't think that's it," she said after a moment's reflection. "Lots of families have been poor. We weren't rich by any means, either. It's something that's inside them. Isn't that a crab on your line?"

One of my lines was moving in the water. I drew it in, and with the net reached down and removed the crab from the creek.

"I think we've got enough," my mother declared.

"Daddy doesn't spend very much time with other people, either," I said.

"That's because he's been in such poor health. Before he took sick he was always doing things. We sometimes used to go out several evenings a week."

"Do you think if he'd taken the Power Company job he'd have started doing that again?"

"I don't know," my mother said. "Here, take this crab off my line, and we'll quit. I've got to steam all these crabs and then pick them."

I scooped up the crab. My mother rose to her feet. "I'm stiff," she said, "I've been sitting still for two hours."

There were so many crabs in the tub that I could barely carry it. "Here, give me one side and you take the other," my mother said. I put the lines in the tub with the crabs, and we walked back up the hills, bearing the tub of crabs between us.

My uncle and my father were seated on the front porch as we came through the gate and into the yard. "Hail the conquering heroes come!" my uncle called to us. "Sound the trumpet, beat on the drum!"

"Bring them on into the pantry," my mother said. "I'll fix them after lunch."

"I'll bring them in when you're ready," I told her. What I wanted to do was run some fresh water over them first. I had read somewhere that if crabs were placed in fresh water for a while, it would make them numb and they would not feel the pain when they were cooked.

I turned on the garden hose and filled the tub half to the top with water. For a few moments the crabs moved about vigorously, then gradually they settled on the bottom. I watched them, and poked at one or two of them with the net handle. They seemed hardly to notice, merely drawing their claws a little closer against their bodies.

My uncle came down the steps to watch what I was doing. "What's the point of that?" he asked.

I explained to him about wanting to make the crabs numb. My uncle laughed. "That's good," he said. "You went down there to the river and you enticed all these innocent crabs into your net, and soon you're going to boil them alive and then eat them up, but you don't want to cause them any pain. That's very thoughtful of you. You remind me of the walrus and the oysters, in *Through the Looking Glass*." He recited some lines:

> 'I weep for you,' the Walrus said;
> 'I deeply sympathize.'
> With sobs and tears he sorted out
> Those of the largest size,
> Holding his pocket handkerchief
> Before his streaming eyes.

"There isn't any sense hurting them any more than you have to," I said.

"That might be so, but if I were one of these crabs, I don't believe I'd be too impressed with your humanitarian zeal."

✳

Aunt Ellen and Uncle Edward arrived not long after six o'clock. I had to go to work, so I was given dinner early. Afterward I sat out on the front porch with everyone. With the exception of my Aunt Marian my father's family were all assembled there. Uncle Ben mixed some of his "Perfidious Albion" cocktails and everyone but my father was sipping them. As I listened to them talking, I thought about what my mother had said about the Kohns being different from other people. She was right; there was a quality of privateness in each of them, even now, as they were gathered together laughing and talking. My Uncle Edward said very little, but when he spoke it was usually to say something funny. Uncle Ben talked considerably more, yet there was a sense, too, that what he said came out of a private depth, so that his comments never revealed all he was thinking, but were rather a kind of selective response.

On the other hand, there was little of this remote quality in my Aunt Ellen. She was the oldest and the most outgoing. Yet she too was different—what she said and did was the product of an attitude toward life that was entirely self-sufficient. It was as if all of them had had to learn, many years ago when they were still children, how to exist within themselves, without the need for others. At the same time, as my mother had remarked when I suggested that the family's early poverty might have been a factor, there was more to it than that. They were, taken together or as individuals, a group of unusual people, out of the ordinary. Seeing them there, the family resemblance was obvious—the high foreheads, prominent straight noses, and deep, melancholy eyes—not even particularly Jewish in appearance. They were a family, all right, but a family made up of very private people, who seemed to look out at the world from a vast interior distance. And for better or worse, I thought, I was one of them.

17.

Friday, the day when the baseball championship would be decided, was bright and sunny. When I woke up that morning I immediately felt my arm and shoulder. I had almost no soreness.

My uncle and my mother went downtown along with my father, and I rode with them as far as the public library. I had finished reading the first volume of the Robert E. Lee biography and was into the second, and I returned it and checked out the two remaining volumes. While I was waiting for the bus at Montague and Rutledge the high school principal, Mr. Strohmeier, came walking by. "Good morning, young man," he said as always, "and how is your good father?" He was fine, I replied, and before he could tell me what I would be if I emulated him, I added that my Uncle Ben was visiting us, assuming that since he had lived across the street from my father's family when they were young, he might be interested.

"Oh yes," he declared, "I recall him very well. He used to be the pitcher on our baseball team. What's he doing now?"

I told him that my uncle was a film writer on the West Coast. "That's very interesting," Mr. Strohmeier replied. "You must take after him, with your interest in writing. And after your uncle Edward, of course." He smiled. "I'll be seeing you in a few weeks." He went on up the street.

The bus arrived and I boarded it. So Uncle Ben had played baseball when he was my age. I wondered whether my father had also played.

When the bus reached Grove Street it had to wait there because the crossing guard rails were down and the warning bells were ringing. The northbound Boll Weevil was just leaving the Seaboard Air Line station. I watched it roll past, pulling a single coach and a baggage car. It had left Savannah early that morning, and was now bound for Hamlet, North Carolina. It would be possible, it occurred to me, instead of traveling aboard the Atlantic Coast Line train next week, to get aboard the Boll Weevil, ride up to Hamlet on it, and from there take one of the main-line Seaboard trains to Richmond. However, I knew that my sister would insist on getting to Richmond the quickest way, which was to board the Coast Line train that left at 1 P.M. and arrived in Richmond a little before nine, and my mother would not take kindly to the notion of our making the trip separately. Meanwhile, the guard rails rose, the warning bells stopped ringing, and traffic along Rutledge Avenue resumed.

When my parents and my uncle arrived home, I described my meeting with Mr. Strohmeier. "Oh, I remember him," my uncle said. "We used to call him Porky."

"Why?"

"Because he was very chubby. His father was a grocer, as I recall."

I asked about the baseball. "We did have a team." He smiled. "Let's see—we called ourselves the St. Phillip's Street Palmettos. We used to play on Saturday afternoons, on Citadel Square."

I asked my father whether he played.

"Not that I remember," he said.

"You were a little too young, I believe," my uncle told him. "Edward played some."

Uncle Ben said that he would come over to Hampton Park to watch our game that afternoon. "Are you going?" he asked my father.

My father shook his head. He seemed startled at the suggestion, as if the notion of attending a baseball game in which I was to play was incomprehensible. "No," he said, "I've got to take my nap."

Shortly before two o'clock I went by for Tommy, and we rode our bicycles to Hampton Park. My uncle would drive over later in my father's car. Tommy was very optimistic. "We'll take them by three runs at least," he declared. "I can hit Joe's curveball any time he throws it." His father was coming, too, he reported, and hastened to add, "He's going to sit up in the stand." I had not so much as seen Mr. Rittenhouse since he ceased serving as our coach.

When we arrived at Hampton Park some of the players on both teams were already there, throwing to each other. Joe Dodge, wearing his felt hat, was loosening up with Johnny Harriman. "You ready for us, Scoop?" he asked.

"I guess so," I replied.

"We're ready too," Joe said.

"You better be," Tommy told him.

Joe laughed.

SOUTHERN ICE EDGES ROSE GARDEN REBELS DESPITE NO-HIT GAME

Walk and Error Negate Fox's Brilliant Performance In Pennant Clincher

By Dennis Clarkson

A no-hit pitching performance by Rose Garden right-hander Junie Fox was not enough to keep Southern Ice from winning its second straight Neighborhood League championship, 1–0, at Hampton Park yesterday.

With the score knotted in the bottom of the seventh and last inning, Fox gave up a base on balls to the Icemen's Donny Trout, who promptly stole second base.

Then, after Red Finklestein was put on base intentionally, pitcher-captain Joe Dodge of the Icemen slapped a potential double-play ground ball to Rose Garden shortstop Tommy Rittenhouse, but second sacker Johnny Harriman's relay to first got by Rebel captain Omar Kohn, rolling all the way to the fence, and Trout came home with the winning run.

Large Crowd Watches

The two teams went into yesterday's contest with identical 8–1 records, and the league championship would go to the winner. A large crowd was on hand to watch the battle for the pennant.

It was a superb pitching duel between Fox, who struck out eleven Icemen and allowed only four base runners, and Dodge, who gave up four hits and one walk while fanning seven Rose Garden batters.

Twice the Rebels advanced runners as far as third base, but to no avail. In the second inning, with one out, Kohn drew a walk, reached third on Jack Marcussohn's double, only to have Dodge strike out Dave Gregg and Billy Maxwell to end the threat.

Fail to Score

In the sixth Fox doubled, and after Johnny Harriman went down swinging, the Rebel hurling ace advanced to third on a fly ball to right field by Kohn. But Dodge again pitched his way out of trouble, getting Marcussohn on a pop fly to second base.

In the bottom of the seventh Fox got two strikes on Trout, the leadoff batter, before issuing a base on balls. The Southern Ice shortstop took off for second on Fox's first pitch to Red Finklestein, and slid in safely under the tag.

After a conference at the mound, the hard-hitting Finklestein was given an intentional pass in order to set up a double play.

Almost Works

The strategy almost paid off when Fox got Dodge to bounce a grounder to shortstop, where Rittenhouse pounced on it and threw to Harriman for the force-out at second.

Harriman then turned and tossed the ball to first base. His throw glanced off Kohn's outstretched mitt and headed for the fence, allowing Trout to cross the plate with the winning tally. The miscue was charged to Kohn.

The game was enlivened in the fourth inning when Rose Garden second baseman Harriman, after being hit in the left shoulder by an errant pitch by Dodge, took out after the Southern Ice pitcher and had to be restrained by his teammates.

Junie and Mac Miller wanted to pitch to Red Finklestein. Tommy Rittenhouse and Johnny Harriman argued that it was better to put him on first base and pitch to Joe Dodge. And I decided in their favor, on the theory that Joe was a slow runner and Red could be doubled up. So we gave Red the base on balls, and tried for the double play, and then I spoiled the whole thing by missing the relay throw.

"Somebody's got to lose," my Uncle Ben said. However, I should have caught the ball. It was a low throw and to my left, but still within my reach. Not only that, but when Jack Marcussohn hit the double to right field in the second inning, I should have been able to score easily from first base. But I was a slow runner, and when I rounded the base Mac Miller, who was coaching at third, had signaled for me to hold up. I might have made it in, but with only one out Mac figured it was better not to take the risk of my being tagged out.

After I let the throw get by me in the last inning and the ball rolled to the fence and Donny Trout scored the winning run for Southern Ice, I walked back to our bench. Junie, whose no-hit game I had ruined, said, "Don't worry about it, Scoop."

Nobody else said anything. There was no need to. The damage had been done, and I had done it.

Mr. Rittenhouse had sat in the bleachers directly behind our bench, and in the fourth inning, when Joe Dodge resumed pitching after his brief scuffle with Johnny Harriman, he beckoned me over and told me that the sleeve on Joe's pitching arm was torn, and that I should protest to the umpire. It was illegal, he said, for a pitcher to wear a garment that distracted the batter's eye. I did not do it. If we had been wearing uniforms it might have been different, but it did not seem right. All he wanted to do, anyway, was to try to upset Joe's concentration. Besides, it was Johnny Harriman who had torn Joe's shirtsleeve during their scuffle.

I went upstairs and took a shower and afterwards went out onto the front porch, where my uncle and my father were sitting.

"That pitcher of yours was mighty good," my uncle said. "He pitched a beautiful game."

"Yes, it wasn't his fault that we lost," I said.

"Your team played very well," my uncle said, "and you almost won."

"We would have won if it hadn't been for me."

"Hold on a minute, now. If you're going to start figuring that way, what about the two batters who struck out when you were at third base? And what about all the batters on your team that didn't even get on base?"

"That's all well and good," I told him, "but if I'd have caught that throw like I should, we wouldn't have lost."

If, I kept wondering—*if* we had let Junie pitch to Red Finklestein, as he wanted to, instead of putting him on base. *If* I'd gotten a better jump from first when Jack Marcussohn hit the double. *If*—

"Let me tell you something that you won't believe," my uncle said. "Some day, years from now, you're going to look back on this game, and you're going to take a great deal of satisfaction from it. And not only that, but you're going to remember how you feel right now, and it's going to amuse you."

The softball game that evening was the last that I would be working before my three-week job was over. The two No. 1 league teams were warming up before the last game of the night when to my surprise I saw Joe Dodge and Johnny Harriman come ambling in across the outfield, together as usual. Joe was still wearing the shirt with the torn sleeve.

"You guys speaking to each other again?" I asked.

"Sure, man," Joe Dodge said.

"We don't let a little thing like a ball game worry us," Johnny added.

"Well, you whipped us, buddy," I told Joe. "You were too much pitcher for us."

"I was lucky," Joe replied.

"You were lucky I was playing first base, all right."

"That wasn't just your fault, Scoop," Johnny Harriman said. "It was a low throw. They should have given me the error, not you."

"It wasn't that much off. I should have had it."

"What the hell difference does it make?" Joe asked. "It was a damn good game, and it could have gone either way."

While we were talking, along came Mac Miller and Junie Fox. There was not enough room for them in the scorer's hut, so they stood outside. After the No. 1 league game was over, we decided, we would go over to Rittenhouse's pharmacy, which always stayed open till midnight, and celebrate the end of the season.

I made Joe and Johnny get out of the hut so they would not distract me from copying my summaries and so I could go with them. When the game was over we waited for a few minutes until the Hampton Park scorekeeper arrived. He gave us all a ride as far as King and Broad streets, and we walked on up King together. Joe told Junie and Mac about the idea we had of entering the Twilight League together next season.

Junie was delighted. "We'll mow 'em down!" he declared. He went through the motion of delivering a fastball. "With me and Joe taking turns on the mound, nobody could touch us. Isn't that right, Scoop?"

"You know it," I answered, using a favorite phrase of his.

We passed by the front entrance of the Charleston Library Society. "What kind of library's that, Scoop?" Joe Dodge asked.

"Just a library, I think."

"I thought the library was down on Rutledge and Montague," Johnny Harriman said.

"That's the free library," I told him. "This one's a private one."

"You mean you have to pay money to use it?"

"I think so."

"I'll take the free one, then," Johnny declared.

Joe Dodge laughed. "You never even use the one at school, man," he told Johnny. "What would you do if you found yourself inside a library? You wouldn't even know how to act."

171

"I'd go find me a book on baseball."

Junie Fox snorted. "Nobody ever learned to play baseball from reading a book. Isn't that right, Scoop?"

"You know it," I said.

Tommy came over the next morning, and as was his way, he was full of second guesses about the game. I let him talk. I wondered whether his father had made the criticisms and he was merely repeating them.

"When are you going to Richmond?" he asked after a while.

"Tuesday. Are you going to New York?"

"No, the trip's off. My old lady had to go to the mountains, to some kind of a sanatorium."

"That's too bad," I said. "How long will she be there?"

"About a month, I guess. That's how long it took last time."

So Mrs. Rittenhouse had been hospitalized before. Her drinking must have been a problem for some time.

"The old man's going to take me on a fishing trip to St. Helena Sound," Tommy said.

"That sounds like fun."

He said nothing for a moment, then, "Want to go to a movie tonight?"

"I'm going out."

He looked at me suspiciously. "You got a date?"

I nodded. I was sure he knew who it was with, and I almost wanted him to make his usual remark about Janice's availability, but this time he had no comment.

We heard the sound of a ship's whistle from back behind Mr. Simons' house, and we went over toward the marsh to look. One of the White Stack tugboats was heading down the Ashley River, and behind it came a small freighter. She was black hulled with a yellow superstructure, and riding low in the water, apparently with a full cargo. We watched her move past.

"I wish I was going with her," Tommy said.

"Where would you want to go?"

"Anywhere," he answered. "I wouldn't care where. Just so it's away from here."

We walked back toward my house. "You want to go to the Municipal League game this afternoon?" I asked.

"Sure."

"I'll be by about one o'clock, then," I said.

"Okay."

Tommy went on home. I had not really intended to go to the game, but I thought he needed something to do. We would probably sit behind home plate and take turns predicting the pitches. He always won, but I didn't mind. I just liked to call the pitches.

18.

Because of the championship game and my Uncle Ben's visit, I had actually given little thought to my date, but as the time drew near I began to get a little anxious. I told myself that this was silly. But this was a *date*, and on Saturday night.

To add to my misgivings, my summer suit, the only one I owned, was over a year old, and when I put it on before dinner the sleeves were up along my wrists, and the cuffs of the trousers did not reach down to the tops of my shoes. If I had only waited until cooler weather I could have worn my winter suit, which fit much better. I began to wish that I had never thought of asking Janice to go to the movies. There was no law that said I had to begin taking out girls just now. I had not known when I was well off.

Yet, at the same time that I entertained all these doubts, I felt an excitement and was proud of myself. I was going on a *date*. On Saturday night, with a girl, to the movies. I had asked her to go with me, and she had accepted. I was a rising senior in high school, and had now begun Going Out With Girls. Or in any event, with *a* girl.

At dinner that evening my imminent mission was very much at the forefront. My mother tended to take the occasion very seriously, and spoke of it with an earnestness that embarrassed me. My uncle seemed amused. What my father thought about it I could not tell. If anything, he appeared to be somewhat embarrassed, too. I did my best to appear unconcerned.

After dinner my uncle called me aside. He took out his wallet and handed me a five-dollar bill. "Here, have a good time," he said.

"I won't need that much money," I protested. "It won't cost more than a couple of dollars."

"You never can tell," my uncle said, blowing a cloud of smoke from his cigar. "Women are expensive creatures."

Before it was time for me to leave, my mother inspected my appearance, made me retie my necktie, and tried to pull my coat sleeves farther down. She also gave me last minute instructions, such as "Now be sure that you compliment her on her appearance," and "Remember that a gentleman always stands until a lady is seated."

Finally it was time to go. "Kiss me goodnight," my mother said. I kissed her on her forehead, and as I did I saw that her eyes were moist. Good Lord, I thought to myself.

I walked down to Janice's house, feeling apprehensive and wishing that instead I were going over to Tommy's, or down to my Uncle Edward's apartment to play music, or almost anywhere else. I went up the front walk, rang the doorbell, and Janice's father came to the door. I was ushered to a seat in the parlor, and Mr. Bryan made conversation about the weather and going back to school soon, until after a few minutes Janice appeared. She was dressed in a dark blue gown, was wearing stockings, and her hair was fixed up. She was carrying a small handbag. She looked attractive, and I recalled how the girls at the press convention had looked several years older when they came down for the dance. It was even more true of Janice.

As we walked toward the bus stop at Rutledge Avenue I felt very self-conscious, and groped for something to say. But Janice chatted away about tennis, school, the movies, shells, and various things, and before long I was telling her about my uncle's visit, and about the baseball game. We got off the bus at King and Wentworth, walked up two blocks to the Gloria Theater, and an usher in uniform and a little round hat conducted us to seats. The main feature was getting underway.

Stagecoach was a good movie. It was about some people, all riding together in a stagecoach in the West, who are attacked by the Apaches. The actors were Thomas Mitchell, who had once appeared in one of my uncle's plays on Broadway, John Carradine, and Donald Meek. For much of the time I forgot all about the occasion and followed the story. At other times, though, I felt quite conscious of sitting there next to Janice in the dark. In the row of seats just ahead of us a man and a girl were cuddled close to each other, with her head on his shoulder. Out of the corner of my eye I glanced at Janice. She seemed absorbed in the picture. Her hand was resting on the arm of the seat next to me, and I thought about reaching over and grasping it. I went so far as to place my hand on the arm of my seat, next to hers, but even though our forearms were touching, I could not bring myself to take hold of her hand.

After the movie was over we walked back down to Rittenhouse's pharmacy, where we took seats at a table near the soda fountain. We ordered Lucky Mondaes, something like an ice-cream soda but larger, with a great deal of thick chocolate fudge syrup. They were called Lucky because if the fountain check had a red star printed on it, the order was free. We worked on the Lucky Mondaes and discussed the movie. While we were talking, in walked Fred Ellison, with a girl I did not know.

They came over to our table. "May we join you?" Fred asked.

"Sure," I said.

The girl's name was Maureen, and she and Janice knew each other. The waitress took their order. Fred and Maureen had also been to see the movie. "I saw you-all leave," Maureen said. We talked about the movie and about going back to school. Fred would be a freshman at Clemson in September. Janice and Maureen appeared to get along well, and I was glad Fred had encountered me here on a date, especially with a girl he knew.

"Can I give you a ride uptown?" Fred asked as we got up to leave. Before I could answer, Janice said, "No thanks, we'll manage all right."

We said goodby and crossed Wentworth Street to wait for the bus. I felt pleased that Janice had preferred to ride home with me on the bus rather than for us to go along with them. A bus rounded the corner of Meeting Street and pulled to a stop. It was mostly empty. We got in and took seats halfway back.

"Maureen seems like a nice girl," I said.

Janice laughed. "Did you notice the way the scarf she was wearing clashed with her blouse?"

"No, I didn't." This reminded me that I had failed to compliment her on her appearance. "That's a very pretty dress you've got on," I said.

She was not as talkative as she had been on the way downtown. But she seemed interested in what I had to say, and I was pleased to be out with her. I talked about my plans for the school newspaper, and about the Robert E. Lee biography, and about fielding a team in the Twilight League next year. When we reached her house I took her up to the door and said goodnight.

I walked the rest of the way up Versailles feeling very satisfied. "Thank you for a lovely evening," she had said, and smiled, when I took her to her door. Well, there would be other such evenings as soon as I returned from Richmond. And next time I would feel more confident, and would take her hand, and perhaps even kiss her good-night, too.

The poker game was still in session when I arrived home. There were cars parked in our driveway, and the light from the windows of the poker room was streaked with smoke. I went up the front steps and into the living room. Although it was close to midnight, my sister was there. She had just returned from a party.

"How did it go?" she asked.

"Okay." I told her about the movie and of stopping at Rittenhouse's Pharmacy afterward, and of our meeting with Fred Ellison and his date.

"Oh, oh!" said my sister.

"What do you mean?"

"Well, Janice was going with him a lot until just before school closed, you know, and then they busted up."

"I didn't know that." Indeed I had not.

I went on up to my room. They had been going steady, and had broken up. So that was it.

I put on my pajamas, and got into bed, turning on my bed light. From the open window I could hear the poker game breaking up, and the participants talking and laughing as they walked toward the automobiles. I made out Mr. Ray Lowell's voice, with his chuckling laugh, and I heard my Uncle Edward say something, and more laughter. Then doors slammed, and engines started up, and the automobiles drove off down Versailles Street. After a few minutes my father and Uncle Ben came up the basement steps. They said a few words, and I heard my uncle come upstairs to the guest room where he was staying. A few minutes later he went to the bathroom off the hall. After he had gone to bed, I thought about the evening.

I had completely missed the significance of what was happening. Instead of being an expression of pleasure in my sole company, as I had smugly assumed, Janice's quick refusal of Fred's offer to give us a ride uptown had been her perfect way of contemptuously declining Fred's company. And on the way back, while I had been talking away, believing that what I was saying was of such vast interest to her, she had no doubt been in a silent rage about Fred, and jealous of Maureen.

177

How naïve I was. And vain. Janice had broken with Fred, and so she had taken whatever was at hand in the way of male company. Better to go to the movies with me than with no one at all.

The bitch! I said aloud. I would show her. Never again would I ask her to go anywhere. As far as I was concerned, she could just go to hell.

The night Seaboard train was crossing the river. I could hear the locomotive pounding away as it headed out onto the trestle, pulling its train of cars. It would be nice to be a locomotive engineer at night, and lean out the window of the cab, high above the drive wheels and gaze down the track as the headlamp illuminated the way up ahead, and watch the woods and bridges and crossroads and towns and cities appear and recede. A railroad engineer always knew where he was going, always had a destination, even if only the next town down the line, or the freight yards.

Damn Fred Ellison!

As usual my anger subsided overnight. The next morning I decided that my reaction to what my sister had said about Fred and Janice had been excessive. After all, my sister was the one who had said that Janice had wanted me to ask her for the date. I had a way of expecting too much of an event or an occasion, or of a person for that matter, and of putting too much importance and significance upon something—and then, at the first intimation that everything was not entirely what I desired it to be, becoming very disappointed and depressed, and blaming everything on myself. Janice had said she had enjoyed the evening. I meant to leave it at that.

19.

My uncle had been with us for four days, and Monday morning he would leave by airplane for the West Coast. Thus far there had been no opportunity for me to talk with him at any length. He must have realized that, for on Sunday afternoon, following dinner, he proposed that we go out for a walk. We set off up Riverside Drive, and then down past the grove to the edge of the marsh. I told him about finding the fossil shells and shark's teeth out on the sandbanks, explaining, however, that other than along the sewer pipe the only access was from behind the Etiwan plant, over a mile away.

"Let's just go out along the pipes, then," he said, and, when I looked dubious, "What's the matter? Do you think I can't walk out there across that pipe?"

"No . . . but . . ."

"I'll make a bet with you," he said. "I'll give you five dollars for every time I fall off the pipe, and you give me fifty cents for every time you do."

I took off my shoes and slung them over my shoulder. Not my uncle; he would keep his shoes on, he said. Whereupon he stepped onto the sewer pipe and walked carefully and with perfect balance out along the rounded surface, all the while smoking a cigar. Without so much as a pause to catch his breath he moved out over the marsh and did not stop until he had reached the other side. As for myself, I proceeded much more slowly, and even with a stick to maintain my balance I lost my footing once and almost toppled in. When I arrived at the sandbank he had been waiting for me for several minutes.

He grinned. "You nearly lost fifty cents," he said.

"I know."

"What you didn't know was that I've got perfect balance. When we get home I'll make another bet with you. I'll bet you that I can stand on one leg, with my arms folded, without moving, twice as long as you can."

"I'm sure you can," I said. Balance was not one of my skills.

I showed him some of the mounds of fossil shells and shark's teeth. He picked out a few shark's teeth and put them in his pocket.

179

"I've got a friend in Carmel who might like to have these," he said.

We walked over to the edge of the river and looked down at the water for a time. There was a sailboat maneuvering a half-mile downstream. "Being out on the water is something that's never interested me very much," he said. "I've never had the urge to go boating or fishing."

"Not even when you were a boy?"

"Not so far as I can recall. Your Uncle Edward and your father used to go fishing occasionally, but not me."

I said that I had never known my father to take any interest in fishing.

"He used to when he was a kid. And he also used to be a very strong swimmer," my uncle said. "I remember once that he and your cousin Sam Brown swam across Breaches' Inlet, between Sullivan's Island and the Isle of Palms. The current there was very strong, and there were signs warning against going in swimming. But they swam right across, side by side."

Now that my uncle had mentioned it, I recalled watching my father swimming far out beyond the breakers at Folly Beach, and then diving through a high wave and coming toward me, with the water streaming from his head and face. It was odd, I thought, that I had never been able to swim, and was afraid of venturing into water over my head, while my father had been so bold a swimmer. "I guess it's because of his operation that he doesn't swim any more," I said.

"No doubt about that," my uncle replied. "The first thing that water attacks is your ears. He couldn't risk anything that might cause an ear infection."

We walked upstream. "I guess you heard about the Power Company," I said.

"Yes, your mother told me about it."

"I wish Daddy could have taken it."

"It's just one of those things," my uncle said. "Your father's had a rough time, and it's been rough on your mother, too."

We continued up the sandbank, our feet making crunching noises in the sand as we stepped along.

"Do you think he'll ever be able to go back into business?" I asked.

"I don't know." He thought for a moment, and blew out a long stream of smoke from his cigar. "I wouldn't think so—for a long time, anyway. You see, with an illness like his, physical recovery isn't the only thing that's involved. The shock to your system doesn't go away just because the wound heals over. I found that out right after the war, when I was in the army hospital. My wounds had healed within a year's time, but it was several years more before I recovered from the shock of having the wounds, and being laid up."

"I don't see what you mean."

"Look at it this way. Suddenly you find yourself disabled. Your body is out of commission. It's a shock to you. You think about it all the time. Everything you do and think seems dominated by the state of your body and your health. And remember, when I was wounded I was just a young man, in my twenties. Whereas your father was in his late thirties when it happened, with a successful business he'd built up over the years, and a family. He lost his health, he lost his business, he almost died—that's not the sort of thing you can just shake off after a little while. It changed his entire life."

We were at the point where the creek cut across the sandbank. "We can wade over," I said.

"What's up there?" my uncle asked.

"More sandbank."

"In that case, let's go sit over by the river on that little rise there."

"The point is," he resumed as we settled down on the dry sand, "a shock like that, physical and mental, turns you in on yourself. Whatever you think about, whatever you do or want to do, you can't get away from it. Do you see what I mean?"

"I believe so."

My uncle lit another cigar. There was enough breeze on the unprotected sandbanks to make him cup his hands about the match flame and concentrate on breathing in quickly, in rapid puffs, to get it going properly. "Okay," he said, "you're a baseball player, let's say. One day you go up to bat, and you get hit in the head by a wild pitch, and you suffer a skull fracture. It's painful, but you make your physical recovery in a few months' time. But when you try to go back to playing, and you come up to bat again, every time the pitcher comes in with a pitch, you instinctively duck away from it, because there's the thought that it could happen again. You have to concentrate not just on hitting the ball, but on forcing yourself not to duck away from the plate, too. You might go on playing for years more, and hit very well, but you'll always have that instinctive reaction, and you'll always have to concentrate on overcoming it every time you come to bat. Do you understand now?"

"Yes, I see what you mean."

I looked far downstream, at the Seaboard trestle that spanned the river. There was a tiny object moving along it, and I realized that it was the southbound Boll Weevil. It was a long way off, and the wind was blowing in that direction, so that I could hear no sound from it. It proceeded very slowly across the trestle, taking its own good time as it headed for Savannah.

"Are you going to play ball next summer, too?" my uncle asked.

I described the plan for entering the Twilight League. "I probably won't play much," I said. "I'll just manage."

"You're fortunate," my uncle said, "to have your afternoons free. When I was your age, the only time I could play was on weekends and holidays."

I told him about the scorekeeping job I had been promised. "That sounds all right," he said. "There weren't any jobs like that when I was starting out. I had to work as a stock boy at Pearlstine's Hardware. I worked eleven hours a day, from seven to six, and half a day on Saturday, and I got five dollars a week."

"How did you get into newspaper work?"

"There was a job open on the *News and Courier*. I applied for it, and so did Sidney Rothenburg." Sidney Rothenburg was now a prominent lawyer in town, who was also an alderman. "We both worked for two months, without a salary, on the understanding that at the end of that time, one of us would be given the job. He had a college education and I didn't, and he got it. But about that time there was an opening on a paper in Birmingham, and they recommended me for it."

"Why did you leave newspaper work?" I asked.

"After a few years it got to be boring. I was doing the same things over and over. To make any money you had to be a deskman, and I got tired of writing headlines and editing copy."

"I like doing that," I said.

"I did, too, at first. And your Uncle Edward's been doing it for years, and he doesn't seem to mind it. It's a matter of taste, I guess. But I'd had enough, and so after I sold a play, I quit."

"Why did Uncle Edward stop writing short stories?"

"I don't know why," he replied. "He just did. You know, I've always felt that it was too bad that Edward didn't get to go to college. I don't think it would have made much difference for me, but I believe it would have for him. He might have been a scholar. That's the kind of mind he has. He was like your grandfather was in some ways."

"What was my grandfather like?"

"Well, it's difficult to say." He thought for a moment. "He was very quiet, shy almost, and he had a good sense of humor, and he liked to read. Of course he wasn't an educated man, you understand. He was very kind hearted. He wasn't really tough enough to be a successful businessman. He used to extend credit to people all the time, and they didn't always pay him."

"What about his father—your grandfather?"

"I don't know anything about him," my uncle said. "Papa never said much about his family. I don't even recall him so much as getting a letter from any of his family over in Europe. I understand that they were religious scholars and teachers—rabbis, I imagine, but Papa himself wasn't very religious. I don't remember him ever going to services, in fact."

I wondered whether this was why neither of my uncles had any interest in religion. As for my own father, there had been a time, after he was sick, when he had begun having us say prayers on Friday evenings before meals, and had even bought some Jewish history books. But he had never read the books, to my knowledge, any more than he ever read any other books, and we had since abandoned the custom of saying prayers. Although he and my mother usually went down to services on Friday night, he was certainly not a deeply religious man.

"I wish I had known my grandfather," I said.

"He died years before you came along," my uncle said. "I was seventeen, and your father was no more than twelve or thirteen. And of course he was sick for years before he died. So I can't say that I really knew him too well. Certainly not as well as you know your father."

My uncle stood up. "We'd better be getting back. Ellen's coming up to see me."

We went back across the sandbanks and to the line of pipe spanning the marsh.

"Are you sure you don't want me to carry you across?" my uncle said.

I laughed. "No, I'll make it all right by myself."

On the way home I thought about what he had said, about how someone recovering from a severe illness was like a batter who had been beaned by a pitch, and who had to concentrate on not ducking away from the ball. In a way, perhaps, that was what my father had been doing all the time.

My uncle would be off for California early in the morning. He would live in his cottage overlooking the ocean and do his writing. He had his own life out there, which sounded like a good one. He had spoken of wanting to give the shark's teeth to a friend, perhaps a woman friend, I thought. Of the three brothers, his career had been the most successful, the one that I might like to emulate. Yet it seemed to me that we were different in important ways. For though I shared, in elementary fashion at least, his interest in writing, there was a resoluteness, a firmness about him that I could never hope to possess, I thought. He identified his objectives and went after them with a confidence in his own abilities. He had perfect balance. In a way, I felt, he was even more solitary than my Uncle Edward, who had at least found a way to be, if not happy, then in any event at rest with himself. My Uncle Ben, for all the comforts of his present life out on the West Coast, could live in a bare cell, or a room at the YMCA, or a hotel room, if that were necessary, in order to pursue his objective.

My father did not have a mere objective; he wanted *life*. And when the blow came that had struck him down he had fought to get up and get going again in the only way he knew, which was, to try and pull himself together again inside himself. It required all his strength.

But where did that leave me?

The night before my sister and I were to depart for Richmond on the train, I read until very late. My Uncle Ben was now aboard an airliner somewhere in the Far West, on his way home to California. I was close to the end of the second volume of the Lee biography. Stonewall Jackson was leading his corps around the Union flank at Chancellorsville, preparatory to attacking Fighting Joe Hooker. The Confederate onslaught was a smashing success, but in the confusion of the night Jackson was wounded by his own men. There followed his struggle for life. At the end, on the last page, he died. I closed the book.

Late at night was my favorite time. First the ball scores—I had already heard them; then the concert from Louisville. The music tonight was by Sibelius. It was not familiar to me, but I liked it. An interesting thing about music was that the more familiar the composition became, the more I liked it—if it was much good in the first place. It was the same, in a way, with reading history. Knowing about something did not necessarily exhaust it. With a good piece of music, it was more interesting when I knew what was coming, because I could wait for it to happen. Just as, each night, I waited for the 1 A.M. Seaboard freight to show up from the west and cross the river. I could already hear it in the distance. I knew every progression of sound, every phase of its journey.

Not once had I ever actually seen the 1 A.M. train. It was a mile distant from our home, and the view was blocked by woods and houses. Some evening I would like to walk over to the Seaboard station and watch it pass by, first the engine, then the freight cars, finally the caboose.

Our trip tomorrow would be aboard an Atlantic Coast Line train. I knew the names of the towns and cities through which it would pass: Florence, Mullins, Fayetteville, Wilson, Rocky Mount, Roanoke Rapids, Virgilina, Petersburg, Richmond. It would have come all the way from Florida—was, indeed, on its way already, somewhere to the south of Jacksonville probably, moving steadily up the coast. Some of the passengers I would see tomorrow when my sister and I went aboard were already on the train now, gazing out of the windows into the dark, or else gone to sleep to the sound of the wheels clicking against the rails.

It was too bad that I could not take a nighttime train to Richmond. I would enjoy lying safely in a Pullman berth as the train sped through the darkness. But a Pullman would be much more expensive, and there would be no pleasure in sitting up in a coach all night long.

I had not had the dream about the nurse trapped inside the flooded train, or the wild-eyed insane woman in the hospital bed, for some time now. And I had not, to my knowledge, gone walking in my sleep again. It would be dreadful if I were to go sleepwalking at my aunt's house in Richmond. But there was no reason to think I would.

I had last visited my aunt and uncle in Richmond for a week back three years earlier, when I was twelve. It was four years before that, in 1931 and 1932, when we had lived in Richmond while my father was in the hospital. I could remember the boys I played with, and the school I attended, but my parents seemed, in my memory, hardly to have been present at all. My father had been in the hospital most of the time, and my mother had been away at the hospital every day, too.

In going back to Richmond for a visit, I would be returning to that time. On my previous trip I had not thought much about it, but this time it would be different. I felt that if I could go back to it, not just in time but in space, to the actual place, then I would be able to find out something.

Then I decided that I was once again about to do what I always did—set myself up to be disappointed. And I told myself that I would do better to try to let the trip to Richmond take care of itself and not try to shape or force it in anticipation beyond what it actually was.

PART FOUR

I once wrote a novel, about twenty years ago, in which, although I drew heavily upon a remembered time and place, almost everything that actually happened in it was made up, invented out of the whole cloth. The following year I was chagrined to find that the New York Times Book Review *had listed it as recommended summer reading under the category of "Memoirs."*

Looking back, I realize that I should have been flattered by the error, for I still hold to the notion that art is highest when it conceals art. And had I not succeeded in making at least one person believe that my little fictional universe had been real?

"It's all done with mirrors." One way to do it is to have the mirrors boldly arranged all along the walls of the fun-house corridors, so that one can take one's pleasure in the distortion, knowing that all the writer can really do, anyway, is to set upon a bough a golden bird that will sing songs to keep a drowsy emperor awake. Another way is to set the mirrors so carefully in the foliage around the playground that no one will even know they are there unless he tries to walk through one of them. I admire the first way the most. But I cannot, for the life of me, do it.

There are various kinds of authenticity in fiction. A novel that sets out to offer the authenticity of memory must offer quite the same kind of scrupulous adherence to the formal demands of fictional patterning that any other kind of novel offers. The terms that matter are those of the inherent imaginative patterns that a remembered sequence of events develops as it unfolds in time. It shapes its own meanings.

Far back along the way, the protagonist of this story took over his own direction. As I rejoin him, therefore, in Richmond, to find out what he will do there, I have only a general idea of what the meaning of what he does is going to be. I anticipate that one of the things he is going to begin to understand is that back in Charleston when he was listening to the Sonata for Piano in A Major on his uncle's phonograph, he was also, without knowing it, hearing the Kol Nidrei. *But I shall not know for sure until he actually does it. My task has long since become principally that of deciphering exactly what it is that he wishes to do.*

20.

There was a picture postcard I had seen from time to time that had always interested me. It bore the legend "Is Two Over One Railroad Fare?" and depicted three railroad locomotives, two of them on trestles, the third at ground level. The city of Richmond, Virginia, the postcard said, was the only place in the world where the trains of three different railroads could pass directly over the same point at the same time. For years I had wanted to see that place. On the final day of my visit to Richmond I set out to find it.

Aunt Maggie and Uncle Charles' home, where my sister and I were staying, was located in the far west end of Richmond. It was a large house with extensive grounds. When my father was sick and we stayed in Richmond, they had lived in a much smaller house in a residential district farther downtown, where the houses were crowded close upon each other and had tiny lawns and fenced-in backyards. But my Uncle Charles was now a prosperous jeweler, and they had since moved to a handsome suburban area with winding roads and wide green lawns. They lived there now with their son Morton and my grandfather and grandmother.

Like my Uncle Charles my grandfather was a jeweler, though not so prosperous. He was a little man with a bald head, and he talked with an accent, for he had been born in what had then been Austro-Hungary. When he came home from his store on the trolley car each evening, he spent all his time in my grandmother's room, at her bedside. My grandmother had been struck by an automobile three years before and had never recovered. The accident had damaged her brain, and thereafter she had steadily declined, until now she had no knowledge of who or where she was. I remembered her as a large woman, but now she was scarcely the size of a little girl, and she lay in her bed all day and all night long, making low, hollow moans when she was not asleep. I had gone in to see her only once, shortly after we arrived, but she did not recognize me or know I was there. All I saw was a small hawklike face above the bed covers, staring straight ahead with wide eyes, while my grandfather sat alongside her bed. She no longer knew him, either. After that I stayed away from her room, and at night when I went to bed shut my door so I could not hear her cries.

My aunt and uncle were very nice people. There were other uncles and aunts, my mother's brothers and their wives; and there were numerous cousins at various removes. Two of my uncles were doctors; the other two were jewelers. They were all very friendly, and my sister and I had dinner with each family in turn. There were also cousins by marriage, the kin of my Uncle Charles, many of whom had come to Richmond only recently from Poland. Their English was not very good, and mostly they talked Yiddish. All my uncles and aunts could speak Yiddish, and everyone found it amusing that my sister and I could neither speak nor understand it. "He's not a real Jew!" one of my Uncle Charles's brothers kept proclaiming of me, laughing loudly; or else, "A Yiddisher mit a Goyisher Kopf!"

They were good humored, and pleasant, and as my mother had said, they were not at all like my father's family in Charleston. For one thing, they were much more sociable and gregarious. They visited each other continually and talked all the time. Their conversation ran to business, family, food, clothes, property, vacations, trips, automobiles, movies, radio programs, and the remarkable doings of their children. They never talked about politics, but sometimes they discussed the news from Europe. When they did, they were no longer garrulous and merry. For if another war came and the Nazis were to invade Poland, they feared for the fate of their relatives there. My Uncle Charles was making strenuous efforts to get others of his family out before war broke out, but the diplomatic process was cruelly slow, and each day's news told of trouble to come.

During the days and nights that my sister and I were in Richmond we were taken sightseeing, to movies, to a vaudeville show, to see Thomas Jefferson's home, Monticello, near Charlottesville. With some of our cousins we went bowling, and one evening I went to see a Piedmont League baseball game at Mayo Island. My cousin Morton was especially nice to me. Of all my relatives in Richmond I liked him best. He was nineteen and a rising senior at the University of Richmond, and he had a car of his own, and took me around in it. One morning we drove downtown to a clothing store, and I was fitted with a new summer suit. My mother had written my aunt and asked that it be done; my father, she said, had noticed that my suit was too small for me, and wanted me to get another. My cousin helped me select a light tan Palm Beach suit.

One evening there was a party. People my own age were there, and there was dancing. The girls I met talked fluently, and asked questions about Charleston and school and other things, but I felt uncomfortable with them. They were no older or farther along in school than I was, yet they seemed more sophisticated, more like adults.

I realized afterward that one reason I had felt strange was that everyone there was Jewish; I mean the boys and girls at the party. For that matter all my aunts and uncles and cousins in Richmond, with the possible exception of my cousin Mortin, seemed to confront almost every aspect of their experience in terms of their Jewishness. In Charleston I seldom thought of my being a Jew as central to my identity. Religious identity simply was not a consideration most of the time. When I thought about it, however, I knew that this was not true for all Jews in Charleston. The young people of the orthodox Jewish congregation had numerous community activities, belonged to Jewish clubs and associations, and were very much wrapped up in being Jews. Not all, of course; there were also some orthodox families who were religious but not narrow socially, and who moved in the same circles as my family.

But it occurred to me that part of the difference between the two families was due to the particular character of my father's family. My mother was certainly right about the Kohns being different. There was a quality about all of them that set them apart, as if an important part of them was separate from the world that most people, Jew and non-Jew, inhabited.

My aunt Ellen had said that back in Europe, both her father's and her mother's families had been scholars and teachers—not in the universities, but in the Jewish religious community. She had once met a woman who had told her that her own father had received his religious instruction from my aunt's grandfather, and that he was one of a well-known family of rabbis and Talmudic scholars. I could well believe it.

I thought of them gathered on our porch before dinner the week before, and I compared that occasion with what I saw of my Richmond aunts, uncles and cousins as they sat around talking and laughing and enjoying each other's company. My Charleston relatives were not merely more quiet and reserved, they were withdrawn. For all their satisfaction at being there with each other, there had been an intensely private quality to each of them. It showed itself most noticeably in their eyes. Their eyes, deepset, blue-green rather than brown, looked out at the world with a kind of sadness, so that although they lighted up in mirth in moments of merriment, they soon grew dark and reserved again.

During the time I was in Richmond I also made several expeditions by myself. I soon found that none of my cousins had any interest whatever in the Civil War. My cousin Morton saw the large, red-bound third volume of Lee's biography that I had brought along to read, and remarked that the author was the editor of the afternoon newspaper in Richmond, but though he, alone of all my cousins, showed an interest in books and even had a bookcase in his room, the Confederacy was not among the subjects that engaged his attention.

One afternoon I went downtown on the Westhampton trolley car and walked over to the White House of the Confederacy, the mansion that Jefferson Davis had occupied during the war. It was now a museum, room after room filled with Confederate relics—pistols, swords, rifles, canteens, uniforms, watches, documents, field glasses, cooking utensils, surgical instruments, flags, photographs, camping equipment—every imaginable kind of equipment needed by an army.

There was a room for each Confederate state. I went immediately to the South Carolina room. Seeing the Palmetto flag spread out, blue and white, in a display case on the wall sent a thrill through me. I examined everything in the room. The family names of the users and donors of the objects on display were familiar to me. I felt a surge of pride. They were South Carolina names.

I visited the other rooms in turn. The Virginia room contained by far the largest collection of relics, and many of them had once been owned by some of the most famous commanders in the war: Lee, Jackson, Stuart, Johnston, A. P. Hill. In one large glass case there was the stuffed body of General Jeb Stuart's war-horse. In another was an officer's gray jacket with a brown stain on it—Dr. Hunter McGuire had worn it while tending the wounds of Stonewall Jackson.

Afterwards I went out onto the rear portico of the building and looked eastward down into the Shockoe Valley. I could see the factories and the network of railroad tracks leading northward from the Main Street Station. There was a long freight train curving northward through the valley, which might well be, I decided, a Seaboard Air Line train. I wondered whether it had passed through Charleston on its way to Richmond and crossed the trestle over the Ashley River. Eastward beyond the hollow of the valley was the area known as Church Hill, and beyond that were the battlefields of the Seven Days' fighting. From where I stood, Jefferson Davis had listened to the booming of the cannon and the rattle of the musketry. What I heard now was the sound of the northbound freight train, the automobiles, trucks, factories, and other noises of the downtown city.

Another afternoon I went to Battle Abbey, a large building located farther uptown on the Boulevard, and saw the massed battle flags and the immense painting, covering an entire wall, of General Lee and his lieutenants. Lee was in the center, mounted upon the gray-white Traveller, and clustered about him were the most famous generals. In a descriptive brochure I looked for the South Carolinians, and found them—Wade Hampton, Anderson, Gregg, and above all, General Longstreet, whom they called "Old Pete" and whom Lee himself spoke of as his "old war horse."

Behind the Battle Abbey, in a park, was another building, a low yellow structure that had once been the Confederate Soldiers' Home. I realized at once that I had seen it before. My father had taken me there, while he was recuperating from his illness. It had been a cold spring day. There was a bench outside the door, and that day two old men, wearing gray uniforms and with long white beards, were sitting on it, canes by their sides, enjoying the sunshine. My father chatted with them for a while, and I shook their hands, which were bony and spotted with age and trembly. I tried to recall what the soldiers had said, but I could not.

Outside in the park were some field pieces, Blakeleys and Napoleons mounted on their frames, with caissons behind. Now I remembered climbing up on one of the cannon, and waving to my father and the two old soldiers in front of the building. It was good to know that I had actually shaken hands with and talked to Confederate veterans.

When was it that I had first become interested in the Civil War? I remembered an occasion when we had come up to Richmond to visit my grandparents, who were living in a house on Auburn Avenue. I had sat out on the front steps, playing with two racing cars that someone had given me, and was repeating over to myself the words *Federals* and *Confederals*. We were the Confederals. This was well before my father had taken ill; I could not have been more than five years old. There was also an occasion in Charleston when I had been told that a Confederate reunion was to be held out in Hampton Park, where I went every afternoon with my nurse. Whether I had seen any Confederates then I could not remember, but I had a dream, almost the earliest I could recall. I was out in the park, at a place where there were oleander bushes and a wire fence, and a large pathway leading through an opening in the fence. At each side of the opening there was a large green post, and as I watched, a file of soldiers, Confederates, silently materialized out of one gatepost, walked one after another across the path, and disappeared into the gatepost opposite.

The parade had taken place two blocks to the north of Battle Abbey that summer. I decided to walk up to Monument Avenue. It was in the direction I would have to go to take the trolley back to my aunt's house. Perhaps I could find the place where my father and I had stood to watch the parade go by.

The police motorcycles had come first, making a deafening din, and then the various military units, including a Norfolk drum-and-bugle corps, wearing scarlet tunics, khaki pants, and shining chrome helmets, and finally the veterans in the open touring cars, and it was then that my father had called out, "Give the old boys a hand!" and the tremendous cheer had come from the crowd. That had been seven years ago. Almost all of those old soldiers who had waved to the crowd from the touring cars seven years ago were dead by now. Supposing that the youngest of them had been fifteen years old in 1865, the last year of the war, that would mean—I counted it up— that no old soldier in that parade could have been less than eighty-two years old that day! For sixty-seven years had gone by since the surrender. I wondered whether, sixty-seven years after the end of the World War, there would be a parade like that for the veterans of 1917–1918, and if there were, whether my Uncle Ben and my father would be around to ride in open cars and be cheered. I found it impossible to picture my Uncle Ben in such a role, but I could easily imagine my father sitting there in an open car, his face wrinkled and old, his hand thin and trembling as he grasped a cane and waved it to the crowd along the sidewalk.

I remembered him with the bandage around his head, walking with a cane, not long after the hospital days. I thought of him as he was now, out in the yard working on the rosebushes, wearing a paint-spattered pair of trousers and an old undershirt with a hole in the back. If he did live to be eighty-five and were to ride in an open car in a World War veterans' parade, would he look very much different? More wrinkled and feeble, perhaps, a little more stooped and frail.

Well, he isn't finished yet, I thought to myself. *Not by a long shot he isn't!*

Now there was no crowd, no parade, only the afternoon traffic moving along Monument Avenue in the early August heat. I walked northward two blocks to Broad Street, crossed it, and waited for the trolley car.

That had been Saturday afternoon. That night my sister and I had gone to have dinner with my mother's youngest brother, my Uncle Paul and his wife Alyce. Afterwards my sister had gone out on a double date. One of the boys she had met at the party asked her to go. It was her first formal date, and she was highly pleased with it and with Richmond. My Aunt Maggie had suggested that I might want to telephone one of the girls I had met at the party and do the same, but I did not want to. Instead I went to the movies with Uncle Paul and Aunt Alyce.

I got back to my Aunt Maggie's house a little after eleven, and I lay in bed reading the Lee biography. From the open windows I could hear, very faintly, the moaning of my grandmother in her room. I thought of closing the window, but it was too hot for that.

After a while, just as in Charleston, I began to make out the sound of a locomotive whistle, to the west. Gradually it drew closer, until I could hear it very plainly. I thought of a story my mother had once told me, of when she had been a little girl in Richmond. There was a railroad engineer who had a special whistle call he blew each night when his train neared town, to let his wife and family know that all was well and he would be home soon. Every night they listened out for it. Then one night the whistle had failed to blow, and the next morning they found out that he had been killed in a train wreck.

To judge from the volume of sound the locomotive I was now hearing must have been much larger than the Seaboard night freight that I heard in Charleston. After the locomotive passed I could hear the steady rolling of cars along rails. It was a very long train, and some time elapsed before it passed out of earshot in the direction of the downtown city. When all was quiet again I listened to hear whether my grandmother was still crying, but I could hear nothing. She must have fallen asleep.

A little later I heard my sister come in, and I went downstairs and listened to her talk about her date. They had gone to a movie, and then to a place called Wakefield's, where they dined on no mere Lucky Mondaes as in Charleston, but on fried chicken, with shoe-string potatoes, hot rolls, and honey. The boy she had dated had asked whether he could write to her. My sister was very excited.

While we were talking my cousin Morton arrived home. I asked him about the trian. What I had heard was a coal train on the Chesapeake and Ohio; the tracks ran alongside the James River no more than a half-mile from the house, through the woods. Not too long ago, he said, he had been about to drive over the river at a bridge at Westham, not far away, when a coal train had come along, and he had to wait while it passed. There were two locomotives at the head of it, and he counted 140 hopper cars loaded with coal before the caboose went by.

That was when I remembered the picture postcard of the trains. I asked my cousin whether he had ever seen the place. He did not remember it, but he said it was almost certain to be located somewhere near the foot of the Shockoe Valley down near the river, below Main Street Station, because that was where the Seaboard trains crossed over the river into the city, and there was also a Southern Railway bridge nearby, while the C&O tracks ran right alongside the river all the way downtown and beyond. "There's no other place where it could be," he said. He found a map of Richmond, and we worked out the location.

The next day was Sunday, and we went to Monticello, but on Monday, the day before time to go back to Charleston, I went downtown and looked for the only place in the whole world where three railroads crossed over the same spot.

21.

It was in the early afternoon that I went. My Aunt Maggie wanted my sister and me to have lunch with her and another aunt at the Miller and Rhoads Tea Room. My sister was still filled with enthusiasm for the date she had gone on, and she and my aunts talked about dates, parties, clothes, and related subjects. While they were talking, they were interrupted by a distinguished-looking elderly man, who came over to our table. He was the rabbi at the reform temple that my aunt's family attended, and when he was introduced to me, his eyes lit up.

"Ah, I remember your father very well!" he declared. "How is he?"

When I told him that my father was in much better health, he went on to tell a story. My father had been in the hospital, and apparently about to die, and the rabbi had come to pray with him the day before his second brain operation.

"He was very ill," he said, "and under sedation, but we read the prayers together. I was about to leave, and I must have looked very sorrowful, because I knew he was in such grave danger. So do you know what your father did? He looked up at me from the hospital bed, and he said, in his weak voice, 'One month from today I'll shoot you a game of craps, at a quarter a throw.' And you know,"—he looked at me and smiled—"he did, and he won fifty cents from me!"

He laughed. "Give him my best," he said, "and tell him the next time he comes to Richmond I want a re-match!"

So that was where the green dice came from.

I told my aunts goodbye, saying that I would come home on the trolley car with my grandfather. I walked down Grace Street to the Capitol, cut across the grounds past the fountain, then down a block to Main Street. I looked eastward, down a long hill to where the elevated railroad tracks crossed over into Main Street Station. That was where I wanted to go. I set off down the hill.

This was the oldest part of Richmond. My cousin Morton had told me something about it when we had driven through, several days earlier. In Civil War times and for decades thereafter, Main Street was the city's principal business mart. Since then the center had shifted westward and northward, and the stores along Broad and Grace streets were now the fashionable shopping area, while Main was the financial and wholesale district. There were large buildings along the street, with imposing façades and entryways, many stories higher than the tallest buildings in Charleston. The street was crowded with cars, trucks, and even some heavy vans with solid rubber tires, while down the center ran a double line of trolley car tracks, with orange and blue trolley cars in view up and down the way. The sidewalks were busy with people, mostly men, some in work clothes and others in handsome summer attire and wearing straw hats. It was a little like Broad Street in Charleston, with its lawyers and bankers and realtors, only much busier and obviously more prosperous and important. Over the entire area was the strong, somewhat harsh odor of raw tobacco from the cigarette factories.

As I walked along, the banks and office buildings began to give way to stores, wholesale businesses for the most part, with old, ornate fronts, and inside, dark interiors and long counters. Again I was reminded of Charleston, along East Bay Street. I came to a newsstand and went in and looked through a rack of postcards until I found one that showed the three locomotives crossing over each other.

Now I was much closer to the station, and the stores along Main Street had become considerably more tawdry. There were clothing stores, shoeshops, hardware stores, jewelers, a few drab-looking restaurants and confectioneries, and several pawnshops with the three gold balls suspended over them. The people on the street no longer included many well-attired businessmen, but for the most part were dressed much more cheaply and sometimes even shabbily. Many were black people.

My plan was to walk southward from the station, keeping as close as I could to the Seaboard trestle, until I arrived at the point where it crossed over the Chesapeake and Ohio tracks, which according to the picture on the postcard would also be elevated above the ground. There, if the photograph were accurate, both trestles would be located directly above the Southern Railway tracks. A narrow street led underneath the Seaboard trestle, so it ought not to be difficult to find the place.

Along the street were some old stores and warehouses, dark and unlovely. Trucks were pulled up alongside the warehouses, several times blocking the sidewalk, so that I had to detour around them. I crossed one street, following underneath the trestle. It was a run-down neighborhood, with a few small factories, vacant lots, and some dilapidated homes, not all of which seemed occupied. At length I came to the end of the street, fronting upon a road, beyond which was open space and what seemed to be some spur trackage, and beyond that a viaduct, which must be the C&O tracks. So all I had to do was to walk several hundred yards over to where the Seaboard trestle curved southwestward and crossed over the C&O viaduct, and I ought to be at the very spot where the three railroads crossed.

But where were the Southern tracks? I looked at the postcard, and realized that what I had thought was a spur track must be the Southern Railway line. But I could see right along it to where it led beneath the C&O viaduct, almost a hundred feet away from the Seaboard trestle. If this were the place, then, the three railroads did not actually cross directly one above the other at all.

I walked toward the C&O viaduct, along the Southern tracks. When I drew closer, I saw that while there might be some way whereby, taken from an angle, a photograph could be made to show the three trains appearing to cross over the same spot, there was no place where they really did.

It was a very hot afternoon. Trucks and automobiles were bumping along the street. If this were the place I had come to see, and it seemed to me that it had to be, then anticipation had greatly exceeded actuality, for what I saw in front of me and around me was a drab-looking area in the industrial part of the city, with some old warehouses across the way and some rubble-strewn lots grown up in weeds, and dirty, ugly steel girders overhead.

The likelihood of even two trains arriving here at the same time was very slight. I should have known. Looking at the postcard I decided that not only had the picture of three trains obviously been contrived, but it omitted the surrounding context—the weeds, dirt, empty lots and debris, the traffic along the road. For someone not looking at a picture postcard but come to see the actuality, however, it was impossible to screen out the context. I tried to frame my hands about my eyes in order to be able to look only at the trestles and track, but it did not work.

Back across the way to the south, toward where the river must lie, there was a wall of high weeds and trees, and some sort of a concrete shed half-encircled in the underbrush. From here, at least, I would be far enough away from the overhead viaduct to be able to see the next big C&O coal train that came along. I went over to it. Just beyond, through thick weeds, I could see a canal, with an oil barge tied up to a float, and beyond that, more underbrush and the foliage of trees, above which, some distance away, were the brick buildings and smoke stacks of a factory. Several blocks to the west was a street of heavy traffic, probably the access to a bridge over the river.

Somewhere near where I stood, I decided, the troops had debarked for the defense of Richmond. I tried to imagine what it must have been like: the little bell-stacked locomotives and wooden coaches, the troops clambering down and forming into ranks to march up the hill toward the capitol. *On to Richmond!* had been the cry of the South Carolina regiments when they boarded those trains in Charleston to travel northward and join the Confederate Army under General Beauregard blocking the southward push of the Federals before the Battle of First Manassas. And here, or somewhere near here, was where the trains had arrived. But that was a long time ago, and there were no signs now that harked back to that day, nothing in view, so far as I could tell, that they would also have seen when they had come here.

I felt the sweat running down under my arms and around my stomach. If a train did not come along soon, I thought, I would not get to see one. I listened for any sound of a steam locomotive approaching through the din of the downtown city. Surely one would show up soon.

Finally I heard the noise of something moving along rails. But it did not sound like a train; there was no noise of a steam locomotive, no exploding pistons and roll of drive wheels, only a low, rumbling that seemed oddly familiar. I waited as whatever it was drew closer, coming from the west.

Then, materializing abruptly from underneath the Seaboard trestle, came a gas-electric coach almost identical with the Boll Weevil back home. It clattered along the elevated tracks, moving slowly, the words *Chesapeake & Ohio* lettered on its side, and clicked on eastward and out of sight.

I began to walk back in the direction of the Main Street Station. It was uphill, and harder going, and I was not only hot but very thirsty.

The heat, the odor of raw tobacco that drenched the air, the weeds and warehouses and old residences and trucks, and brick walls with fading Coca-Cola and Domino Cigarette signs on them, and the grimy girders of the trestle overhead, seemed dreary in their heavy stolidity. Somewhere in the distance I now heard the whistle of a steam locomotive. But I would not go back for it.

Across Main Street, a block up the way, was a confectionery of some sort. I would go in and get something cool to drink. I walked along by the shabby store fronts with their cheap finery, and passed a pawnshop with its gold balls overhead, its window display loaded with watches, binoculars, knives, diamond rings, and other objects taken in hock.

Jews.

And what are you?

Hadn't my mother's family come out of just this neighborhood? My aunt had said that my grandfather once had his store at 15th and Main, just a block or two from where I was, and that they had lived above it, though it had been "a much nicer neighborhood back then." When my mother was my age she had probably lived within several hundred yards of the very spot where I was walking. And if my father's family were indeed so different, more complex and remote and withdrawn, it was certainly not because they were not equally Jewish. Quite the contrary. In Europe they had been teachers, scholars— *rabbis.*

I went into the confectionery, ordered a lemonade, and sat down at a table over against the side wall. The room was dimly lighted and had a sour smell. An electric clock on the wall, with *Pepsi-Cola* across its face, showed 4:19. Behind the counter the woman who had served me was washing some dishes. There was a mirror behind the counter, with a Budweiser Beer slogan in frosted lettering along the top. In front of the counter were some high, wire-backed stools, two of which were occupied by men in railroad workclothes, drinking beer. The floor was covered with brown linoleum. Toward the rear of the room were several pinball machines and a chrome-and-colored-glass jukebox. A floor fan droned away. At least I was in out of the sun. The two men at the counter were talking about an automobile that someone they knew had bought.

I sipped my drink slowly. I was tired, and it was a relief to be able to sit down and rest. I should have known better, I thought, than to come off on a fool's errand like this, down into the dregs of Richmond. In a way it was fitting, though. I had gone in search of a picture postcard view of a place where three railroad locomotives crossed, marvelously, simultaneously, over the same spot of ground, and had seen only a little gas-electric coach like those I saw every day at home, and ended up, hot and tired, not two blocks from where my mother had once lived.

My father's world was not at all like this. But neither, for that matter, was my mother's. For had not she and her family emerged from this neighborhood, refusing to stay trapped in its ugliness?

Moreover, it was because I was my father's son that I was here, for I could not imagine any of my numerous cousins and relatives on my mother's side of the family being so impractical as to spend an afternoon doing what I had done today. It would be something that my uncles might do, though—or even my father, who had, after all, taken me to see the old soldiers.

A door to the street opened and a girl came in, who looked to be about twelve or thirteen years old. She ordered a pint of butter pecan ice cream. When my mother was that age, she might have come into this place, or a place like it, and bought ice cream, just as that girl was doing. I watched the girl—rather short, sallow-faced, with stringy blond hair, ordinary looking, as she waited for her purchase and then left. No, my mother would not have looked like that at any time, or dressed like that, or stood there like that, vacant-faced and listless.

My mother had had a hard winter and spring, and she had said some things to me that she had not meant, or not in the way they sounded. It was because she remembered this neighborhood, even though it may have been nicer then, that she had been so intent upon making me get a job, earn money, show myself to be capable of protecting myself from this kind of place. She did not understand that if I could ever do that, I would have to do it in my own way and not the way that her father and her brothers had done it. But that was because theirs was the only way that she understood, and not because she did not love me.

I felt better. I finished the lemonade and went back onto the street. It would be an hour and a half before my grandfather would be departing for home. Instead of returning back up Main Street and across to Broad, I would walk north along the side of the railroad station and the trainyard, and then cross westward on Broad Street. It was still quite hot, but the drink and the rest had refreshed me.

I passed a large open-air market, with many stalls and bins. Although it was late in the afternoon, numerous people were still moving about the market area, inspecting the wares being sold there. I imagined my grandfather and grandmother marketing here, purchasing chickens, meat, vegetables, fruit for the family, just as these people were now doing. Trucks were drawn up along the street, and some wagons with mules and horses in harness. There was a scent of rotting produce, mixed oddly with the pervading aroma from the tobacco factories and the heady smell of coal smoke emanating from a grimy switch engine that was shunting cars in the trainyard. I looked up at the locomotive as it chugged back and forth. It seemed to be engaged in making up the consist for an outbound passenger train, perhaps a C&O train that would soon be speeding westward, bound for the mountains and beyond. That was another trip that I intended to make some day.

I was on the eastern side of the Shockoe Valley, walking along past warehouses and Railway Express sheds. Across the network of tracks to the west, now that I was at eye level with the yard, I could see the State Capitol and the buildings and steeples of downtown Richmond, up on the hill. I tried to imagine how it would have looked during Civil War days. Many of the buildings would have been there then, I thought, though others, including all the high office buildings along Main Street, were more recent than that.

It was an imposing city. But my home was in Charleston. Yet if that were so, why had I come here today? And why was I always dreaming of other places, wishing that I could, like my Uncle Ben, go off to the Northeast, the West? I thought of a French teacher I had in my sophomore year who assigned me a passage to translate aloud in class that contained the phrase *le juif errant*. After I had gone through it, he asked me whether I knew who the Wandering Jew was. When I said that I did not know, he became exasperated, and said to the class, "For God's sake, do any of you know who Jesus Christ himself is?"

Some time later I found that Jack Marcussohn was assigned precisely the same passage in his class, and when he too failed to identify the Wandering Jew, the teacher had responded in exactly the same way. Evidently the teacher had seen to it that a Jewish boy would be given that passage to translate aloud, in order to embarrass him. The teacher, who was not a native of Charleston, sometime later propositioned a male teacher in the faculty lounge and received a bloody nose for his pains. A little later, after getting involved in some kind of scandal in town, he left Charleston.

It was time to turn west on Broad Street and walk up the hill. It would be a long climb, first across a bridge that spanned the railroad tracks, then on up the slope to my grandfather's store. It was after five o'clock by now, and the street was crowded with automobiles leaving the business district. Broad Street stretched from up on Church Hill all the way west to the city limits and beyond. It was a very long street.

Longstreet and Wade Hampton and the South Carolinians had come to help defend this city.

If you lived in a place and you liked it, it became your place, so that everything that ever happened to it became part of you. So that if, like my Uncle Ben, I was fated to be the Wandering Jew, it was not because I did not have a home, but because of the way I looked at the world.

As I got halfway across the bridge, above the tracks, a passenger train pulled out of the station. I stopped to look down at it as it labored toward me, the locomotive moving slowly as the drive wheels bore down onto the flanged rails in order to get the string of coaches moving. It was northward bound. Then, as it drew nearer, until it was almost directly below where I stood, I was startled to see another locomotive come sailing out from underneath the bridge, inbound with a long string of coaches. The northbound train, driving hard to get under way, had made so much noise that I had not heard the southbound train arriving. It swept past, moving easily, and as the two locomotives passed each other below me, the drive wheels and pistons seemed to unite in a kind of rhythmic collaboration, the outbound train sending powerful, spaced notes, the inbound locomotive clipping along much more easily and its percussion light and rapid, sounding behind and around the other, as in counterpoint. The air rang with the rhythm, and the long, low, accompanying roll of the trailing coaches along the rails.

I watched the inbound train pull to a stop alongside the station, a long way off from me, then I resumed my walk up the hill. Why should I not go where I pleased, just so long as the trains ran in both directions? *For God's sake why not?*

I walked on, feeling, as I so often did after watching a train go by or hearing a piece of music played, that something had happened, and, though I was not at all sure what it was, that it was important.

I still had a long way to climb before I would reach the crest of the Broad Street hill, and I walked slowly. By the time I cleared the bridge, I was tired. If I passed a drugstore or a confectionery, I thought, I would buy another cold drink. Next to me was a large gray building, however, and I saw no sign of any place nearby where I could buy one.

So, hot and with my legs aching and my feet feeling heavy and weary, I walked onward, and drew alongside the entrance to the gray building, and I looked up and saw a set of tall brown wooden doors, and a brass plaque with a name.

All morning long we had waited, watching the hands of the clock travel slowly around the dial, so slowly that it was only when I turned away for a while and then back again that the minute hand seemed to have moved at all. I looked at picture books, played on the rug with cars and lead soldiers and the new red boat my uncle had bought for me, taking care not to get myself dirty. My father had gone away a long time ago; for months he had been away in the hospital. Since then my sister and I had stayed with the nurse all day until my mother came home at dinnertime. Early the week before there had been several nights when she had not come back at all, and the nurse had given us dinner and put us to bed and heard our prayers. My uncles and aunts from Charleston had come to see us. On the third evening my mother returned, looking very tired, but smiling, and told us that my father was going to get well again. Every morning after that I asked, "Can we go to see him today?"

but had been told, "No, not today. Soon." Now, at last, we were going.

Finally it came time for lunch, and then the nurse scrubbed the dirt off my hands and face and knees, and we changed into the clothes that ordinarily we wore only to Sabbath school. Then we went out onto the front porch and waited until my mother arrived in a taxicab, and we ran to the sidewalk and climbed in with her.

It was a long way downtown, but at last we were passing Capitol Square where George Washington sat on his horse high in the air, and then several more blocks, and the taxicab pulled to a stop at the curb. We were standing outside a large gray building, with a brass plaque on one side of the doorway that read MEMORIAL HOSPITAL. We went in through the tall brown doors, through a large room where many people were waiting, past a counter behind which there were nurses in gray and white uniforms who nodded to my mother, until we came to an elevator. The black man who operated it closed the sliding door behind us, and he turned a handle and the elevator began rising.

"What you got there?" he asked me, pointing to the red wooden boat.

"A Clyde Liner," I told him. "It's named the Algonquin. I'm going to show it to my daddy."

"Well, ain't that nice?" the black man said.

The elevator stopped, the black man opened the sliding door for us, and we stepped out into another hallway, not so dark as the one downstairs. There were nurses and several men dressed in white suits, who smiled at us as we walked along. I looked into some of the open doorways and could see sick people in beds. I wanted to hurry as fast as I could, but I made myself keep pace with my mother and sister.

Then we came to one doorway and my mother stopped and took us by the hand, and we went inside the room. A very high bed was over by the windows, and next to it a table with flowers. Nearby there was a dresser, also with flowers on it. In the bed, propped upon pillows, was someone with a white bandage all about his head. Only his face was showing.

"Go over and say hello to your Daddy," my mother said.

Now I felt very shy and timid. I walked toward the bed, holding the red boat out in front of me.

"Step a little closer," my mother told me. "Don't be afraid."

I went nearer to the edge of the bed, which came almost up to my chest, and my father reached out his arm and placed it about my shoulders. The arm was thin, and it was shaking a little. The light coming through the windows was so bright that I could hardly see. He drew me close to the bed, toward him, and when he spoke it was in a strange-sounding voice.

"Come here, my son," he said.